IN THE CITY

OF PIGS

ANDRÉ FORGET

IN THE CITY

OF PIGS

RARE
MACHINES

Publisher: Scott Fraser | Acquiring editor: Julie Mannell | Editor: Russell Smith
Cover designer: David Drummond
Cover images: water: shutterstock.com/kryzhov; bubbles: shutterstock.com/Alena Ohneva; organ: shutterstock.com/MAD.vertise

Library and Archives Canada Cataloguing in Publication

Title: In the city of pigs / André Forget.
Names: Forget, André (Novelist), author.
Identifiers: Canadiana (print) 20210300507 | Canadiana (ebook) 20210300515 | ISBN 9781459749085 (softcover) | ISBN 9781459749092 (PDF) | ISBN 9781459749108 (EPUB)
Subjects: LCGFT: Novels.
Classification: LCC PS8611.O753 I5 2022 | DDC C813/.6—dc23

We acknowledge the support of the Canada Council for the Arts and the Ontario Arts Council for our publishing program. We also acknowledge the financial support of the Government of Ontario, through the Ontario Book Publishing Tax Credit and Ontario Creates, and the Government of Canada.

Care has been taken to trace the ownership of copyright material used in this book. The author and the publisher welcome any information enabling them to rectify any references or credits in subsequent editions.

The publisher is not responsible for websites or their content unless they are owned by the publisher.

Printed and bound in Canada.

Rare Machines, an imprint of Dundurn Press
1382 Queen Street East
Toronto, Ontario, Canada M4L 1C9
dundurn.com, @dundurnpress 𝕏 f ☺

For Jean-Pierre

My words appear to leave you cold;
Poor babes, I will not be your scolder:
Reflect, the Devil, he is old,
To understand him, best grow older

— Goethe, *Faust, Part Two*

FIRST MOVEMENT

THE CITY
OF PIGS

I HAVE NOTHING to say about Montreal. I remember only
the slow inevitability of the train pulling out of Central Station,
the benevolent red glow of the Five Roses sign, the whiteness
of the year's first snow sprinkling the trackside. Montreal was
a dream from which I awoke as we sped past the Lake of Two
Mountains, a patchwork of brown nocturnal memories, a pud-
dle of piss turning to steam on the sidewalk.

We left the last suburbs behind us. The beverage cart came
by, and I ordered a drink. The porter flipped open the tab of
the beer can with a disdainful thumb. I could tell he thought
I was a train drunk. He didn't understand that this was not

a thoughtless or routine drink, but a drink laden with ritual meaning, drunk to memorialize the end of a catastrophe — and not, therefore, subject to the usual conventions governing alcohol consumption. He placed the can on the tray in front of me, covered by a superfluous plastic cup, and I felt only pity.

Outside the window, dead fields lay under a dusting of snow so fine the darkness of the furrowed earth was still visible. It was the last day of November. Laptops snapped open around me and my fellow passengers pulled up their spreadsheets and quarterly reports. I had no work to do. I turned to the window and listened to Glenn Gould's recording of the Brahms intermezzi on my phone; I was in a sentimental mood, and nothing has ever been more sentimental than Gould's fingers landing on the opening chords of that E-flat Major intermezzo. There was nothing outside the window but farmers' fields and ditches and forests. Occasionally, a small town's asphalt roofs and dejected steeples passed by. The only indication we were leaving one unhappy province and entering another was the signposts: towns named for polysyllabic saints gave way to towns named for colonial administrators. And yet I couldn't look away. Montreal had died for me so the rest of the world could come alive.

I hadn't been to Toronto in years. But the city had, over the past months, taken on a dense significance in my mind. This was not because of Gould and his delicate E-flat Major intermezzo. Gould's Toronto had disappeared decades ago, buried under condo towers and chain pharmacies. If anything, the more or less complete erasure of the city Gould had known made it possible to imagine moving there. Toronto attracted me in direct proportion to the claustrophobia and disgust I felt walking the streets of Montreal. The city as it existed in my mind was an elaborate perversion, a glassy necropolis where skinny men in Tiger of Sweden suits ran free beneath a sky refracted in coloured glass. A vulgar and frictionless place, a city that could now never produce a Gould.

My fellow passengers were staring at their screens, sleek in their cotton blazers and wool ties. Their proximity thrilled me. I wanted to follow these people into their twelfth-floor condos and watch them send one last email while leaning against Formica-topped islands, drinking glasses of twenty-dollar chianti. To wait outside their bathroom doors while they listened to alt-pop and brushed their teeth. To watch them get two pages into some CBC-recommended novel before going back to their phones and eventually falling asleep nestled amid enormous pillows. The lives of these people seemed impossibly exotic. Perhaps I, too, might find a middle-management job at a bank where I would spend my days denying people loans. My face would grow smooth from shaving, I would get a gym membership, and I would invite sophisticated older women to join me at the symphony. I would surprise them with charming anecdotes about the lives of German baroque composers and smile mysteriously when they asked me where I'd learned such things. Soothed by these fantasies and calmed by the gentle rocking of the train, I fell into a light sleep somewhere west of Kingston.

The snow had turned to rain by the time we got to Toronto. I stepped out onto a platform that smelled of diesel and rusting metal. Descending into the warren of corridors and half-finished hallways beneath the station, the people I had been watching with such curiosity became hunched and ordinary, diminished by arrival. It took me several attempts to locate the exit.

When I finally emerged from the underground, I found myself on a large plaza bounded on one side by the blank facade of Union Station and on the other by an ostentatious hotel. There was a line of taxis waiting with lit lanterns. I walked up the main avenue, away from the station, suitcase banging against my leg. The pavements were slippery beneath my feet. Everything seemed to be closed.

I had thought to catch a streetcar a few blocks north, but the misting rain turned into a proper downpour. Cold water trickled down the inside of my collar. I took shelter in a construction passageway and waved my arm at a passing cab. The address I had been given meant nothing to me, but the driver wordlessly pulled away from the curb and into the stream of traffic heading west. He was following a foreign-language program on the radio with great interest. We drove down narrow corridors threaded between tall towers whose sides glowed black and orange in the darkness, through blinking intersections and echoing boulevards. The skyscrapers gave way to older, more human architecture. The streets became cheerful and welcoming, lined with boutiques and restaurants that had the kind of expensively dirty look that marks a cresting wave of gentrification.

After blocks of parks and promenades and increasingly dingy bars, the driver pulled up beside a storefront. It was completely empty save for an old soccer ball that had what appeared to be a cactus growing out of it. A series of numerals and diacritical marks were plastered over the entrance. He looked back at me expectantly, and I gathered that we had arrived. I paid the fare and stepped into the rain with my suitcase. There was a black door with a tarnished lion's-head knocker beside the mysterious shop, and above the lintel was the address I'd been given. The handle wouldn't open, and the number I had been told to call when I arrived went straight to voice mail. The rain was falling more softly, now, and the wet asphalt mirrored the golden light of the street lamps into a yellow sky. I sat on my suitcase in the shelter of the awning and sent a text. The minutes ticked past.

I was almost resigned to a night in the park when I heard a clatter of steps and the turning of a deadbolt. The door swung open, and framed in the darkness was a man wearing a pair of old sweatpants and a T-shirt advertising a sinister-looking hot dog franchise. He blinked unhappily in the cold, started to speak, and then cleared his throat and tried again.

"It's not the first, is it?" he asked, in a way that suggested he was aware of the date.

I nodded silently.

"Are you sure?"

"Yes," I said. "I mean, technically. The arrangement I made with Charles … he said I could arrive evening of the thirtieth. I was under the impression he'd cleared that with you."

"Uh huh."

"I'm Alexander Otkazov. I believe we corresponded about me subletting the apartment?" This was more a statement than a question, but I was standing on an unknown street in a strange city with everything I owned packed in a suitcase, and I hesitated to make the point more forcefully.

"That was probably in the email, wasn't it?"

"I … believe so."

"Right. Okay. Well, come in, then." He led me up a narrow flight of stairs that terminated in a dark room. The man gestured to a short hallway leading to the front of the building. "You're in the room at the end. That was Charles's. I'm at the back. Sasha is next to you. Washroom is on the other side of the kitchen. I'm working early tomorrow morning, but I can show you around the rest of the place in the evening. Or Sasha can. Or you can show yourself around. It's not a big apartment. I'm Ted, by the way," he said, extending his hand.

I shook it, and felt calluses on his upper palm and on the pads of his fingers. "Pleasure to meet you, Ted."

"Make yourself comfortable. Or whatever."

Ted disappeared into the darkness at the back of the apartment and I carried my suitcases to my room. It was completely bare, with a bay window overlooking the street. I took off my coat and laid a towel on the floor beside one of the walls, padding the pile with a few sweaters, and lay down. The ceiling was covered in whorls of textured plaster. The pale, periodic chime of a streetcar bell rang outside the window. I listened to the mechanical shudder of great metal bodies stopping and starting until, somewhere in the depths of the night, I fell asleep.

II

I AWOKE THE next morning to pale light shining through the dirty glass of the window, illuminating things I had not noticed in the dark. The walls were cracked and discoloured, cross-hatched with scratches and lines where furniture had been moved and repositioned and moved again. The closet doors hung at odd angles, and there was a slant to the floor that inclined me toward the wall. These imperfections had a comforting effect. However much money there was in Toronto, the neighbourhood I had moved into was marked by a reassuring kind of decay.

I might have stayed there in the crook of the floor the entire morning had the need to use a washroom not impressed itself on me. The hallway was stygian after the winter light, and I didn't notice until I was halfway through the living room that I was not alone. Stretched out under a blanket on a green paisley divan, there was a woman reading a magazine.

"Good morning," she said, looking up. "Welcome to Toronto." The woman's dark eyes were framed by a square-cut bob, and she was wearing a crimson housecoat that looked like it had come from a period drama. She did not seem surprised to see me.

"Are you Sasha?"

"Yes."

"I'm Alexander."

"I know."

"You got the email, then?"

"I got the email."

Sasha returned to her magazine and I made my way to the bathroom. It was covered in beige ceramic tile, and there were intricate arabesques of mould on the ceiling. The toilet didn't flush very well, and I detected the unhappy scent of rotting drywall. A variety of male and female grooming products were arrayed on every available surface.

"Do you want some coffee?" Sasha asked when I emerged. "You can help yourself." She gestured toward a half-full French press on the counter.

On the stove next to it, a very large stainless-steel pot was bubbling with a brownish liquid that smelled agricultural. I poured a cup of coffee and sat down on the only other piece of furniture in the living room, a sort of low bank of mattress foam covered in an afghan, mounted on what appeared to be milk crates. The coffee tasted much better than I expected it to.

"Sorry about that," Sasha said, looking up from her magazine. "Ted built it last summer. He's become very attached to it. I don't want you to get the impression we can't afford a second couch. Ted just prefers to make his own furniture. It's his name on the lease, so ..."

"It's quite comfortable."

"I'd be careful with that kind of politeness. He might insist on building you a bed."

"I do need a bed, actually. Charles hadn't mentioned ..."

"Yeah, I think he actually meant to leave you some furniture. But the bed he was using belonged to an, uh, ex, or something, and she came by to pick it up a couple of weeks ago. I'd take a careful look at Ted's bed before you take him up on any carpentry offers."

As it turned out, Ted had put his skills to work on a number of domestic construction projects. The living room was smaller than it had seemed the night before, a series of shelves in fantastical geometric shapes hanging from the walls and suspended from the ceiling using hooks and rope. It opened onto an equally small kitchen done in blue Mediterranean tilework. Most of the shelves were empty. Sasha encouraged me to use as much room as I wanted.

"He found this old turntable and hi-fi system by the side of the street last summer and decided he was going to get into record collecting, and built all these shelves to store the records he was going to buy. But he only picked up, like, four albums, by bands his university friends were in, and then lost interest. That's all we really listen to. So if you've got books or records or whatever, feel free. I've been using them to store back issues of *Vogue*. Trying to raise the tone around here, you know? Did you bring any records? That's a shame. I'm getting a bit sick of Ted's 'collection,' to be honest."

Sasha slid gracefully from the divan and tied the belt of her dressing gown around her narrow waist. In her slippers, she was nearly as tall as I was. She had the purposeful walk of someone used to running things.

The apartment was a long, narrow rectangle, with rooms stacked back from the street one behind the other. The main living area divided mine and Sasha's rooms at the front from Ted's at the back. A narrow corridor running beside Ted's room connected these common spaces to a long rooftop patio that opened onto the back alley. An extensive network of gardens had been built along the cinder block parapets of the rooftop, and out of these poured a jungle of dead vegetable matter. Plastic planter pots dotted the concrete deck, and here and there could be seen the withered remains of tomato plants clinging grimly to bamboo stakes. A large trough of earth running along the back wall of the roof had a tree growing out of it.

"It's paradise in the summer," said Sasha, leading me back inside, "so long as you don't mind the raccoons or the rats or the smell of bad meat. The dumpster out back belongs to the butcher's next door. We throw our garbage in there at night. Otherwise we'd have to buy bags from the city."

Sasha's main job was waiting tables at a restaurant, but she also reviewed art shows for one of the local newspapers. She had moved in with Ted the year before after a breakup had forced her out of a third-floor loft in one of the cooler retrofitted warehouse buildings off Queen West. ("It was the best apartment I've ever lived in. Sean was absolutely not the best boyfriend I've ever had, but this apartment ... You're from Montreal, so maybe you don't understand.") Sasha and Ted had done fine art degrees at the same university, but she'd stopped booking shows a couple of years after graduation because she was tired of writing explanatory essays. ("I made an abstract painting. It uses a lot of red. Do I really need to pretend it's a meditation on menstrual blood and the Catholic Church? I mean, Jesus Christ.") She was quick to explain that she wasn't planning on staying in the apartment long. In fact, she was constantly on the lookout for new places: it was just hard to argue with the rent. ("Four hundred and fifty for a bedroom, with a back roof, a decent kitchen, and three excellent bars within a two-minute walk. Take that into account, and living with Ted really isn't so bad.")

"So what's your thing?" she asked, taking a seat by the kitchen window and lighting a cigarette. "You a sculptor? A DJ?"

"Not really."

"Does that mean you have, like, an 'artistic practice' that you never actually do? Or do you mean you're actually not an artist, and know Charles through axe-throwing or something?"

"I don't know Charles through axe-throwing."

"Yeah, you don't seem like the type."

"I trained as a pianist."

"Right."

"It didn't work out." I coughed politely. I wasn't generally opposed to smoking indoors, but Sasha had forgotten to open the window, and the kitchen had quickly filled with a yellowy haze.

Sasha began frantically jerking the window up with one hand and waving the clouds of smoke into the narrow alley between our building and the next.

"I always forget to do that," she said apologetically. She slid the pack of cigarettes across the table. "Help yourself. It'll give your lungs a chance to build up some resistance."

We sat by the window, smoking, and I gave an abbreviated version of how I had come to leave Montreal. Sasha was inquisitive but easily bored, and before long the conversation moved on to other things. I was grateful. Sasha was beautiful in an aristocratic way that was both intimidating and vaguely asexual, and she had a kind of energetic detachment that made me feel like I was being interviewed for an extremely cool job I wasn't qualified for. It was very stimulating.

"So you don't, like, have work or anything?" Sasha finally asked, after I finished explaining that I no longer had any real confidence in the potential of contemporary art music to radically expand the horizons of piano repertoire in particular, and the Western musical tradition in general.

"Not exactly."

"Charles sort of suggested you had a few things lined up. He said rent wasn't going to be an issue."

"It won't be."

"Right. The thing is, this city has a way of eating into your savings account. Not to put too fine a point on it. I can put in a word for you with the manager at the place where I'm working, if you decide you want to supplement your revenue stream. It's a kind of high-end brunch spot down on King Street. The tips are good, everything else is bad. But I make more in two months serving three shifts a week there than I used to make working an entire semester as a sessional instructor. So, you know, think about it."

Sasha had said all this so matter-of-factly that it was hard to tell whether she was concerned about the possibility of my skipping out on the rent or was merely being polite. I told her I'd let her know. She briskly explained a few further elements of housekeeping to me, including that I was under no circumstances to eat any of Ted's jam, and stubbed out her cigarette on a saucer and flicked it into the alley. Wrapping her housecoat tightly around her shoulders, she returned to the divan and took up her magazine. I sat at the window until the last ribbon of smoke disappeared.

III

—————◆—————

IN THE DAYS that followed, I established a routine of rewarding leisure. I slept until late in the morning, and in the afternoon took long walks through the West End and down to the lakefront. The weather, though cold, lacked the vicious edge I had gotten used to in Montreal. Each day brought new diversions. I explored the boutiques of Queen West and the last remaining Maltese cafés of the Junction; I cut my way through the stench of new money and Catholic nostalgia on Roncesvalles and Little Italy; I watched the swans beat each other for crusts of bread by the breakwater. I became acquainted with the midnight world of Ossington Avenue. My senses seemed sharper, the world denser and more textured. Those frosty December days were not without their anxieties, but I still remember very clearly certain details from those walks — the scrollwork on a pair of wooden corbels on an old house in Kensington Market, the knot of sparrows nesting in a bush of witch hazel. I almost felt happy.

Ted got home from work at seven o'clock most nights, and the majority of Sasha's restaurant shifts were for brunch. In the evening we would gather in the kitchen and listen to one of Ted's four records and talk about what had or had not happened to us that day. Ted had a connoisseur's attitude toward beer, and the endless pots bubbling on the stovetop were the mash for his homebrew. We drank out of mason jars while Ted led me point by point through the beer-making process, and what distinguished a Pilsner from a lager. Sasha didn't bother to feign interest. She'd heard all this before, and she considered beer to be calorically wasteful. Her preference was for extremely dirty martinis made with cheap gin and expensive vermouth.

Sasha was one of the few Torontonians actually born there. Her parents had emigrated from Hong Kong in the 1980s, and during their first decade in Toronto established a small design firm specializing in print advertising in English and Cantonese. Their venture was so successful that when their only daughter had completed her primary education, she was sent to an Anglican boarding school somewhere in Forest Hill, as a day student. This was followed by a brief stint at the University of Toronto, where she picked up and dropped a variety of subjects in quick succession, eventually receiving a degree in drawing and painting at OCAD.

Unfortunately, her parents' business had fallen victim to the irreversible collapse in fortunes that hit the newspaper industry in the first years of the 2000s. They salvaged parts of the company and pivoted to digital work, but the relationships they had built up with Chinese- and English-language newspapers were dealt a near-fatal blow. By the time Sasha graduated, she had taken a job at a diner to cover her tuition fees. She came out of these experiences a confirmed atheist with a pronounced, if largely performative, sympathy for the tenets of Marxism-Leninism and an abiding hatred for "rich fucks."

Most of this I pieced together on my own. Sasha didn't like talking about her life before university, a reticence made only more remarkable by the total candour with which she shared stories from her adulthood. At OCAD, the repressed Protestantism of her early life had flowered into the healthy bonhomie of a party girl. At twenty-five she had met a minor art critic from Paris on the train to Montreal. They fell in love when he asked if the Quebecois couple sitting across from them also sounded like peasants to her. She returned to Canada at twenty-seven, disillusioned as much with art as with the Frenchman. She took a job at the restaurant to make rent and started to take writing more seriously. ("If that idiot could build a career off of blowing cigarette smoke in people's faces and declaring things to be '*dérivée*,' so can I," she explained.)

All through those final weeks of December, we spent our nights smoking on the back roof, watching the lights go on in the neighbouring apartments, the slow change of the colours on the CN Tower off in the distance. I found myself able to think about Montreal without wincing. I even started telling little jokes about my life there. To my own great shock and surprise, my plan seemed to have worked.

IV

REALITY CAME CRASHING in with the new year. Filled with disgust after a particularly costly night of shouting at Sasha and Ted over a live band at the Cameron House, I faced the music and looked at my bank balance. The mocking little numbers on my phone told me, in no uncertain terms, that I needed to start working again. I had a cigarette with Sasha that evening and delicately suggested I might not turn down the prospect of a job if one was available.

"It's a bad time of year, Alexander," she said, blowing smoke out through her perfect nostrils. "You know what the number-one financial resolution people make in January is? Spend less money eating out. And I don't know if you've noticed, but the weather makes that kind of easy. It doesn't last, of course, but we're definitely in belt-tightening season."

"I thought that might be the case."

"You should have said something last month. We were hiring before Christmas."

"Right."

"Are you going to be able to make rent?"

"Don't worry about it."

"That's not encouraging. Look, one of the barbacks was caught doing coke in the main dining room after his shift ended, so they might decide to replace him. The head manager likes me these days. Give me your résumé and I'll put in a good word."

I crafted a CV so inflated it was almost fictitious, and waited for a phone call. It came a couple of days later: a neutral-sounding voice asked if I could come in for an interview, and I rushed down to Liberty Village, hair still wet from the shower.

As in so many of the old industrial neighbourhoods, where the solid manufacturing economy of the twentieth century had given way to the steroidal finance capitalism of the twenty-first, attempts to preserve Liberty Village's architecture only rendered it ridiculous. Sheer glass fragments jutted precipitously out of the roofs of three-storey brick shopfronts. Brand-new English pubs designed to look as though they'd been built in the nineteenth century sat cheek to jowl with the corrugated steel of squat box stores. Everything was scrubbed and new and extremely well lit. I felt like a trespasser in someone else's erotic dream. The restaurant was in a converted warehouse standing on a rise off Atlantic Avenue, overlooking the rail line that curved gently into the heart of the city. A broad flight of concrete steps led up from street level, and beside it a ramp rose in thoughtful cutbacks to an elevated promenade that ran beside a showroom selling fast furniture marketed to the upwardly mobile. I made my way up the stairs, shoes crunching over the salt that covered every surface. The people of Toronto, I surmised, were extremely litigious about ice fall incidents.

Inside, the restaurant had the unnerving look of a place that had been designed to pass off thrift as good taste. The ceiling was impossibly high, and under the painted steel girders, all kinds of flowing bits of fabric were suspended from steel wires — intended, perhaps, to make the space feel less cavernous. The colour scheme was a blend of light pastels and heavy charcoal, and the seating appeared to have been designed by a sex pervert who wanted to maximize patrons' discomfort in ways that would make them suggestible to arcane forms of depravity. It was completely empty.

I hadn't been waiting long when a young woman emerged from behind a curtain near the front vestibule. She ushered me around a corner to the bar, where another young woman, even taller and skinnier than the first, was slowly shredding a piece of celery with a potato peeler. She nodded at me with calculated neutrality. I'd barely had the chance to get uncomfortable when a third woman appeared suddenly from a set of swinging doors and told the celery shredder to make two lattes.

"Do you like lattes?" she asked in the faintest Berliner accent.

"A latte would be —"

"I'd love a beer, of course, but it's not five o'clock yet."

"That's —"

"Just a bit of fun, of course! We try not to drink on the job here," she said, giving the celery shredder an exaggerated and slightly deranged wink. The celery shredder tightened the muscles of her mouth in a way that was, technically, a smile. "Sasha said you're looking for a job. Do you have any restaurant experience?"

I pushed my résumé across the bar, and she glanced over it quickly.

"You're from Montreal, I take it?"

"Most recently."

"Good city for restaurants."

"Yeah."

"Based on this, I assume you've tended bar."

I thought it best to let her assume what she wanted. I had spent a lot of time in bars, after all, and a lot of time making drinks, and, for a few disastrous months, had even been employed as a dishwasher. I felt this was close enough to being a bartender.

"Only for six months, though!" the woman said, as if she was catching me out in something. "Unfortunately, we can't hire you to work behind the bar with this experience. But we do have an opening for a steward. We'd need you for two weekend shifts to start, plus one weeknight. You'd be working for minimum plus a cut of the tips. How does that sound? Does that sound good? We'd need a commitment right away. Can you make a commitment?"

I made a commitment. By the time I walked back out into the ice and the salt and the wind, the darkness had set in completely and I'd been booked for a training shift. I bought myself a bottle of the good Canadian Club on the way back to the apartment.

Sasha was waiting for me with an empty glass. "I'd offer my congratulations," she said, "but it's unlikely you'll be thanking me for this in two months."

V

IT ISN'T POSSIBLE to really know a city without working in it. Not because work forces you to interact with unpleasant people you would otherwise avoid (which can easily be managed by hanging around an art gallery or going to the beach), but because a city is essentially a massive production line, and only by entering its infernal machinery can you see how it operates. This was the main reason I'd avoided having a job whenever possible: there are things I preferred not to know. The work I had, reluctantly, picked up over the years — playing music, teaching piano lessons, freelance writing — allowed me to remain aloof and mobile, retaining the illusion of freedom.

I liked jobs where I was paid to make a very specific contribution. Jobs with titles like "head of product acquisition" or "customer relations associate" had, until very recently, left me with a sense of incipient dread.

Working at a restaurant was far from ideal. But it was a low-investment way of paying the bills. And unlike my peers, whose more purely North American pedigree allowed them the illusion that art is subversive, I understood very well that musicians are always in a basically symbiotic relationship with the ruling class. I might have preferred playing piano to pouring drinks, but I was not stupid enough to believe these were fundamentally different things.

After I got over the initial humiliation, being a steward was rather peaceful, compared with other jobs in the restaurant. The premise was so absurdly simple (carrying food to customers, carting away dirty dishes) that I quickly learned to dissociate from all the people yelling at me. It became a very pure experience of time. Packing up a plate of fifteen-dollar French fries for a customer so they could throw them out the next morning took about two and a half minutes. Clearing, cleaning, and resetting a high-top took around three minutes, if the napkins hadn't already been folded. Do these two tasks back to back, and I'd killed five whole minutes. If I needed to clear a four-person dinner immediately after, that was another five minutes, which meant I'd be one-sixth of a way through the hour, or one-thirtieth of the way through a five-hour shift. So long as I avoided thinking about it in the scope of my life, it wasn't at all depressing.

Of course, moving things about was only a small part of the job. Most of it was managing the anxieties of the servers, the manager, the kitchen staff, the customers, and anyone else who might wander in. This, too, was a matter of mental discipline: all I needed to do was pretend I was not doing what I was doing — or, rather, that I was not the one doing it. I was not myself, but a character in a film whose only interest lay in doing the task assigned. The entire service economy rested on these kinds of wilful imaginative acts: the customer entered the restaurant hungry, ill-tempered, looking for an experience that would be nourishing, convenient, and socially pleasing. They put themselves at the mercy of strangers who touched their food, recorded how much they ate and drank, handled their dirty napkins, cleaned up their spills, and generally judged them on their breeding, table manners, and generosity. The psychic strain involved in engaging in this practice week after week, year after year, would have been enormous if the diners weren't able to convince themselves that the person serving them was a social inferior whose opinion didn't really matter.

Having thus been put into the position of the subordinate, the server or steward was faced with the problem of how to retain their dignity, which could be done only by creating some kind of distance between themselves as a worker and themselves as a person. Money was at the heart of this relationship not only because money was the lubricant that facilitated the exchange, but because it served as a justification. The fact that our customers had money, and I wanted money, gave me licence to debase myself in all kinds of ways. At the same time, it allowed the customer to not feel that they were, in fact, debasing me. Money hovered over these routine encounters like a dense fog, an essential veil that allowed us all to preserve some measure of self-respect.

And where there was money, there was sex. The servers fluttered and pouted and told dirty jokes, the kitchen resembled a never-ending stag party, and grabbing one's crotch was an established way of answering a question. The bawdiness was alienating and exciting. I couldn't remember the last time I'd slept with someone (there had been many patchy nights during those bleak final months in Montreal; some of the things I remembered were probably dreams, and some of the things I thought were dreams might, perhaps, have happened). But even at the best of times, sex, for me, was basically meteorological: it came into my life with the same unpredictable regularity as an ice storm, and left about the same amount of damage in its wake. I understood that the sexual economy could be manipulated, that with enough charm and attention you could talk someone into bed, but this seemed an achievement on par with splitting the atom. And so I kept my distance from the restaurant's hypogeal erotic currents, and left as soon as my shift was over.

This changed on a Tuesday evening in February, when I burst into the dish pit with a tub full of dirty china to find a tall, muscular individual with brown skin and a pencil-thin moustache polishing glassware and singing to himself. He was the most beautiful man I'd ever seen.

"*Notte e giorno faticar, per chi nulla sa gradir, piova e vento sopportar, mangier male e mal dormer.*" He swirled a bit of linen around the inside of a wineglass before pausing for the big line: "*Voglio far il gentiluomo!*"

"*Che tumulto,*" I said, sliding the dishes onto one of the side tables.

He stopped polishing his glass and looked at me suspiciously. "You're not Italian, are you?"

"God, no."

"A musician, then."

"In another life."

"I hope I can rely on you not to tell anyone what that aria is about."

"It's Leporello talking about how much he likes his job."

"Yeah, exactly," said the singer, going back to his polishing.

"My name's Alexander," I said.

"Sev," he said, flipping the cloth over his shoulder and shaking my hand. "You'll never believe the conversation I just had with one of the sous-chefs. He asked if I was practising for a musical. A musical! I have two master's degrees."

"Most people don't even have one master's degree."

"Exactly. Like I'm going to perform in a fucking musical."

I started polishing a wineglass. There was something about Sev that made me immediately want to be liked by him. "Is that your polishing aria?" I asked.

"It's whatever I want it to be. I'm playing Leporello in a chamber production this spring, so as you can imagine ..."

"Of course."

"Are you working on anything right now?"

"Oh, I've left all that behind. I don't even own a piano anymore."

"I didn't know that was possible."

"Lots of people don't own pianos."

"Yeah, I mean the other part. Like, one day you just decided you didn't want to play music? How does that work."

"It's a long story."

"I'll bet it is. Don't tell it to me, though. I can't deal with that kind of chaotic energy right now."

I picked up another glass and started polishing. There were a lot of glasses, and the manager had told me the lull wouldn't last forever, but Sev had stopped working and seemed slightly agitated.

"Just to be clear, you're still *into* music, right? You still listen to it? This isn't some weird religious thing?"

"Definitely not a religious thing. It's just the playing I've given up. I'm actually listening to a lot of Feldman these days. People talk a lot about the more overtly experimental work, you know, the big sixties and seventies pieces, but his early piano and chamber work in the forties and fifties, it's really —"

"Feldman who?"

"— quite bad. Morton Feldman. The New York School guy."

"Sorry, dude, but all that shit sucks. Putting microphones on cacti? Grow up."

"There's more to it than that."

"Sure there is," Sev said, attacking the next wineglass. "Scores with colours instead of notes. Performances where you don't actually play anything. I'm not some kind of conservative freak, but as a singer, it all stops being interesting to me after Britten. I mean, I *understand* it. Dodecaphony, serialism, all that stuff. But for Christ's sake, give me something to work with. Give me a character! Strauss, Berg … you can push the envelope musically without giving up on the psychology, the narrative. And I'd argue that we still haven't completely even exhausted the possibilities of the good old Classical eighteenth century. Especially not now, when decadence is again —"

I didn't find out what decadence was again, because Sev's speech was interrupted by the appearance of our manager, who hissed something about how hands were needed to deliver a plate of sliders.

Sev jerked his chin in the direction of the door and kept polishing.

"Can't you do it? I'm still figuring the situation out here."

"I've been here longer than you."

I picked up the plates from the chef's station and headed out to the floor, where a number of people were already quite mad at me.

When the tables had been reset for the next day and the glasses were gleaming on their shelves, the floor manager invited everyone to have a drink at the bar. Sev told me to try the Rioja, and picked up his discourse on modern music exactly where he'd left off.

"My point is that for all the emphasis on the twentieth-century break, I think there's a lot that can still be learned from the Classical period. Take the economics of music: if you wanted to compose or play back then, you basically needed to sell your soul. To the church, to the aristocracy, to any rich slaver who could pay you. Sound familiar? And speaking purely musically, it was a period of revolutionary change, right? You had Old Bach and Young Bach, the baroque and the Classical, the exhaustion with counterpoint. The movement toward a new kind of secular individualism, freedom from the church and its superstitions. A shift in the ideological weather between generations. It's very fertile ground."

"It was then, at least."

"It can be again … I'm sorry, I've forgotten your name."

"Alexander."

"Alexander. Is it okay if I call you Alex?"

"No, I'd prefer —"

"The eighteenth century is extremely good, Alex, and I'd take twenty-four bars of a Mozart sonata over an entire opera by Debussy any day."

I was about to disagree, but found myself unable to. I hated *Pelléas et Mélisande*. "It depends on which Mozart sonata we're talking about," I said, trying to affect a thoughtful attitude. "But we may have to agree to disagree."

"Bullshit. Tell you what, Tafelmusik is doing a double feature tomorrow night, Mozart's Fortieth and Forty-First, back to back. Tickets are so cheap they're basically free. If you come out of the performance thinking the eighteenth century is a wash, I'll buy you a drink."

I was not in the position to turn down a free drink. Sev gulped down the last of his wine in a very satisfied way and told me to text him the following afternoon. As I put on my coat in the foyer, I could see the skinny bartender smiling as she poured him another glass.

VI

IT SNOWED OVERNIGHT, but the weather turned and by afternoon the slush in the streets had been whipped into a foul meringue. I soon regretted having left my apartment. For reasons that remained opaque to me, every homeowner in Toronto was responsible for clearing the patch of sidewalk directly abutting their house. As these homes were owned by people so rich they traversed the city via levitation, my shoes were white with salt and a film of sand had worked its way into my socks by the time I reached the concert hall. An old man took my ticket at the door and pointed me toward the foyer. Inside, the faces were either craggy with age or ghoulishly young and fashionable. It was unclear where I was meant to sit, or whether any kind of seat assignment system did, in fact, exist. This was Sev's fault, and I was eager to find him so he could see just how much I had been put through.

But then there was a tap on my shoulder, and all of a sudden he was introducing me to a group of old friends he'd just happened to run into, and I had to start laughing and smiling along with the people who had, until moments ago, filled me with anxiety and revulsion. Sev introduced me as a disillusioned pianist, and explained that he had wagered I wouldn't be able to make it through the performance without having my jaded and adolescent prejudice against Mozart exposed for the affectation it was. I responded by making energetic and entirely insincere pronouncements about how music had, in general, only gotten better, and how music of the Classical period was actually deeply degrading to the listener and should be studied strictly as a historical folly, like rockabilly or the Crusades. My blather was cut mercifully short by a discreet usher who told us things were about to get started.

I understood what Sev had been talking about as soon as the music began. The famous opening measures were played with surprising hesitation and pathos, and when the twenty-eighth bar came, it was like a great sun rose over the stage. The musicians were vibrating out of their seats. They played like they'd never heard the hackneyed old progression before, and were discovering for the first time the layers of feeling latent within a simple G Minor scale. It was fun. So fun, in fact, that I didn't mind being reintroduced to all the same old cynical tricks. Or perhaps I just felt generous. Grateful to be at a concert with people I hadn't known forever, people who weren't from Montreal.

These positive feelings created a degree of awkwardness at
the intermission; I felt it necessary, for the sake of appearances,
to pretend I had hated everything. But Sev's friends were good-
natured enough to play along by heaping abuse on me, accusing
me of being an unreconstructed ideologue, a cloth-eared snob
who had long since lost interest in music as a performed thing
and cared about it only as a set of ideas that corresponded with
my own blinkered and ultimately academic view of the world.

When we returned to our seats and the Forty-First began, I
was accustomed enough to the extraordinary level of musician-
ship on display to be reminded of what I found so unpleasant
in Mozart. There was clearly a great intelligence behind the
music, but it was the intelligence of a professional charmer who
expected his audience to be distracted by baubles. Like any con-
jurer, he knew exactly when a darker progression could be used
to add the illusion of depth. But these detours were meant only
to titillate: Mozart glided through his world like a courtier,
seeing the violence and filth but never letting it colour his art.
I refused to be delighted by the breathtaking fugato at the end.

The lights went up and everyone started frantically clap-
ping. The orchestra bowed so many times I began to worry
that the timpanist, who was rather fat, would collapse onto
his drums. I made a concession to manners by rising to my
feet to applaud (it is a well-known fact that in Toronto, even
a symphony performed by deaf orangutans would be entitled
to a standing ovation, so long as at least half of the orangutans
showed up). But I could feel Sev's eyes on me the entire time,
and when we left the concert hall, he insisted I had been converted to his way of seeing things by the vigour of the *molto
allegro*, and invited us all to retire to the Bedford Academy for
a drink.

The Bedford Academy turned out to be an old house north of St. George Station that had, at some indeterminate point, been turned into a bifurcated pub. The front half was tastefully lined with leather-bound books (upon closer inspection, these were revealed to be the proceedings of the Law Society of Upper Canada), while the back half was laid out like a sports bar, with large televisions and framed pictures of curvaceous bums. The server, perhaps doing some quick calculations about our tipping capabilities, suggested we would be most comfortable at a long table jammed under a poster of naked women whose backs had been painted to resemble Pink Floyd albums.

I was seated next to a sad-looking man named Liam, who immediately started talking about the tuning of the instruments, a subject of particular interest to him. Apparently, the performance could not be considered a success from a strictly historical perspective because the orchestra had been tuned to concert pitch. He spoke with a bleating home counties accent, and had the kind of round English face that looks like a bowl of porridge an unwell person has spat into. I looked around the table with a sinking feeling. At the far end, Sev was leaning in to hear what a woman with an exquisite Persian nose (introduced to me as Nousha) had to say about some recent scandal. I wondered if I had been positioned to contain Liam — or, worse, if we had been positioned to contain each other.

"Of course, tuning is only one aspect of a performance. Possibly not even the most important one for most audience members, ha ha. But we must remember that the notion of tuning to four hundred and forty hertz is a modern innovation, one that cannot but distort our experience of pre-nineteenth-century music. We may laugh at Verdi and his four thirty-two hertz, but did you know that Mozart's tuning fork produced a tone at four twenty-one point six hertz, a difference of nearly a semitone? Everything flows from tuning — timbre, pitch, tonal warmth, et cetera — so to claim that you are offering an *authentic* performance and then tuning everything to concert pitch is, I think you'll agree, misleading at best. And this is not, of course, merely a theoretical question! E-flat and G create completely different sonic worlds. We know this from experience, of course, but it isn't *merely* experiential. It's a scientific truth. The sound waves of different keys operate at different frequencies and create different patterns, as has been shown using experiments with water, which I'm sure you've heard about. But what do keys rely on? What is the underlying physical reality that makes 'C Minor' a coherent sonic structure? Tuning. So, by the transitive property, tuning alters our experience of keys, which in turn creates a different experience of music. Now, if the conductor had opted to use baroque tuning, at four-fifteen hertz, this would have rectified some of these problems. But not, of course, all of them, insofar as the experience of listening to music in the eighteenth century (and perhaps more importantly, performing it) was significantly more chaotic, pitch-wise, than it is today. Merely replacing one standard tuning with another standard tuning does little to bring us closer to the conditions under which the music was originally experienced."

"That's fascinating. I wonder —"

"Which is why — you'll pardon me for interrupting, but I am getting to my central point here, and I don't mean to be immodest, but I do think it is a significant and even radical point, given the current debates happening in musicology and performance theory, and a point that could go a long way toward correcting some of the misconceptions about 'progress' in music and the meaning of the avant-garde in a post-minimalist, post-aleatoric world. Which is to say that the real missed opportunity this evening was to confront the audience with the true revolutionary potential of the past, to deconstruct (as you fans of the postmodern love to say) the baroque tradition not by disrupting continuity or tonality or introducing elements of randomness or engaging in mathematical experiments, but by performing the music on the instruments it would originally have been performed on, sung in the style it originally would have been sung in, using a different tuning for each piece, and demanding that the audience acknowledge that this is what historically faithful performance really means. It would be much ruder and more unsettling for the subscribers than whatever it is Fera Civitatem is trying to do."

"I'm sorry, what's that?"

"That radical Twitter musicologist you people love so much."

"Sorry?"

"The person who organizes those guerrilla performances in old warehouses and bricked-up theatres. They wrote that extremely boring social media manifesto about creating new experiences of music for the twenty-first century."

"I'm new here. And I'm not on Twitter."

"Oh really? Well, it's all nonsense."

"What's all nonsense?" Nousha had turned to us and was looking at Liam confrontationally.

"You know what I'm talking about."

"If you keep obsessing over radicals like this, people are going to start making assumptions."

"They're not radical *enough* is the problem."

"I'm sorry to interrupt," I said, "but could someone tell me what this is about?"

The individual conversations that had been humming along grew quiet. Sev looked somewhat put out.

"It's this new 'experimental' 'collective' ... well, not exactly experimental —" Sev began before he was interrupted by Nousha.

"About a year ago, some anonymous Twitter account announced that there would be a completely new staging of *Salome*. Whoever was running the account said it was the voice of a new music collective who were going to 'revolutionize how audiences interact with opera,' or something like that. The big plan was to put on these guerilla concerts in warehouses and abandoned theatres and shipyards and stuff. People who wanted to attend needed to sign up to receive an announcement on the day of the performance, telling them to go to such-and-such an address. I guess a lot of people thought it was a pretty fun idea, and the first one was a big success. There were all these crazy cellphone videos of the show going around afterward. It looked really wild. And the people who went said it was actually way above what they were expecting, musically speaking. But then they ruffled feathers by putting up this big manifesto about how performance of classical music has grown stagnant and reactionary and today's composers need to rediscover the libidinal side of music. Pretty harmless stuff, if you think about it."

"It was barely coherent postmodern bullshit straight from an undergrad seminar, hardly worth —"

"Would you be surprised to hear that Sev didn't approve?" Nousha said, interrupting him with an ironic smile. "A lot of people didn't approve, actually, but the group, or collective, or whatever it was put on another show last spring, in this old theatre on Spadina. It's got a grocery store or something on the main floor. I don't know how they managed it, but they broke into the back door and anyone who'd signed up to attend was snuck in by the organizers. People who went said the music was like nothing they'd ever heard — they took a bunch of early modern material and played it through about fifteen different synthesizers and an old harmonium to create this primitive, hypnotic effect. People were dancing like it was a rave."

"That wasn't the only way it resembled a rave," Sev added.

"What do you mean?"

"Ever been to a rave?"

"Sure."

"Well, there you go. Basically Gomorrah."

"Sev wasn't there," said Nousha, "so his opinion doesn't count. Most of the people I know who went had a good time. I'm not sure it's really doing all that much for classical music, but if the kids want to enjoy themselves, who is it hurting? It's not like they're throwing Molotov cocktails through the windows of Roy Thomson Hall."

"That's where you're wrong, though!" said Sev, now quite animated. "If they just want to throw a party and do a bit of MDMA, it wouldn't matter. What I object to is the idea that somehow this *hedonism* is morally or spiritually meaningful, that it brings out something in the music that concert halls have suppressed. The whole point of concert halls is to be sedate and unstimulating, so the music speaks for itself."

Liam, who had periodically attempted to establish a beachhead in the conversation, broke through Sev's monologue with a quavering point of his own.

"As I said before — and as I have, if you'll pardon me, been trying to say for the past while — if we take these people's manifesto at face value, we must confront the fundamentally conservative nature of this call to establish an alternate space of musical experiment. It is not the manifesto of revolutionists, but of quietists. Why not retake the concert halls themselves?"

A silence, perhaps thoughtful, overtook the table. A great many sips were simultaneously taken. Nousha asked whether he was suggesting some kind of stockholder takeover or a literal armed rebellion, Liam began offering a stuttering clarification, and the conversation fragmented along a half-dozen different trajectories. I thumbed beer foam from my upper lip and realized with some surprise that I was enjoying myself.

VII

———

I WOKE LATE the next morning. Little golden bars of light fell across the walls of my room, and above me an abandoned spiderweb hung tenuously from a whorl of plaster, moving whenever a disturbance in the air caught its folds. I had grasped something important in my sleep. Though it was now forgotten, a residue of meaning and purpose remained. I pulled the curtains and sat down at my desk. The temperature had dropped again overnight, and the clarity of the frozen street awoke feelings keen and analytic. I opened my laptop.

I had looked up Fera Civitatem when I got home the night before. It truly was anonymous: neither the address itself nor the associated webpage had any information about who was behind the project. Even the promotional photographs and video clips were shot and edited in such a way as to make it impossible to make out faces or even general racial or ethnic markers. In the wash of vermilion light, there was only form and outline, and a seething threnody. This was surprising; if there is one thing classical music performers and composers share, it is an insatiable desire to be listed prominently in official programs. It might be possible to put together a roster of musicians of this calibre willing to perform for free, or to embrace a more club-like atmosphere, but not if they weren't getting formal recognition.

There was also the question of the venue. Nousha had said the concert took place in an old theatre on Spadina, and so far as I could tell, there was only one place it could have been: the old Oren Theatre at the corner of Spadina and Dundas. A brief bout of Googling revealed that the building was now slated for demolition. The previous owner, Chinatown Fruit and Vegetable, had sold the property to a developer after an incident the CBC described as "a break-in that raised questions about neighbourhood safety." The *Toronto Star* was more explicit: "Chinatown Fruit and Vegetable agreed to sell the defunct Oren Theatre to the Kilbride Development Corporation after a rave led to electrical damage and two overdoses." Fera Civitatem, it would seem, had earned its name.

It had been some time since I had thought of anything as a story. But working at a restaurant reminded me that there were hard and less hard ways of making money, and, all things considered, writing about music was one of the less hard ones. The magazine piece I'd written about the Société de musique contemporaine du Québec had paid for my train ticket out of

Montreal and my first month's rent. Whatever my intentions had been when I arrived in Toronto, I began to wonder if it wasn't okay (mature, even) to venture back into this world, now that I was clear-eyed and free of illusions. More to the point (I told myself), as long as music meant Montreal and Montreal music, I would remain a prisoner. As I watched a dog urinate on a lamppost, it occurred to me that the only chance I had of severing the psychic connection was to symbolically revisit the scene of my trauma by immersing myself in music again, equipped this time with the wisdom garnered during my previous descent into the underworld. Imagining it this way cheered me up a bit. Writing about Fera Civitatem was actually a psychologically necessary step in my emancipation from the past.

I brought the matter up with Sev at our next shift together, but he brushed me off rather coldly — so coldly that I might have been hurt, were I not immediately absorbed by the mathematically impossible task of balancing several large plates of eggs on various parts of my arm so a table of wolfish social media influencers would all get their food at the same precise moment. When I had time to reflect, I felt a little foolish. I didn't know Sev all that well, and the concerts obviously meant something very specific and maddening to him. If I wanted us to be friends, it might be better to start on a more agreeable foot. And perhaps there were better ways to get in touch with the people who would be able to tell me more.

Polishing the last of the glassware later that night, I mentioned to Sev how much I'd enjoyed the concert and asked him what he thought of Joseph Losey's *Don Giovanni*, which I untruthfully told him I'd just rewatched. This topic carried us through setting the tables, the staff drink, and out into the street when the lights had finally been turned out. We walked east along King, the wind whipping a curtain of fine snow from the overpass. I felt a certain unplaceable affection for Sev; I was glad we were walking together through this cold, late-winter evening. There was a playful and ever-present edge of irony in his talk, an ambiguity of phrasing and tone that made me want to watch his mouth as he spoke, to judge his meaning by the curve of his lips. And yet, ebullient as he was, he had a gentle way of moving through the world. The hardness that had come to the surface was, I began to suspect, simply proof of the fundamental respect he had for the people around him. It wasn't until we'd walked all the way up to Dundas that I realized I had no idea where he lived.

"Oh, I'm in the Annex," he said cheerfully. "I usually take the streetcar, but I figured you'd like some company." He walked off into the darkness whistling "Madamina" as I waited for the light to change.

Back in my room, I opened my laptop and navigated to Fera Civitatem's website. It was laid out on a basic template, the kind you get free from a digital publishing outfit. The landing page consisted of a clean bullet-point list of what were presumably recent concerts (the last one, which had taken place on October 22, 2014, was "The Garden of Earthly Delights"). The sidebar menu had only three entries. I clicked through to "About" and read the manifesto again.

> Our music is sick, and it has sickened us. We pitch between hieratic abjection and narcissistic consumerism on an ocean of our own vomit. We slurp back the pablum fed to us through wet gums; we fill our bellies with syrup and heavy cream and shit our guts out in the bleak hours of the afternoon.

We reach with quivering fingers to hit the space bar on our laptop; we want to hear "Ode to Joy" again. Every year we drag ourselves through the city's reek and filth to Roy Thomson, to Koerner Hall, to the Winter Garden Theatre, to the Four Seasons Centre, praying that this season's sugary confections will give us relief. We creep away self-soiled and half-asleep. We listen to the train howling and screeching through the underground. We remember having liked art, once.

Our music is sick, and it has sickened us. We have forgotten that it is vicious and cruel; we have pulled its teeth and mutilated its genitals, and painted our academies red with its blood. As a consequence, our music has become very obedient. We wonder where it goes at night. We try to forget the glottal whimpers we hear in the darkness at the bottom of the garden. We sometimes feel our music is watching us very quietly. We aren't sure if it remembers when we worshipped it as a god. We try to coax out a hosanna, but the taste of bile rises in our throats.

Our music is sick, and it has sickened us. We have fallen into syphilitic reveries. The only way to recover our health is through a cleansing fever. We must be exorcised. The body must dance as if palsied, and we must let ourselves be bruised and beaten by music that snarls at the whip and refuses the comfort of the cage. We must let our music run wild. We must learn to be afraid of it again. We must let it bite us and become rabid. We must sink into the fever to rise again.

Fera Civitatem is the fever. We will intoxicate you and leave you cleansed.

I opened the window to let in some fresh air. What nonsense. The fact that the group had given themselves a Latin name made the whole thing seem even more ludicrous. Had I not known that it had already sparked a passionate response from at least some elements of the music scene, it would have struck me as juvenile, the kind of thing a group of teenagers might do for a school project. But the Instagram and Twitter posts scrolling down along the sidebar bore witness to its popularity.

I'd been initially sympathetic to Sev's assessment. The criticisms these people were making could be made about anything. No concrete argument or program was put forward. No attempt was made to distinguish what actually made them different from any other music company. The language was flatulent and ostentatious; whoever had written it seemed very pleased with themselves. But this led me to the root of the problem: if they were this lost up their own assholes, why didn't they take credit for it? Hucksterism is hardly looked down on in art music. Controversies launch careers. It was hard to believe anyone capable of writing like this was sincere, but it was also hard to imagine that someone so insincere would carry on a time-consuming anonymous bit for so long. The only logical conclusion was that they were playing it straight. But who could be sincere about this kind of thing? They'd have to be delusional.

Delusional, or — and this was the conclusion to which I began circling closer and closer on that mild February afternoon — possessed of a great deal of time and money.

VIII

———

MONEY WAS SOMETHING much on my mind in those days. It was hard to avoid. Working in Liberty Village, I was becoming aware of the subtle gradations of wealth. Successful professionals enjoying a Sunday morning off were different from the start-up crowd, who were different in turn from new-media types. Our restaurant wasn't patronized by the truly powerful, but our demographic was distinguished by an aggressive identification with the cultural and political elite. They made their careers out of connecting people, managing brands, poaching ideas, researching new shades of pink. They could squeeze money out of the margins but they couldn't conjure it out of thin air. A million dollars was still serious money for them. Occasionally, I walked out the swinging door that divided the front of house from the steaming kitchen and caught sight of an aging character actor or B-list singer at one of the plush banquettes at the far end of the dining room. More frequently, I delivered food to a table of vaguely familiar faces only to realize later that they all worked for one of the porn studios the next building over.

Because my duties consisted of bringing things to people's tables and taking them away, I had plenty of opportunities to eavesdrop. You can hear a lot, reaching between elbows to extract smudged mimosa flutes: about what films were being shot in the warehouses of Leslieville, which start-up had received Y Combinator funding, how dramatically the quality of cocaine available in Toronto had decreased over the past couple of years. The information was not, for the most part, useful to me, but it had the cumulative effect of making me wonder whether I might one day be the served rather than the server. In such close physical proximity to people who could barely conjugate their verbs and yet carelessly ran up five-hundred-dollar tabs for breakfasts that were, when you got right down to it, just eggs, flour, pork belly, and booze, it was hard to believe I couldn't find myself in their position if I only applied myself. And yet at the same time, I felt a deep revulsion for these careless and vapid people, their brand mergers, their houseboat threesomes.

I had thought of the rich as another species, a kind of rare fungus that reproduces asexually. The idea that I could be wealthy — that, indeed, I could have been wealthy *already* had I simply made better choices — was vertiginous. When I served tables of young people whose parents or grandparents had come from the far corners of the globe, I couldn't help thinking that my own origins were not so different. It was just that they had judged their odds in the worlds of management and administration and gambled accordingly, and I had wasted my youth behind a keyboard, sweating over all the sounds that could be wrung out of the A-sharp above Middle C.

It had been different in Montreal. Not because Montreal was poorer than Toronto (although it was), but because snobbery had insulated me against it. Until very near the end, I had hung on to the belief that art had its own kind of aristocracy. What was disconcerting about the sideways glimpses into the lives of the successful that the restaurant provided was its libidinal effect, the way it stimulated and aroused desires I had long been too apathetic to feel. If I disliked the entitled and immaculately groomed tech CEOs who crowded in every Saturday morning, it was not because I believed myself superior to them, but because I envied their simplicity. To desire nothing more than to spend Saturday mornings eating pancakes next to women with very successful Instagram accounts seemed a fundamentally healthy approach to life. I had wasted my first twenty-five years believing the things I liked were better than the things other people liked, and now those other people nodded politely as I cleared the half-eaten plates off their tables. I would never have been so magnanimous had our positions been reversed.

This was a difficult subject to broach with my co-workers. Sasha seemed to believe in a vague way that in the not-so-distant future, a great number of our guests would pay an extremely high price for their rudeness in the form of struggle-sessions and revolutionary tribunals. For Sev, on the other hand, the restaurant really was a temporary thing: his father was a Turkish architect and his mother was from some minor branch of a wealthy British Columbian timber family. He'd spent the first years of his life bouncing around the Mediterranean, gone to school in Vancouver, and summered at Salt Spring Island and the Bodrum marina. His work at the restaurant was just a way of making a little extra money on the side before the summer festival season, after which he hoped (with good reason) to start singing full time. From the acute discomfort he took whenever the topic of resources came up, he seemed eager to come across as just another bohemian working to make rent. He was so unflappably neutral-to-positive about the job that admitting to the hooded avarice I felt was impossible.

And so it was a great surprise when, laden with dirty dishes, I pushed through the swinging door to find Sev anxiously craning his neck around to stare at the corner table.

"You wouldn't mind delivering this salmon benedict to that couple at fifteen, would you?" he quickly asked, gesturing at two plates piled high with poached eggs and hollandaise sauce, cooling on the counter.

"Not if you'll finish clearing off twenty."

"I'm afraid I can't do that."

I had already picked up the plates and was halfway out the door before his refusal registered. By the time I reached table fifteen, I had decided to take offence. The couple sitting there seemed unremarkable. The woman was rather well dressed for a Saturday brunch, and had the kind of experienced beauty that manifested itself in delicate lines on the forehead and in the corners of the eyes. The man was tall and large and exuded a leonine virility so dense and pungent it hung in the air like cologne. They received their plates graciously, and even made eye contact when I asked if they wanted pepper (they were, of course, well bred enough to refuse).

"What was all that about?" I asked when I returned to the dish station stacked high with the last of the glasses from table twenty. Sev was busying himself with some unnecessary polishing and looked very uncomfortable.

"There are lines a professional cannot cross."

"Uh huh."

"You can't serve someone breakfast on a Saturday morning and expect them to take you seriously at a rehearsal on Tuesday night."

"They're music people?"

"They're the Standishes, if that name means anything to you. He works in finance or something like that and gives a lot of money to the Canadian Opera Company. She used to be a well-known coloratura. Still plays minor roles here and there, though I think she's mostly active in the philanthropy side now. They're not the kind of people I want to have associating me with wet salad."

"They seemed nice."

"I'll bet they did."

"Do you think they'd recognize you?"

"I don't know if you mean that to come off the way it does, but I've met them socially, if that's what you're asking. I do have a career outside of this job. I was personally congratulated by Mrs. Standish on my Don Alfonso last year."

"I'm sorry, I didn't realize ..."

"Look, it's not a big deal. Thanks for taking out the order."

I took refuge in the dining hall, where plates of bacon and spinach needed to be delivered, and tables needed to be cleared, and it was easy to retreat behind the uniform and become a supporting character again. The man and woman at table fifteen lingered over their benedict, and left deep in conversation. Sev emerged from the backroom as if nothing had happened.

"Do you want to go to a party tonight?" he asked at the end of the shift, while we were having our customary drink at the bar.

I reflected on the two inches of beer I had left in my glass, and concluded that was very much what I'd like to do. "What kind of party?"

"I have a friend who just moved into a place in Forest Hill. There'll be a lot of music people there."

"Is this a bring-your-own-beer kind of thing?"

"These are wine people."

"Right."

Sev gave me his address and told me to swing by in a cab later that evening so we could drive up together. I picked up a bottle of burgundy on the way home and had a long and wasteful shower. When I emerged, Sasha was eating a head of lettuce and carving off slices of pecorino for herself at the kitchen table.

"What a fucking day, right?" she said, munching her way through a leaf of romaine. Sasha worked as a hostess, and generally finished up a half-hour before everyone else. "For a while there I thought I was going to have to serve those fuckers in the late-morning rush peeled grapes with my very own fingers to shut them up. It's like, yeah, there's limited space, *sir*, you should have come early like all the other business psychos who can't go a day without complaining to someone's manager. I mean, Jesus. You got a date tonight? You spent enough time in that shower."

"Sev invited me to a party."

"I love parties."

"I can ask if you can come along. I mean, he invited me, so I can't imagine it would be a problem. It's a housewarming for some festival director."

"A festival director?"

"Yeah, some guy. Do you want me to check?"

"And where is it?"

"Forest Hill."

At the words *Forest Hill*, Sasha's face took on a blank expression. I could see that something about what I had said was bothering her, but when I pressed the question, she curtly told me that Forest Hill was full of cunts and she'd never met a festival director who wasn't a pervert and she was probably too tired for a party anyway, come to think of it.

I left Sasha to her salad and put on Ligeti's *Atmosphères* while I dressed. The dissonant promise of the woodwinds and brass was arousing. I hadn't been to a party in months. I put on a white cotton button-up and dark jeans, which I hoped would make me seem unremarkable. As the deep satanic horns of the Berlin Philharmonic blended with the brushed piano wires, I was struck by a certain rise in spirits, a stirring and hardening of forces that made it difficult to stand. I hadn't felt such a sweet convergence in months.

IX

"I FORGOT TO ask if Sasha wanted to come," Sev said as he settled into the taxi beside me. "I hope you mentioned it to her."

"I did."

"She busy or something?"

"Said it was a bit far to go for a party."

"Forest Hill? Fuck, it's not like we're going to Scarborough. And she knows Sean quite well, too, as I recall."

"She seemed a bit funny about it, actually, like, she was open to the idea, and then ..."

"You know, now that I think about it, there might be some history there. Oops. Toronto seems like a big city when you arrive, and then it just starts shrinking ..."

"Every city is like that."

"You think so? Do people in New York feel this way?"

"Probably."

"God, I hope not. The whole point of a city that size is to have a little anonymity."

"You could always move to Scarborough, right?"

"Well, I dated a guy from Brimley once. I'm sure I'd always be bumping into his cousins on the subway."

The taxi dipped under a railway line and sped up a broad avenue toward the heights above the old city, where the smug crust of wealth was impenetrable in the darkness. Here, even the apartment buildings were romantic, their handsome profiles looking out over the street like indulgent patriarchs. We had passed into a part of the city unfamiliar to me, a neighbourhood of tall stone houses. It would have been impossible to say how old most of these mansions actually were. They had the blank look of buildings that are regularly scrubbed clean with money.

We pulled up beside a long wall. An iron gate opened onto a courtyard, where a number of cars were parked in front of an imposing building that curled around a flagstone drive. It was solid red brick, built in the gothic revival style, but the mellow illumination of a dozen hidden wells made it seem diaphanous, as if it was floating above the ground.

When we stepped out of the cab, the silence was nearly perfect.

"I'd expected it to be smaller," Sev said as we made our way between the BMWs.

We paused for a moment at the door before Sev pressed down the latch and walked in. We hadn't had time to remove our things when a slender man with a scruffy brown beard clapped Sev on the shoulder and reached around to shake his hand.

"How the fuck are you, man?" he said.

"Oh, I'm good," said Sev, one arm still caught awkwardly in his coat sleeve. "Congratulations on the move, Sean — the place looks incredible. This is Alexander, by the way. He's ... well, I guess you'd say he's a critic, primarily —"

"Isn't everyone! Glad to meet you, glad you could make it out to this little housewarming, glad Sev didn't bore you to death on the way. No, don't worry, I'm just fucking with you. We love Sev. Such a mind, such a detailed knowledge of music. And such pipes! Look at that beautiful chest — show him, Sev, stand up straight. His body's like a fucking organ, isn't it? A goddamn masterpiece. Total breath control. Maybe later tonight, you can give us that duet you did with Jessica last summer. What was it, *Barber of Seville?* Sorry, yeah, *Così fan tutte*, what was I thinking! Anyway, Jessica's somewhere here. But let's get that organ warmed up first. There's some people you'll probably want to meet ..."

Sean led Sev into a large, low-ceilinged living room. I followed behind, not knowing what else to do. Standing in little knots in corners and beside bookcases or sitting on the sleek grey furniture at the front of the room, the gathering seemed to consist mostly of fashionable types in their late twenties to early forties, with a few grey heads scattered in among them. Chatting amiably to Sev about the perks of the new house, Sean brought us to a large table at the back covered in bottles and plates of food. He made a big show of whipping up each of us a cocktail tailored to what he judged our particular tastes to be. Sev was handed a boulevardier in a heavy square glass; apparently, I looked like I wanted a Moscow mule. I pretended not to be insulted.

Sean swept Sev off to talk to a group of people sitting by the fireplace. The ginger from the cocktail stung my lips, and I faced the unenviable choice of hanging about the bar like a creep or trying to elbow my way into someone else's conversation. I loved parties, in theory. But in the same way you forget how uncomfortable it is to walk in wet shoes until you step in a pothole, I never seemed to remember the deadliness of that first sober hour until it was upon me. I tried to appear relaxed and collected and nonchalant as I scanned the room for people in the same position as me, people who didn't know anyone too well, people abandoned by those who'd brought them. The fireplace circle was certainly not an option; nothing but middle-aged men in perfect physical shape, laughing at Sev's jokes. At the front of the room, a group of women in complicated outfits were reclining on the furniture and drinking wine. I folded my arms and looked at the large piece of art mounted on the wall above the bar. At first glance, it seemed to be a large mandala, the kind of geometric figure you might see in a kaleidoscope. Upon closer examination I saw that it was made up of hundreds of obscene little photographs.

"She doesn't look very comfortable, does she?" A balding man in a rumpled jacket had sidled up to pour himself a glass of Scotch and soda at the bar. "But maybe that's just how such things go these days."

"Sorry, who do you mean?"

"The woman in the miniatures. Or the women, I should say. When I see something like that, all I can think of is the elasticity of youth. Once it's gone, it's gone."

"They do seem very, uh, limber."

"Is this an interest of yours?"

"What, erotica?"

"Modern art."

"Oh. Not particularly."

"You just seemed very taken by it."

I began to stutter something about how I hadn't realized what I was looking at, but the man waved my explanations away.

"Don't worry about it. Have you been abandoned by our host? That's often the way at these parties. Everyone's trying to get an angle on the latest thing. Eventually it gets to be an obligation. But then nobody forced me to come. It's just that you never know what you'll overhear, and I worry that staying home with a bottle of Malbec will be dereliction of duty. I feel such a great obligation."

"Right."

"There's so much to keep up with these days. I can't shake the feeling that I'm missing out. I don't know how Sean does it, his fingers in so many different pies. I have this calendar I keep on my desk, you know, and every day I have to add something new to it. Even four months in advance, I've got all these little notes. The summer is almost completely booked."

The man looked glum, and had already made significant progress on his drink.

"So what do you do?" I asked. "Are you in the arts?"

"Oh yes, yes. You could certainly say that. You could say I've been working in the arts my whole life. And yet I haven't produced any art myself. Isn't that funny? Surely there's a joke in there somewhere. I'm like one of those Greek statues holding up the, you know, the roof on the temple. You understand what I mean?"

"The Caryatids?"

"Maybe. Yes. That sounds right. I've spent my whole life just standing there, holding up the roof. Though it doesn't feel like that, of course — if anything, I feel like I'm always in motion, never getting a day's rest. Yes, I seem to have latched on to the wrong metaphor there."

"Don't worry about it," I said nervously. He was starting to look rather misty-eyed. "Administration is such important work. So thankless, and quite difficult, too, I'd imagine ..."

"An administrator! Yes, that's true. I am constantly administrating things. Without my guidance, my attention to the little details, the whole structure that artists treat as a backdrop to their brilliance would fall apart. But I suppose that's true for all editors. The great burden, so much of it hidden from view. People see the finished product and think it was created by a big team, but it's just me, all of it's me. Or almost all of it. I'm not really qualified to handle layout issues, you understand — we hire someone else for that. A freelancer. She's very good, though I have to coordinate things with her, too — another thing I have to administrate, now that I think of it."

"I'm sorry, I didn't realize you were ..."

"Yes, yes. I've been an editor for twenty-five years now. All at the same magazine! And we've seen changes — my God, have we seen changes. And between you and me, mostly not for the better. Back in the nineties, it was so easy to sell advertisements. Every season, the offers just came flooding in; every company wanted their full-colour poster in the September issue. You weren't even selling them, really, you were just taking calls and collecting people's money. We had a proper staff then. Now they say, oh, but it's so much easier to run a magazine, you have the computer, you do everything on the computer. But they don't see the financials, do they? Revenues dropped like a stone a few years back, all because of online. It's the social media. Everything's gone to the social media. But try explaining that to a young person, they just tell you that you need to figure out how to make social media work for you. But tell me this," here he straightened up to deliver a well-rehearsed syllogism, "if I'm not losing money, why are these social media companies making so much of it? Their money came from somewhere, and I can tell you exactly where: from *Classical Modern!*"

"That's a great magazine," I said dishonestly.

"Well, thank you. Sorry, I'm Henry Zimmermann. The editor-in-chief. Though editor-in-chief is a rather inflated title, I sometimes think. Chief of what? Myself and a handful of freelancers? Not exactly David Walmsley. But I do my best. And yourself, are you a musician?"

"Not exactly. Or not anymore. I was. I've actually been transitioning to writing."

"Novels, stories, that kind of thing?"

"More like reviews, features ..."

"Yes, well, if you're ever interested in trying your hand at something for us, we're always looking. There, you see, this is exactly how these conversations are supposed to go — you start by talking about Sean's questionable art, and by the end you've offered someone a job. It's remarkable how he spins his webs. But I must refresh myself, I'm afraid." He turned to the bar and caught sight of Sean gliding across the room toward us. "Speak of the devil, and he will come to you."

Sean took my elbow and pulled me aside. "Do you like drugs, Alexander?"

I looked at Zimmermann, but he was occupied with his drink. "Well, I —"

"Don't stand on ceremony. We have some very good coke. And some ketamine. Weed, of course. Various, you know, pills. Et cetera. Anything you want."

"Thanks."

"And it isn't that shitty coke you find everywhere else these days. It's the real fucking thing."

"I guess I wouldn't say no to a line."

"That's the spirit."

Sean led me up a wide staircase to the second floor, into a darker and more intimate room where a group of men with beards and women in extremely high-waisted jeans were gathered around a glass table. This group seemed younger, and by the looks of it they had already consumed quite a bit of coke. And yet the atmosphere lacked the general edge of desperation I had come to associate with the drug during my Montreal years, that manic feeling that comes when everyone is trying to ensure they get as much as possible up their nose before the supply runs out.

"This is Alex," said Sean, as a woman with impossibly long black hair handed me a rolled-up five-dollar bill and gestured for me to join her on the couch.

I snorted like a bull and felt a delicious tingle as it entered my nose.

"What do you do, Alex?" asked the woman. She pulled the hair back from her face, and I realized that she was alarmingly, mathematically beautiful. Her cheekbones formed two exquisite scalene triangles united in sublime harmony by a delicate pointed chin. Her eyes were set deep in her face, like well shafts beside a perfect aquiline nose. Her forehead was like a sail full of wind.

"I'm a music critic," I said, trying to see where Sean had disappeared to. "And actually I prefer to go by —"

"Oh, very cool. Cool shit. What are you listening to these days, then?"

"This and that."

"Sure, but like, what were you listening to, like, on the way over here."

"I took a cab with a friend, actually, and —"

"Are you fucking with me, Alex?"

"Well, I've been getting into Kopatchinskaja's *Ligeti* and *Bartók*. And that Prokofiev she did last year. Sometimes you've just got to believe the hype, right?"

She leaned over to do the next line, her hair covering her face like a curtain from behind which certain snuffling noises emerged.

"I thought her Bartók was a bit showy," she said when she straightened up again. "Want some more?" She gestured at the table.

Not being sure what to say, I took her up on the offer and cut a slim little line out of the pile. I'd assumed she wouldn't know who Kopatchinskaja was.

"Are you a musician?" I asked, haltingly, as raw white energy bloomed behind my eyeballs.

"I'm doing my B.Mus."

"Right."

"How do you know Sean?"

"I don't, really. I was invited along by a friend of his. A colleague. I mean, a singer I know."

"Well, Sean certainly likes his musicians. I don't mean to be rude, but if you're a journalist, who do you write for?"

"I'm a freelancer. Just moved here from Montreal."

"But you must do your freelancing somewhere. What do you cover? Where did your last piece come out? Or are you a critic in the way that these guys are composers?" She jerked her chin at the group of well-dressed young men sitting at the far end of the table, each of whom was simultaneously offering his own disconnected monologue on the best restaurants in the West End.

"I wrote about the SMCQ earlier this year for *Chomedey*, if you're familiar with that magazine. And I do reviews for the CBC whenever they'll take them."

"Anything you're working on now?"

Somewhere within, the remnants of my ego stirred, and I answered as casually as I could. "I've got a long read in the works, actually. I've been researching Fera Civitatem, that group that does those exciting underground concerts people are so worked up about on social media."

As soon as I said the words *Fera Civitatem*, her entire affect changed. She tucked her hair behind her ear and conjured a glass of wine from beneath the coffee table. She looked alert and focused, like she was expecting me to say something more.

"I think it's a really interesting example of the classical world meeting pop music," I continued, "akin to the way Copland and Stravinsky borrowed from jazz in the thirties. And, of course, such an interesting comment on the commodification of music vis-à-vis the concert hall experience."

"Where have you pitched it?"

"A couple of places have expressed interest," this was, of course, untrue, "but I'm waiting until they announce their next show before I really try to hammer out something solid. I mean, it's the kind of piece that really needs to hang on a particular performance, doesn't it? I wasn't around for 'The Garden of Earthly Delights.'"

"How interesting. Are you interviewing anyone for it?"

"I assumed I'd just grab someone at the show. Not exactly forthcoming about personal details, are they?"

"I might be able to help you with that."

"You know someone who's involved?"

"You could say that."

"Maybe we can meet later to talk about it."

"That's rather forward."

"I'm sorry, I didn't mean to suggest ..."

"What?"

"I mean, I clearly gave the wrong impression."

"What impression might that be?"

"That I was hitting on you."

"Are you?"

"No."

"Why not?"

"Well, I, uh ..."

"I'm sorry, I'll stop tormenting you. The way you're blushing answers my question. Yes, let's meet up later on, somewhere with fewer distractions."

She handed me her phone and directed me to enter my number, then called me so I'd have hers.

"What's your name?" I asked when it came through.

"Why do you want to know?"

"You know mine."

"I suppose that's true, Alex," she said, and turned back to the slowly shrinking mound of white powder on the table. Something in the way she enthusiastically snorted up the next line suggested our conversation was, to my relief, over.

Invincible light flowed through my limbs as I walked downstairs to the bar. I was vibrating at high and sacred frequencies.

The art seemed more pleasing and the people much kindlier than they'd been earlier that the evening. More guests had arrived, and I suddenly had no trouble at all inserting myself into conversations. I had heard of everyone and everything; I was a fountain of bons mots. The people I shook hands with were sophisticated, relaxed, open to new ideas, brimming with intelligent conversation. My opinions provoked passionate but engaging responses. There was a great deal of laughter. When my mouth began to feel dry, I drank more wine.

At some point, I found myself sitting on a couch next to Sev. He had undone the top two buttons of his shirt. I began to explain to him why composers in Quebec were so much more willing to take chances than Anglophone Canadians, when he cut me off.

"I'm in the middle of a conversation, Alex." Beside him a man wearing a paisley scarf came into focus, someone who had obviously been saying something when I interrupted.

"I'm so sorry. So, so sorry. That was very rude. I don't know what's gotten into me …"

"Alex has just moved here from Montreal," said Sev, as if by way of explanation.

Something dropped into place and I felt suddenly foolish. I shook the man's hand and retreated down the hallway. Large as the house seemed from the outside, the rooms had a claustrophobic quality. The place was a warren of little closets and antechambers and staircases with low ceilings and few windows. In the large, renovated kitchen at the back, people were milling about over food. I helped myself to some shrimp and followed the servants' staircase up to the second floor. After some twists and turns, I found myself in an empty room. Floor-to-ceiling bookshelves lined the walls. A large desk looked out over the snowy lawn. My heart had settled into a curious rhythm, and my hands were damp. I looked at the titles arrayed before me. Everything very predictable. Popular novels, classics, some general history, economics, quite a few expensive art books, and the kind of cultural criticism you'd expect someone like Sean to be into. Lots of Hitchens and Paglia. An entire wall was devoted to memoirs, biographies, and popular studies of famous events in classical music. It was the collection of a man who never visited a bookstore without buying something.

"Theresa tells me you're interested in Fera Civitatem."

I turned to see the host, Sean, standing in the doorway, scratching his little beard. With him was an older gentleman who seemed familiar but unplaceable.

"Who?"

"The girl I just introduced you to. I figured you two would get along. She's got a very bright future ahead of her. Or she will, if she plays her hand right! Anyway, she's a good friend, and Fera is a mutual fascination of ours. I hadn't realized you were a fan, as well."

"It's just such an interesting concept, you know?"

"Oh yes, we know!" said the older gentleman, in a bass so craggy and sonorous it conjured up images of salt spray and Hebridean rock, though the accent was Canadian. "We see so little that is genuinely new here, so little that isn't an inferior copy ... In its bones, Toronto is still a provincial city. One doesn't need to condone every aspect of the Fera project — there is a degree of recklessness, admittedly, in some of their performances — to find it refreshing. I had the good fortune of being young in the sixties, you understand, and it delights me to see some of that anarchic energy resurrected after these decades of irony and earnestness."

"My apologies," I said, rather bewildered, "but have we met before?"

"I, at least, don't believe we've had the pleasure of a formal introduction," the man said, graciously extending his hand. "Lionel Standish. And you are?"

"Alexander Otkazov," I said, realizing as I did that I had served him lunch earlier that day.

"And where are you from, Alexander?"

"Montreal."

"Aha, yes." He grinned, looking at Sean knowingly. "Though perhaps not originally?"

"I don't think any of us are from here originally," I said, trying to match his playful tone.

For some reason, both of them found this rather funny. Sean grabbed my shoulder and gave it a jocular shake.

"Lionel is actually from an old Toronto family. One of the prettiest patches of Rosedale is named after them, if you can believe it. Who was it, Lionel — was it your great-great-grandfather built that hideous old pile? Bet he bought the land cheap, too."

Lionel chuckled and nodded, one hand tucked into a pocket below his bulging stomach, the other holding the stem of his wineglass. "All ancient history, I assure you," he said. "When the first of us arrived, Rosedale was nothing but a hill covered in trees. We saw our opportunities where they lay, we invested wisely, and in time we made it bloom. Though I'm told it took a bit of work. 'Roses have thorns, and silver fountains mud,' as I'm sure you know. Of course," he added ponderously, "we were also lucky."

"I guess my ancestors just weren't hard-working enough to buy half of North York when it was a woodlot," Sean said.

"Plenty of other families that were just as lucky have squandered their good fortune," Lionel responded, not entirely without malice. "We're just joking, of course," he said, turning back to me. "Sean is someone I rely on greatly for his insight — into music, and into other things. We both have a great passion for the arts — all the arts, though music is especially dear to me. My wife was an opera singer, once, as you may have heard. Now, if you wouldn't mind, we do have one or two matters to discuss in private ..."

I nodded and tried to muster a friendly grin. I regretted not having refreshed my drink earlier. At the door, I looked back to see Lionel's large head bent low, Sean whispering into a hairy ear. The laughter was completely gone from their eyes.

Down a large corridor, I could hear the sound of voices. I followed them until I was once again in the room where I'd met Theresa. A small crowd was still gathered around the table, but I didn't recognize anyone. Based on the pungent smell, the new drug of choice seemed to be marijuana. On a side table, there was a large water pipe with several hoses coming off it, and a haze of vapour in the air. Someone had opened a window and a cool draft lightened the oppressive atmosphere. Music was playing, a melancholy electronic beat underneath something cloying and Russian that sounded very much like Rimsky-Korsakov. A space had been cleared for dancing. A few people were swaying awkwardly. I sat down on the couch and accepted a mouthpiece when it was offered. The conversation around me was impenetrable, but it felt good to sink into the expensive upholstery. Perhaps Theresa would be back. The man sitting next to me started to tell me about his new album, and I nodded congenially and let the comfortable leaden weight of *cannabis indica* sink into my bones.

At some point I looked up and noticed that Sev had joined the dancers. He moved gracefully but with a certain reserve, his forearms bent at right angles to the ground, his hips pivoting gently back and forth. He looked seraphic, as though he alone understood the meaning of the music. I felt a yearning to join him. Instead, I pushed myself up and out of the couch and went downstairs. The crowd had thinned, and those who remained were on the younger side. The liveliness of the early part of the evening had been replaced by a feeling of intimacy and trust. I poured myself a glass of water and balanced it out with a Scotch. It was well past midnight. I downed the Scotch and poured another, thought for a moment, and poured a glass of wine, as well. I brought both back up to the second floor. The music had picked up, the dancehall Rimsky-Korsakov replaced with a kind of Hungarian waltz. Sev whirled on his toes and twisted his torso in time with the music, and when I handed him the glass of wine, he cocked his body so that we were at an acute angle to each other. The music slowed for a measure, and we counted the beats with the balls of our feet.

I don't know how long it took for the water pipe to burn itself out, and the music to stop, and the room to empty. When the lights came on, Sev's shirt was sheer, his chest muscles clearly defined beneath the cotton.

"I'll call a cab," he said.

I nodded and went in search of a washroom. None of the doors I opened led to a toilet, and eventually I found myself back in the doorway of the book-lined room. Two bodies, one standing above the other, were illuminated by the desk lamp. Theresa leaning back against the desk, her face turned rapturously to the ceiling. Sean's hand around her throat. I retreated back down to the front entrance, where Sev was pulling on his shoes.

We stepped together into the night air. A taxi was waiting inside the gates.

On the way back to the Annex, Sev and I sat in a companionable silence. The dark tangle of streets passed by the window, and then suddenly we were on the main avenue again, speeding toward the lip of the ancient lakeshore that divides midtown from the rest of Toronto. Far away, the blinking golden lights of the financial district hung weightlessly between earth and sky.

"How did Sean make his money?" I asked.

"You don't want to know."

X

———◆———

I WAS WALKING home from work up Dovercourt Road several days after the party when the Pärt I was listening to was interrupted by the ping of a text message. I didn't recognize the number.

—*Saw you walking and waved. You didn't see me? :(*

I pulled out my headphones and looked around. The street was deserted. I put the phone back in my pocket and kept walking through the uncleared snow. I'd gotten a new number when I moved, and it was entirely possible the text had been intended for someone else. But when I reached Dundas, my phone pinged again.

—Don't be rude Alex.

I stood at the corner and looked back down the street, and then, absurdly, up into the sky. It was snowing again. The city was grey. Everyone who was out seemed to have somewhere to go. I turned the phone sound off and made my way home, trying very hard to think of who among the people who had my number might find this funny.

I sat down at my desk with a cup of coffee. The baseboard heater had been going all day, but the room was frigid (except for the small space under my desk, which was uncomfortably hot). I checked my phone and saw four unread messages.

—Don't be alarmed

—I saw you from my window

—You can't guess who this is?

—You really shouldn't give out your # at parties if this is how you respond to being texted!

I sat back, feeling very stupid. Over the course of the next few minutes, I composed several acerbic responses and deleted them all.

*—You got me! Afraid I didn't see you wave. As for the rest …
let's just say I have a bad imagination.*

I barely had time to put the phone down before she texted back.

—We'll see about that

I stared at the message preview at the top of my screen. I had the distinct impression I was being mocked. Before I could open the text, it was joined by a second.

—I'm at the Communist's Daughter. Are you going to let me drink alone?

I responded:

—That would be very rude. Be there in a half-hour.

It turned out that Theresa was not alone. When I arrived, I found her deep in conversation with the woman behind the bar, and it wasn't until she turned to take my order that Theresa acknowledged my existence with an ironic nod. The bar itself was cramped and cluttered, a narrow box that seemed to be mostly chairs and countertop. It succeeded at feeling louche in a specifically *fin de siècle* way. All the stools at the bar were taken, so I leaned awkwardly beside Theresa and waited for my lager.

"I read your piece in *Chomedey*."

"Oh?"

"Yes."

"What did you think?"

"You seem very pleased with your vocabulary."

"You'd be surprised how much of that gets added at the editing stage."

"Did they also add the bit where you talked about how great a job Marie-Claude Langevin is doing as head of the Institute for Sound Studies?"

"No, that was me."

"A bit gratuitous, don't you think?"

"She is doing a great job. She's one of the best apologists for experimental music this country has. And you'll recall that I did mention the incident at St. Joseph's. You can't say I wasn't willing to talk about the, uh, controversies."

"That's not what I meant."

"Well, what did you mean?"

"The thing is that Langevin is thinking way too *small*. The St. Joseph's incident, the fire, the goats, the maimings ... it's the only interesting thing she's done, and it was a complete accident! I can't stand these Boomer radicals who think that putting on a big show makes up for all this shitty, unimaginative music that hasn't moved an inch since the eighties. I was hoping you agreed. But if you can say nice things about Langevin, who is such a *fucking* dullard ..."

"I was being tactful," I interjected, blood up, cock starting to come alive. "The readers of *Chomedey* think Milton Babbitt is pretty cutting edge; I just wanted to nudge them toward concerts where meeting the composer afterward would be physically possible. This is a really conservative country when it comes to art, you know? How would I even write an essay critiquing Langevin for not being avant-garde enough when I'd first have to explain to the editors that people kept composing music after John Cage died."

Theresa launched into a monologue about how bad criticism leads to bad art, and how reviewers have a responsibility to treat their audiences with a modicum of respect if the general tenor of the conversation was ever to be improved. As it was, I had simply used my platform to shower weak praise on a hack who would use the unearned notoriety the incident bestowed on her to score a few more grants. She concluded by coyly suggesting that if Langevin had only *meant* to set fire to St. Joseph's Church, the whole project might have had some dignity.

"Is that what you think Fera Civitatem is trying to do?" I asked.

Theresa had been slouching casually against the bar, her legs twisted into a complicated pretzel beneath the countertop. But she straightened up, as if the real work had now begun. A table had opened up at the back, and she suggested we move for the sake of privacy. A candle burned between us, casting intimate little shadows around the transcendent geometry of her face.

"I wouldn't feel comfortable speaking for the organizers. 'I'm just a fan,' she said. But I will say this: one thing art has always struggled with — not artists as individuals, but art as this thing we 'consume' — is the line that must not be crossed, the line between the fantasy and everyday reality. In theory, operas like *Salome* or *Orfeo* are about the transgression of that line, right? They're about desires that go out of bounds, which is why we like them so much. But even though they're all about excess, when we stage them, we tame all that wild energy. Like, we make sure no one actually gets seduced by the 'Dance of the Seven Veils.' You can get a kick out of perversity so long as you're not actually a pervert. Successful artists have always understood that it's about getting close to the line without actually crossing it. Audiences will accept everything as long as the transgression remains symbolic, as long as you don't actually do anything wrong. But for us, in the twenty-first century, when no one's shocked by anything anymore, that line is the last taboo."

"So if Salome actually does a striptease instead of pretending to do a striptease, we're breaking barriers?"

"It's not just about sex. Sex is just the easiest way to explain it. When I experienced Fera for the first time, everything suddenly made sense. Nothing new is going to come out of a university, or a government funding body. We've reached the end of what we can do by playing around with mathematical formulas or new tunings or fresh vocalization styles, or cosplaying as monks, or 'discovering' non-Western music traditions. I know the people who are involved in putting these concerts on. I've met the composers — yes, the music was written by a group, that much is basically public knowledge, though of course they are rather private and are trying to keep their identities hidden. That's the whole point, actually. No recordings, no auditoriums, no publishing the sheet music so the concerts can be reproduced aseptically anywhere in the world by anyone with money to pay the licence. We have to cut the cord. Musically. Institutionally. Experientially. Once we cut the cord, everything will be possible. Fera have accepted that their work is effervescent, the musicians know that what they're playing is going to be heard only once, so everything matters more. And the audience can tell. You don't have to burn down a church to get their attention. Not that I'm against that kind of thing, as long as it's on purpose."

There was something deeply annoying to me about this speech, but I found myself unable to articulate exactly what it was. I wanted to say that institutions are harder to kill than we might think, that there are limits to boundary-pushing as an aesthetic ideal. But when I looked into her eyes, all of my opinions about the death of the author and temporary autonomous zones seemed stupid and obvious, so I asked the even stupider and more obvious question that had been on my mind all evening: Who was cutting the cheques?

Theresa smirked and leaned back against the wall. She gestured at my empty glass questioningly and signalled to the bartender, who lovingly gave her the finger before pulling another couple of pints. It wasn't until the drink was firmly in her hand that Theresa responded. I wondered if she was buying time.

"There's a simple answer to that question. Once the project got off the ground, Fera found that there are actually quite a few people interested in paying for these concerts, not least the concertgoers themselves. You do know that outside your rarefied bubble of classical music, there is an actual music industry, right? That makes money by selling a product people want, rather than by browbeating them into going to the opera or the symphony by telling them it's an ennobling cultural experience? Every time I've gone to a Fera show, I've paid for my ticket. And like any other concert, refreshments are sold. It's a little more complicated, of course, because none of this is happening in regular spaces, but you'd be surprised to find out how much money you can bring in by performing music in a way that's stimulating and arousing and dangerous, rather than just educational.

"The other part, which I'm sure you've figured out on your own by now, is that there's not a lot of overhead. All equipment is owned by Fera — the instruments belong to the performers. They don't have to rent space. No venue is trying to get its cut. That definitely comes with its own risks, but wouldn't you know it, the risk is part of the appeal! I swear to God there were people at 'Garden of Earthly Delights' who were there because they *wanted* it to get busted. It would have been exciting. Obviously care has to be taken in setting up the concerts, and care has to be taken to make sure that no one who isn't supposed to be there is sent the password. But I think people intuitively understand that it's a very pure thing. Especially in this city, where everything interesting is being bulldozed or turned into a condo, and people don't even know these bizarre little theatres exist."

"You're making a lot of compelling points."

"Am I?" she said, smiling sarcastically. "I'm glad to hear that."

"But what about the collateral damage? There was a bit of fallout from that last concert, if I'm not mistaken. Overdoses, arson. The grocer had to sell the building. I mean, this is all technically illegal — I assume that's why no one's written about this before?"

"Lots of things are illegal. Cocaine, for example. But breaking the law is part of the fun! Sure, yeah, things got a bit carried away, and I know the Fera people feel bad about what happened to the Chinese Vegetable Stand, or whatever it was. But it's not like they were robbed. They got the fair market price."

"That's not what I heard."

"And about the overdoses, you should know — everything turned out okay, it was at the end of the night, an ambulance was called, no one died. That kind of thing happens all the time. If someone ODs at a club, do you hold the DJ responsible? The whole point of what Fera is doing is that there's risk involved. People know that going in. You can't do this kind of thing if you need to worry about permits and liquor licensing and safe capacity guidelines. It would fundamentally violate the spirit of the thing."

The candle between us had guttered out, the cheap paraffin wax hardening into opacity. I relit it, thinking about Lionel Standish and the nineteen-sixties. He was right: it had been a very long time since art was in the anarchy business. Veins harden, sclerosis sets in, ideas fall out of fashion or live a half-life as dogma. Fera Civitatem would follow the same course. Everything has already happened. But even if you know the story, it's still more interesting to watch from the front row.

"I do want to write about this," I said, catching Theresa's eye. "I don't know who for, yet — obviously I'm still building my relationships here — but would it be fair to say that you're willing to help me get in touch with the, uh, Fera people, if the pitch is accepted? I imagine they'll want to stay anonymous, but if there's a way of arranging an interview ..."

"You want me to be your go-between?"

"Or you could just give me an email I could reach them at."

"I think it's better if I serve as your go-between. Certainly more fun for me!"

"Whatever you prefer. Do you have an idea when the next show might be?"

"Yes, but I'm not going to tell you. Why don't we continue the conversation?" she said, as I started to get up. "Conversation can be fun, you know. It doesn't just need to be an exchange of information. Here you are, having a drink with a beautiful woman, talking about music in a bar that once appeared in a Sheila Heti novel. You could be enjoying the moment! Instead you're talking about getting someone's email like you've got somewhere to be tomorrow. Do you have somewhere to be tomorrow?"

"Strictly speaking, no."

"That's what I thought. It's only just past nine o'clock. By the time you've finished that beer, maybe you'll even start flirting with me again."

"You're very eccentric, Theresa."

"I'm so flattered! No one's said that about me in weeks."

"Don't take this the wrong way, but it might take more than a couple of drinks to get there. First, I need to ask if you've spent much time in Montreal ..."

I don't know if it was after either the third drink or the fourth, but eventually we found ourselves standing on the corner, Theresa drawing her wool coat close around her body. In my not-quite-drunken mind, she appeared as a long, dark *aleph* against the salt-white city, and the bell of desire began to ring insistently inside my chest.

XI

I UNDERSTAND THAT for some people, sex is a matter of arithmetic. Lists are kept in notebooks tabulating the raw data of one's erotic life: twenty-two conquests in vaginal intercourse, twenty-six in cunnilingus, forty in fellatio, thirteen in anal sex, one threesome, some overlap in partners between categories. Traditionally, the keeping of these accounts has been considered a masculine activity, Don Giovanni's carefully compiled list of 2,065 sexual encounters across Europe and the Mediterranean being perhaps the most famous. Women must keep lists of their own, although perhaps less neurotically. Or more neurotically — I don't know. I've never asked.

Regardless, these lists serve a variety of functions: bolstering the ego, commemorating the progress of sexual maturity, serving as a sort of aide-memoire to bring to mind obscure or uniquely pleasurable encounters. On a more unconscious level, they prove that sex is not (at least, not for the people who keep lists) a biological process as straightforward as blowing one's nose.

I had my own list, although it was not long enough to have ever bothered writing down. The list that mattered to me was more personal, less tangible than a series of names, dates, erotic specifics. It was a list of the times I had watched a woman decide to sleep with me. These moments were far more important than the sex itself, which was usually just a blur of body parts and odd bits of scenery: what never lost its vividness was the singular, almost religious experience of watching a woman give a little shake of her shoulders, of seeing a certain resolution drift across her eyes. These moments were especially precious when things never progressed any further, when a woman changed her mind, or events intervened, or there simply wasn't time. The fragile understanding was all the more erotic for having gone unfulfilled.

With Theresa, the moment came under a street lamp at the corner of Argyle. Small pellets of ice were blowing in with the storm clouds off the lake, and the frozen city around us was covered in a brittle, silvery skin. My hands dug into the pockets of my overcoat. When I leaned down to kiss her, she held back, smiling, and cupped my cheek in her palm.

"That's more like it," she said. "You'd better come up."

She apologized for the state of her apartment and poured us both a glass of bourbon. She lived alone on the second floor of a house owned by an old Portuguese widow who was, Theresa assured me, deaf. I drank the bourbon obediently. I couldn't stop staring at her neck, at its gently creased skin the colour of honey, at the architectural harmony of her shoulders and collarbone, at the sweeping, modernist line of her jaw.

"Do you miss Montreal?" she asked me.

"No," I said.

"I sometimes wish I'd moved there. I've lived in Toronto my whole life. The biggest change I made was leaving Greektown."

"I haven't met very many people who were born here."

"Now you can say you've met one more."

"I guess that explains why you're so aggressive."

"There are nicer ways to say that."

"It's good that you're aggressive."

"Would you be here if I wasn't?"

She had finished her bourbon, and was leaning back against the kitchen counter with her hips thrust forward. I deposited my glass in the sink and stood in front of her. Even then, I might have said good night and made my way home, had I not seen a shuddering of fast blood in the large vein in her neck, and noticed the shallowness of her breathing, and seen that she, too, had not been entirely sure what would come next.

I took her cheek in my hand like she had taken mine and tasted the last of the bourbon on her lips. She lifted her hands to my chest and slid them up to my collarbone, holding me there for a moment. I lifted her onto the counter. Her mouth was small and active, nipping and biting, the muscular little tongue penetrating my lips and darting away. Beneath her shirt I felt every knob of her spine, the ripple of ribs under her skin. The heat between her legs was radiant, humid, aestival. She ran her fingers through my hair, and grabbed hold, and pulled me back, and her lips crept down. With her other hand she opened my belt. I was hard and constrained against the lip of the counter, and I gasped as she pulled me free and took me in the warmth of her palm. But when she slid the skin back and exposed me completely, she did so with great tenderness.

Still, involuntarily, I stepped back. She laughed at my confusion. I pinned her gently to the cabinet with my hand, feeling each breath she sucked in. Her eyes were ecstatic. Her nipples twitched alive when they met the cool air, but I could not look away from the crease of skin where her jeans met the flesh of her stomach. I unbuttoned them slowly, and slowly I drew them from her legs. She lifted her bum off the counter to make it easier. I was shaking, sick with the particular kind of desire that rises from the stomach before the animal part of sex begins. There they were, her delicate little lips wearing their mysterious smile. She watched me, her back arched against the cabinets.

The kitchen floor hadn't been swept. I could feel the grit through my pants as I knelt, kissing my way up her leg. I breathed in deeply the scent of soap and sweat and cunt, and ran my tongue down her prickly mound. When I finally placed my mouth against the softest part of her body, I felt her shudder. She grabbed my hair and held me still. I could see the angry red blush where a razor had recently passed.

"It's sensitive," she said. "It's okay, it's just sensitive."

Her words settled something inside me, and my cock grew harder as I watched a bead of moisture roll down her stomach.

"It's okay," she said, relaxing her fingers against my scalp and gently pulling me forward. "It's okay, it's okay, it's okay, it's okay."

XII

———————

THE NEXT MORNING, the city was covered in frost, and I walked home through unshovelled sidewalks and wet, clumping snow. As I removed my shoes at the top of the stairs, Sasha lowered her magazine and grinned at me from the chaise longue.

"Did you get lucky?"

"Who knows," I said, and went to bed.

I woke hours later, in the red light of a March afternoon. Snow had built up on the window ledge, and cars crept uneasily through the streets below. The smell of sex rose from my unwashed body. As sometimes happens when waking from daytime sleep, I was filled with a strange calm. I made my-self a cup of coffee and opened my email. There was one new message, from Theresa Lykaios. It had no subject, and when I opened it there was but a single line of text followed by a link.

And you said you had a bad imagination. Thanks for the drinks.

The link took me to the Fera Civitatem website. Blood flushed beneath my scalp as I realized what I was looking at. Across the top of the page, in clear black letters, was spelled out a title and date:

The City of Pigs
11/04/15

What will be their way of life? Will they not produce corn, and wine, and clothes, and shoes, and build houses for themselves? And when they are housed, they will work, in summer, commonly, stripped and bare-foot, but in winter substantially clothed and shod. They will feed on barley-meal and flour of wheat, baking and kneading them, making noble cakes and loaves; these they will serve up on a mat of reeds or on clean leaves, themselves reclining the while upon beds strewn with yew or myrtle. And they and their children will feast, drinking of the wine which they have made, wearing garlands on their heads, and hymning the praises of the gods, in happy converse with one another. And they will take care that their families do not exceed their means; having an eye to poverty or war.

But, said Glaucon, you have not given them a relish to their meal.

— Plato, *The Republic*, Book II

Let us imagine a city. An unrecognizable city, free from wealth or want, where the citizens are noble enough to love simplicity. In this city, the wind blows in from the lake and stirs the gardens of the people, spreading the perfume of apple blossoms and lilac over those who sleep long in the heat of the day. Winter nights are spent intoxicated with smoke and spiced wine, chanting the deep mysteries.

It is only in this city that love is possible. Without avarice, free from kings and bishops and their bloody nightmares of hierarchy and domination, its streets are filled with a true eroticism. Care and respect for the entwining of bodies is the only religion, and it is worshipped with a true liturgy. A liturgy of music and dance so perfect it transcends the union of two souls that is the foundation of all other cities — the dyad of master and slave — to unite every worshipper in a climax of becoming.

Some have called this a city of pigs, a bestial city. They say its citizens feed and rut like swine, cut off from divine images and laws, following only the dictates of nature. Where, the priests and economists and government ministers say, are the finer things in life? Where are the featherbeds and rich sauces, the slave's deference and the peasant's groan? They have bulldozed and paved over this ancient city, and buried it to sleep beneath churches and courthouses.

Have you had enough relish yet? Are you ready to descend into the City of Pigs?

There was a video embedded underneath. A shaky, darkened image came to life when I clicked "play." From a background of electronic static, a high, thin tone emerged, a violin that began to play a repetitive motif. The camera moved through a darkened space. Flashes of red and blue illuminated a hunched-over figure moving in a circle around some large dark mass in the centre of the room. The violin was joined by an echoing viola and cello, and the camera spun around the circling bodies and then went black. A figure appeared, bathed in red light, holding a whip, and when the whip cracked, the strings and electronic fuzz cut out altogether and a chorus of voices began to sing, sustaining what sounded like a C Minor 7th chord, but corrupted and dark; stacked thirds organized in a way that I couldn't quite place. A pulsing dance began to play, and staccato purple light revealed a pile of writhing naked limbs. The pace grew faster, the light matching the beat, until the screen finally cut to black and a card with the title and date appeared.

I sat back in my chair and played it again. The music was fairly ordinary, up until the big reveal, but the camerawork and editing were highly professional. It was not immediately clear to me how any of this connected directly with the curious text. But in its own way, it answered any remaining questions I had. It was all too impressive. There was no way DIY art punks were responsible for this. The production was too slick, the audio too good. And after the legal risk they'd already exposed themselves to, advertising the date seemed reckless.

I opened the *Classical Modern* website. The landing page looked as though it had been designed in 2009, and was dominated by a highly professional shot of Itzhak Perlman playing violin and looking extremely constipated. There was a horizontal slider below the main story containing the headline *Celeste Andrews Wows Winnipeg With Concert at Centennial Hall*. I was about to click the *Submissions* tab when the next ad in the slider glided across the screen. It was an advertisement for a job at the magazine. A full-time position with a "competitive" salary.

I clicked through. Applicants with experience in classical music were encouraged to send in a CV and writing portfolio, before the deadline at the end of the month. I wasn't sure what "competitive" meant, and my conversation with Zimmermann had left me with a distinct impression of the magazine's philosophy — one that was confirmed as I began reading through the main stories from its last issue. There wouldn't be much room for digressions about Plato, and nor would there be much interest in the more politically charged ideas Theresa had put forward.

I started the painful process of cobbling together a pitch, which culminated in an anxious smoke break. When I returned, the words I had written made me slightly uneasy. I could imagine exactly how Theresa's mouth would twitch up in derision as she read them. There was nothing in what I'd said about the necessity of exploding the old forms or moving beyond the static audience-musician-composer relationship that had become engrained over the past two hundred years. If anything, the pitch I had prepared was a step in the opposite direction, a digestible take that domesticated Fera Civitatem's experiment, asserting that however radical they seemed, these concerts actually belonged alongside the comfortably genteel productions that ran mechanically each passing season. It was an apology for the excess, not a celebration of it.

But iconoclasm is easy when you have everything or nothing, and I was neither desperate nor comfortable enough to fantasize about burning it all down. The only thing standing between me and never having to clear another table again was my willingness to adopt a slightly different angle in my coverage of a concert that, in the grand scheme of things, meant less than nothing. The decision was quite easy in the end, given that there was no way to monetize Theresa's approval.

XIII

———

THERESA REMAINED SILENT for a week, and aside from a brief response to thank her for the email, I made no effort to contact her. She had taken the initiative; I thought it best to let her keep it. But when the text came on a Monday afternoon, I felt a small muscle deep inside me unclench. She had talked to the Fera people, and they were interested. Could I meet her for a drink at the same bar as before? We agreed to eight o'clock. I was five minutes early; she was fifteen minutes late. Her lips were painted bright red, she had a little brown bruise high on her neck, and she was eager to talk business.

"Quite a promotional video, wasn't it? They're really stepping up the game for this one," she said, polishing off a good part of her old-fashioned in a single go. "Want to reach a broader audience while still maintaining the more intimate vibe. As you probably gathered from the announcement, they're really interested in this idea of the pig as an exemplary kind of creature. I don't know if you went back and read the relevant sections of *The Republic* (you've read *The Republic*, right?), but Socrates really doesn't think the city of pigs is a bad place. It's focused on basic needs and living more harmoniously, without a violent hierarchy, which he sort of implicitly approves of. I guess you could say it's uncivilized in the best sense of the word. In English it sounds ironic, of course, because we basically only use the word 'pig' to talk about cops, gluttons, capitalists, that kind of thing. I mean, from a Judeo-Islamic perspective, pigs are unclean and to be avoided. But that's exactly the point: the concert is about imagining this idea of a pre-Abrahamic city, a pagan city that isn't contaminated by Christianity or capitalism or feudalism or any of that shit. A city where, you know, sensuality is embraced and nothing is unclean and people can just live with each other naturally in a society that isn't constantly trying to force them into these predetermined roles."

"A golden age, if you will."

"Exactly."

"It sounds ambitious."

"Well, yes. But it's a continuation of what they were exploring in 'The Garden of Earthly Delights.' A lot of the same themes. I mean, the music is completely new," she added quickly, "but it's fair to say it's going to build on what they've done in previous shows. It's just taking the themes of deconstruction of capitalism and Western reason that were implicit in the earlier concerts and making them a lot clearer."

"Do you know where it's going to be performed?"

"No, not yet."

"You must have some idea. There's only so many boarded-up theatres in Toronto."

"But there's an almost unlimited number of derelict factories. Believe me, Fera is a long-term project, and they've thought through that particular problem. I can't say anything for certain, obviously, but I suspect they'll need to find a bigger space than last time. There's more interest. The production requires more room. Another round?" she said, gesturing to my glass, which wasn't empty.

"Sure, I —"

"Great. Two old-fashioneds, please. Have you pitched the piece yet?"

"I sent the email earlier this week."

"Good. Ideally, it would come out pretty soon afterward. They were a bit cagey about press after the first shows, but I think they've realized what they're doing is really important. The word needs to get out."

"I'll see what I can do."

"Thanks. Actually, why am I thanking you? This is a good scoop. I'm doing you a favour."

"You are."

"I know! You're really lucky Sean introduced us. You'd still be polishing wineglasses with absolutely no hope of an inside track on this."

"Yes, well, I'm very grateful."

"You don't sound very grateful."

"What do you want me to do, get down on my knees?"

"You know, that's not a bad idea. As I recall, it's a pose you do a lot with. You know how to work the angle."

"Actually, that was something I wanted to ask you, Theresa."

"You mean what happened the last time we saw each other?"

"Yes."

"I had a lot of fun, and it was nice getting to know you a little better."

"Right. Yeah. It was lovely. I guess what I'm wondering is, like, in your mind, how, uh, how does tonight end?"

"However you want it to."

"And if I want it to end the way the last one did?"

Theresa's red lips tugged up in the corners, creating gentle creases in her cheeks, something between a grin and a smirk. Her eyes had settled on something just past my shoulder before locking back onto mine. She took a long, leisurely sip from her drink before answering.

"Look, I'd be happy to have you over again. We can see where things go. But don't expect me to start sending you sweet little texts before bed every night."

"I'm most productive between ten and two, so that's not something you should worry about. I'll generally be working at that hour." Her mouth had now opened into a proper smile, and I felt a vertiginous drop inside my chest. I took a drink to have something to do with my hands. "So, like, do you want to get out of here?"

"No," she said. "I want another drink. You can tell me about your work, if you want to, and I can explain the major shortcomings of this country's approach to classical music education. We can have a nice civilized evening out together, like friends do, and then we can get out of here."

I nodded silently. I was smiling, too.

XIV

―――――――――

IN THE WEEKS that followed, I became familiar with Theresa's apartment. We saw each other regularly, although not often and not for very long. As is often the case with relationships that begin in large cities, there were parts of Theresa's life I knew quite well, and parts that were completely opaque. We usually talked of music. Her tastes ran to the bombastic and the provocative, and her views on the tradition were strictly contrarian: she insisted, poker-faced, that the greatest pianist who ever lived was Erik Satie. I knew she was studying music history, and I knew she regretted having chosen the University of Toronto, and would prefer to be living in the States. But about where her money came from, or if she had brothers and sisters, or whether she'd been raised religious, or if her parents were immigrants, I knew nothing. I suspected I wasn't the only one making regular midnight trips past the Portuguese widow's door to Theresa's cheerful little kitchen and dark, mysterious bedroom. We were both happy to avoid the subject.

I could accept the boundaries that had been put in place in part because of the agility and wit of her conversation. She spoke with absolute confidence, able to grasp immediately the root of any difference in opinion between us. I understood the world as a slow accretion of often-contradictory facts that took on definite proportions only over time. For Theresa, outlines seemed to appear immediately, as if lit by lightning. When she turned her attention to me, it was like being caught in a searchlight, illuminated in a way that was erotic and thrilling.

In other ways, of course, she was an ordinary person. She was fastidious about keeping her bread in a breadbox, but sometimes piled her dishes in the sink for days without washing them. She had a magnet on her fridge of herself as a first-grader. She farted delicately after sex and pretended it was a squeaking bedspring. The more time I spent in her apartment, the more these small things made it possible to believe this was not a brief and meaningless collision of bodies. Late at night, after she had cleaned the residue of my cum off her stomach in the bathroom, her ordinariness met my own. She rested her head on my arm and I dreamed of the future.

XV

IN MARCH, IN Toronto, there are days when the temperature rises so high it feels like a god has tilted the earth back on its axis, flooding the shores of Lake Ontario in Caribbean light, and there are days when the winds come suddenly in from the north, glazing the city in ice. The weather was particularly treacherous that first spring. I had gotten used to the consistent severity of Montreal, the way the snow and darkness suddenly disappeared sometime in April, to be replaced in a couple of weeks by humid greenery. Whenever it got warm, I optimistically switched out my winter jacket for a wool blazer. Ted found this extremely funny; he wore the same enormous corduroy overcoat regardless of the weather. But at the beginning of April, the forces of light made their final breakthrough and the city woke up to the first truly hot day of the year. Sasha and I opened every window and door in the apartment to entice the wind. We washed the stairs and swept the floors and bought stone fruits and melons and rum. Sev dropped by with white wine and seltzer, a sprig of mint in his pocket. Ted came home from work with a bottle of Scotch and a box of *decimos*. As the evening light burnished the windows of every building in the West End red gold, we smoked and drank in the slowly cooling air. It was a proper idyll, at least until the conversation came round to Sean Porter.

It was Sev who brought him up, in an offhand remark about the Great Lakes Opera Company. Sean was a member of the board, and Sev was hoping this connection would be advantageous: he had an audition booked for the end of the month. Perhaps he had forgotten that there was history between Sean and Sasha. Perhaps he, like the rest of us, was just too far in his cups.

"I'd be careful about relying on Sean too much," Sasha said. She was slouched down in a deck chair, her feet resting on the electric heater Ted had hooked up. "He only helps people who can help him. And even then."

Sev, who was in high spirits, laughed and said he had a pretty good idea of who Sean was.

"Be careful, saying things like that. If you really know who Sean is, you'll want to maintain plausible deniability."

"Do you mean the app thing? Everyone knows about *that.* CTV covered it, for fuck's sake. Not that I'm excusing the behaviour — like, it was obviously a shit-heel move."

"No, I don't mean the app thing."

I looked at Ted, who seemed to be following the conversation just fine.

"I'm sorry," I said, "but I don't know anything about the app thing."

"Just a little scandal," said Sev. "Or what passes for a scandal in Toronto. Sean Porter's first business was some kind of online marketplace app. It started out as a completely legitimate business, but a couple of years ago it came out that it was mostly being using for drug trafficking, prostitution, that kind of thing. Obviously, that raised legal issues, and there was some kind of inquiry. Sean said he'd been misled by his business partner, who was overseeing the regulatory side of things — or whatever the technical term for that is. He'd already cashed out, sold his stake a few months before the shit hit the fan. I think he ended up testifying against the company, talked about how lax the corporate culture was, you know, lots of boozy meetings, not a lot of concern about who was actually using the service. He made it sound like that's why he left. The other guy ended up getting slapped with a fine, the app got shut down, a bunch of sex workers had their private information leaked. A few people got picked up for dealing. Real nasty business."

"Slippery as a fucking eel," Sasha said around a mouthful of smoke.

"Some people — Sasha included, I guess — thought he knew a lot more about what was going on than he admitted."

"He knew exactly where the money was coming from."

"The Crown was unable to prove that," said Sev, almost apologetically.

"I was living with the fucker."

"I'm sorry, Sasha. I didn't mean to suggest … I'm not try-ing to defend the guy, right, I'm just telling Alex the story as I understand it."

"You don't know the fucking half of it. Sean knew what kind of business he was in from day one. How do you think he was getting his drugs? How do you think he was getting his dick wet?"

Sev was looking quite intently at the cherry on the end of his cigar. It had burned unevenly, and the ash was bowed out, the flame eating up the side of the rolled leaf.

"I don't have to like the guy to work with him."

"Yeah, yeah. I know. And I'm the crazy ex-girlfriend. You know, he told me everything, all the little secrets. He was never ashamed. That I will grant him. He never pretended to be any-thing other than what he was — at least not in private, at least not to me. He just made it sound like this was the only way to live, complete freedom, no pretending, no bourgeois morality. Like getting his friends to fuck me in the ass was a revolution-ary act. That's his charisma, his little magic trick. You go along with it because you believe it might actually be true. Everyone else is the greater fool."

The sun had long since set, and the only light on the roof was the glow of the electric heater. Ted poured out the rest of the Scotch. Sev flicked his cigar into the alley.

"I don't know what to say."

Sasha tottered to her feet, and Sev stood up to steady her. "Don't you worry, Sev. Sing your little heart out. You get the part, you don't get the part, it's all the same. I'm going to bed."

XVI

THERESA INVITED ME to her apartment a few nights later. She had some exciting news to share, and wanted me to come over as soon as possible. The stretch of Dundas Street between our houses was pointed straight into the heart of the city, the towers rising into the evening air like glittering stalagmites. But I was focused on visualizing the curve of Theresa's golden-brown hip, a horizon that receded no matter how ardently I approached.

I texted Theresa when I got to her building, but there was no response. I tried the knob and found it was unlocked. I walked upstairs and removed my shoes on the landing, and as

I slid them off, I heard a voice, not hers, on the other side of the door. I quietly put my shoes back on and retreated to the sidewalk. I lit a cigarette and walked a few dozen metres up the street and pulled out my phone. I felt extremely stupid.

It took three cigarettes before I saw someone emerge from Theresa's house, by which point I was not at all surprised to see who it was. For a moment, I was tempted to walk over and shake his hand and make a coarse comment, something filthy and degrading to both of us. Instead, I walked up the street with my back turned so he wouldn't see me smoking on the street, like a dog waiting outside a supermarket. My phone began to ring. It was Theresa.

"Where are you?" she asked.

"I'm just up the street."

"I thought you got here, like, fifteen minutes ago."

"I did."

"So why are you still up the street? I left the door unlocked." From my silence, she could tell I was taken aback. "Did you not try the handle?"

"Uh, no. I've just been out here, smoking."

"Okay, well, I'm sorry about that. But you really should have tried the handle instead of lurking out there like a creep."

I did feel like a creep. Why had I been so perturbed by the fact that she had someone over? There would have been nothing unusual about it. Maybe Theresa had meant for Sean and I to run into each other. But if she had, surely she would have responded more promptly and invited me in; she always kept her phone near at hand. She must have seen my text. When I climbed the stairs, I found her wearing a housecoat and drinking champagne by the kitchen window. The gown fell loosely from her shoulders, exposing the inner slopes of her breasts.

When she stood to pour me a glass, the thick cotton hung lazily about her legs.

"What's the occasion?" I said, as the bubbles tickled my nostrils.

She smiled and invited me to sit across from her. "'The City of Pigs.' They've got a location, the equipment's set to go, the musicians are ready. Everyone's getting chills. It's a whole new frontier."

"Really."

"This is a big deal for you, too. Your debutante's ball. Play your cards right, and you might end up going home with a rich gentleman."

"Just what I've always dreamed of."

"Don't be sarcastic. I'm really excited about how all this has come together. I've got goosebumps," she said, extending her arm to me.

"I can see that. These rich gentlemen never give you something for nothing, though."

"Right. But in this case, holding up your end of the bargain means doing something you ostensibly love. That's what we're talking about, right?"

"Yeah."

"Have more champagne."

I had more champagne, and we went to bed. She walked slowly in front of me, reaching up and letting her hair fall down her back. In the hallway, she shrugged off her housecoat. It fell around her feet, leaving the golden pillar of her body completely exposed. The flesh of her buttocks was red, and there were angry marks up and down her back. She watched my face over her shoulder.

"Do you see anything you like?"

I caressed the glowing patch of skin below the flare of her waist. It was very warm. I ran my hands gently up her rib cage and around her breasts. They rose like two halves of a pomegranate. She pressed gingerly against my pelvis.

"Is it sore?" I asked.

"Yes."

XVII

THE CONCERT FELL on the second Saturday in April. I was filled with a certain unease, a quickness of breath that came on me when I thought about the heat rising from Theresa's buttocks. I had caught a glimpse of something unpleasant inside myself, something aggressive and sadistic; I enjoyed feeling the poison waters closing above my head.

At eight o'clock, after I'd showered and drunk a pot of coffee, I received a text message from an unknown number. I responded with the code I'd been given when I purchased my ticket (Theresa had told me what to do) and walked down to the small park on Queen Street between nine and ten, to wait for further instructions.

A small knot of people had already gathered by a young maple near the path. I didn't recognize anyone, but when I said the word *Fera*, there was a round of nods. I hadn't been there ten minutes when a young man in a leather jacket appeared and told us to follow him. He asked each of us in turn if we were cops, which I assumed was part of the theatre, before leading us down a side street and around an office building, then into an alley that ran behind a row of houses. Everything felt very conspiratorial, but the whiff of transgression was tempered by the knowledge that, however naughty it might seem, nothing very bad could possibly happen. We'd bought tickets, after all.

A large brick building loomed at the end of the alley. A fire escape ran in zigzags up to the roof. Our guide led us wordlessly up to the first landing and knocked three times on a metal door that had no handle. It was opened by a young woman, also wearing a leather jacket, who escorted us through a series of cramped hallways and corridors to a large, unlit space that smelled of dust and sweat and perfume. As my eyes adjusted to the darkness, I realized that I was standing beneath some kind of mezzanine. I stepped past the row of shadowy pillars in front of me and a cavernous space opened up. Here and there I could see strings of glowing green lights, and around me dozens of whispered conversations came together to create the sound of a buried sea.

The pillars of the mezzanine curved gently inward. Ghostly faces flitted past, and the lights blinked from the deeper darkness beneath its shadow. As I grew closer, I realized that the blinking effect was created by a crowd of people milling around a makeshift bar. A small hand-lettered sign saying *$5* hung

above the counter. There was no other information. I took out
a ten-dollar bill and tried to get the attention of one of the
bartenders. They had necklaces of green glowsticks hanging
against their chests.

"What are you serving?" I whispered, when my turn came.

"It's five dollars," they said, pointing up at the sign.

"What's five dollars?" I asked.

"The price you must pay for a drink."

"Right, but what's the drink?"

"The Nectar of the Gods."

"Okay, but what is it really."

"We cannot say." A hint of irritation had crept into the
bartender's voice.

"I have allergies."

"Are you allergic to anything in sangria?"

"No."

"Then you should be fine."

"Great, give me two."

I drank one of the sangrias directly. It was shocking to
think that, somewhere just a few blocks from my apartment,
this enormous concert hall had been sitting empty for months.
When had it been built, and for what purpose, and how long
would it last? The cranes had begun to march north from
Liberty Village. New condos were going up on the corner of
Queen and Dovercourt. It seemed inevitable that such an un-
productive space would soon find itself slated for destruction.
There would be no record that this evening had ever happened,
that a concert had been held in spite of the safety pedants and
scolds and permit-grubbers. The music would live for a while in
people's memories, but in time (if Theresa was to be believed)
it, too, would be erased. And this was what the composers and

volunteers and musicians were willing to risk fines and court orders for. In spite of all the absurd posturing, perhaps filling this doomed theatre with mystery and young life for a few hours was not such an ignoble thing.

Again I wondered who was really paying for all this. Lying in bed with Theresa two nights before, I had tried to get her to disclose some information about what, exactly, I could expect. But she had just told me to read Book II of Plato's *Republic* again, which hadn't proved any more helpful the second time around. There was a great deal of talk about justice, and whether or not the best situation would be to behave unjustly while keeping the appearance of being an upright person. Then Socrates started talking about the beautiful city, the city where people lived simply and met their needs in uncomplicated ways. But Glaucon found this city too crude, fit only for swine, and told Socrates to be more realistic.

In theory, this squared well enough with the concert description. But I was left with a few nagging doubts. Socrates had given up on his beautiful city rather easily, after all, as if it were more a rhetorical gesture than an actual ideal. Later in the book, he certainly seemed happy enough with a stratified society, with philosopher kings at the top and foreign slaves down in the muck where they'd always been. It was as though the city of pigs was a kind of fantasy, an ideal of such unworldly beauty that no reasonable person could believe in it. But then perhaps I was reading too much into things. It was just a concert.

My train of thought was derailed when an ear-splitting shriek echoed without warning from somewhere in the depths of the theatre. The sound started out viciously high, a sudden, agonizing blast of pure noise settling into a kind of morbid buzz. When it finally died away, my heart was pounding and

I'd spilled sangria all over myself. The burst of sound was followed by a silence that carried on so long as to become unnerving. The audience began to whisper again, but as the sound of hushed voices increased in volume and pitch, it became clear that the whispers of the crowd had been joined by the hum of strings. From the mezzanine above, a blue light crept up the dome of the hall. The contours of the room became clearer. At the front was a stage that held a large, solid mass, a kind of squat cylinder or raised disc. The music of the strings became a kind of dreadful static, unsettling precisely because it was organic, like the crunch of a hand slammed in a car door.

The noise reached an unbearable excess, and there was a sudden electrifying *crack*. A narrow red spotlight turned on directly above the cylinder, revealing a figure dressed completely in black and carrying a bullwhip. A piano started to play somewhere up in the mezzanine, and it was joined by another and then another placed at points around the room. Each played a complex tonal figure in staccato bursts, less melody than percussion. A kettledrum added to the din with a series of cascading triplets. Because the musicians seemed to be half a beat or so behind each other, the music was filled with strange, unpleasant echoes, a cacophonous effect that was magnified by the size of the hall and the distance between the instruments. I had no idea how they were keeping time, or if they were even trying to keep time. The collision of sound made it nearly impossible to identify a signature. Tonally it was chaos, but as the piece went on, a certain inexorable pattern emerged. The rhythms of the timpani became more regular. The piano melodies simplified into chord progressions. Something like a beat appeared, and the stupefying noise coalesced into a mechanical grunt and shudder.

It was at this point that the figure in the centre of the stage cracked its whip again, and a series of dull thuds and clanks were heard in rough time with the music. Grey light filtered in from the wings, illuminating two lines of figures in simple tunics marching with long poles in their hands. Every step the figures took, the poles were raised and then hammered into the stage. The clanking sound came from the manacles and chains binding their hands and feet. One column snaked around behind the cylinder and the other curled in front of it, eventually taking their places in a ring around the structure. The whip cracked again, and the poles were slotted into holes in the sides of the cylinder. Each manacled figure took their place in front of their pole and began to slowly push forward, as if turning the spokes of a great wheel. The pianos, which were now playing in concert, were joined by the strings in a dodecaphonic fugue.

As the figures marched slowly around the circle, something remarkable happened. The top of the cylinder, which had seemed flat, slowly began to rise. The figure in the centre was pushed higher and higher into the air on a central pillar, ascending toward the spotlight above. Steps began to appear around the pillar as it rose, covered in mounds of fruit and olives and bread, great wheels of cheese and demijohns of wine. When the marchers completed their first revolution, the brash menace of a trombone could be heard issuing a long, low note that slowly rose in pitch and then burst into staccato broadsides that played a counterpoint to the beat of the drums. The cylinder was now a ziggurat, the figure with the whip a kind of heroic statue. The trombones and pianos began to add harmonies and counterpoint, giving the music a new emotional complexity. There was something of Strauss about it, and something, too, of Berg — yearning shaded into terror.

There was movement in the middle of the room, a group of people pushing and shoving through the audience. As the knot of bodies moved toward the front of the hall, it became clear they were following some kind of choreography. They slid fluidly over the lip of the stage and took their places in front of the manacled figures pushing the poles. They wore the same simple tunics, but a disproportionate number of them seemed to be female. A struggle ensued, a pushing match in which the newcomers strove to halt the advance while the prisoners kept doggedly moving forward. The high, fluttering trill of a clarinet danced above the swelling waves of the symphonic poem, joined by oboes and bassoons. The brass howled louder, but the woodwinds grew in strength as the newcomers slowly began to prevail, turning the screw back. The figure on the pillar became agitated, snapping the whip over the heads of the people below, but then his arm jerked back, arrested in the middle of the arc, the whip caught on something above the stage. He hung on to the whip as the pillar dropped out from below his feet, trying to climb it up to the light. Below, the manacled figures joined the newcomers and all together began to bring the ziggurat slowly down. After a climactic series of sustained notes, the horns expired in a long, agonizing chord, and the body flailing above the stage dropped sickeningly, the whip tangled into a noose.

All that was left was the clarinet, its melody, somewhere between a dance and a dirge, echoing above the quiet hall. The figures onstage stared at each other in shock. The sound of the clarinet was high but rich, and in time it was joined by a violin. As the intertwining harmonies played, the newcomers unclasped the manacles from their partners' hands. The rest of the strings and woodwinds joined in one at a time, rising from the silence to provide a glowing cushion of sound. When each of the figures onstage was free, a dancer leaped up onto one of the poles, like a gymnast on a balance beam. She unfurled her arm and reached out toward the nearest step, where a pile of fruit spilled out of a cornucopia. Her outstretched fingers grasped a bright red apple. Facing the audience, she raised it above her head. The rest of the dancers fell back, as if afraid of what was going to happen, but when she put it to her lips and took a bite, the entire orchestra gave voice to a magnificently twisted C Minor 7th chord and the stage was bathed in golden light. The chord hung in the air for a moment, the tableau frozen. She slowly brought the apple down from her mouth and, kneeling on the pole, offered it to a man standing before her. He bit into it, and the orchestra came roaring to life again with a vast, rippling moonrise in D-sharp.

The dancers began to climb up the platforms, tossing food down to those below. Coming out of the powerful single chord, the orchestra struck up a dance. A demijohn was opened and wine poured from the top of the ziggurat onto the dancers below, who waved goblets to catch it. The golden light on the stage was tinged with the blue of the mezzanine until a soft forest green emerged. The dancers began to carry fruit into the audience, and suddenly there were people bearing palanquins covered in grapes and large, many-hosed water pipes through the crowd, inviting anyone who wanted to breathe in the vapour. I took one of the hoses and sucked in the smoke until my lungs were full. It tasted of mint and rosewater and marijuana.

The dance continued through several variations, a different section of the orchestra taking the lead on each one. The music was filled with rich harmonies, but it was not without tension, and as the food and smoke made their way through the room, the melodic centre collapsed and shifted into a kind of seductive march. At the same time, the cheerful green began to grow deeper and bluer, its yellows dampening until the hall was lit in a dusky phosphorescence of sapphire and purple.

Someone grabbed my elbow. It was Theresa. She wore the same simple tunic as the dancers, and she was smiling mischievously. She held something out to me and whispered, "Take, and eat." I reached down. It was small and dry in my hand. Only when it was in my mouth and the rubbery texture of fungus crossed my tongue did I realize what I had eaten.

Around me, dozens of other women and men in tunics were moving through the room with baskets. Some took what they were given, others did not. My mouth felt dry, and I wished I had something to drink. Theresa was gone. I pushed my way through the crowd to the bar, which was now thronged with people. I was starting to feel quite strange. The light grew thicker and heavier. I slid my five dollars onto the counter and took the drink.

The march had morphed into a tarantella, and the dancers, who had placed their palanquins at cardinal points of the hall, now cleared a space in the middle of the room and began to gyrate in a circle, pulling audience members in to join them. The space became thronged with bodies. Audience members leaned against pillars, smoking, or watched from the deep shadows beneath the mezzanine. As the pace picked up, I was pulled into the interlocking circles of dancers in the middle of the room. I downed my drink and began to stamp and sway along with everyone else. Limbs flew around me, and clouds of hair, and the room was spinning. The violins howled a Neapolitan melody, and the music crossed some invisible barrier and entered its third modulation, something dark and sinister that spoke of forgotten religions and Neanderthal caves. Voices sounded from the edges of the room, chanting unrecognizable syllables, and the sweating bodies of the dancers curled in toward the centre of the hall. I retreated behind a pillar, and watched as they began a kind of deranged kalinka in the middle of the room, swaying and spinning and kicking as the audience clapped along. The music was a rapidly shifting interplay between clarinet, piano, and viola, and the chanting that flowed behind it was all diminished sevenths and minor thirds, a curtain of water falling over rock.

The floor of the hall was now an empty space, a hole surrounded by a rigid ring of bodies whipping and thrusting as they circled the centre. The spotlight flashed on again, and I could see two figures facing each other on the stage, the dancer who had given the apple and the dancer who had taken it. They were completely naked. The man reached out his hand to the woman and they began a rigid, almost violent tango, the man's penis swinging and slapping about in time with the music. They reached the lip of the stage, turned to the audience, and fell forward face first. They were caught by the interlaced arms of two pairs of dancers and thrown in the air, and when they fell back to the floorboards they landed in perfect form. They moved gracefully through the circle in contrary motion, as if they were stalking each other, the pace increasing, and the dancers around them moved in an ever-tightening circle, forcing the couple closer and closer. The music was aching and insistent, an impossible circle of harmonic tensions in duple time. My own heart had begun beating out of control, and every limb of every dancer hung very clearly in the light. The circle was just a crowd of bodies, the man and the woman caught in the middle, the rhythm and the dancers falling on each other in a mass of arms and hair and beads of sweat, in an impossible, unmistakably sexual rhythm.

The din was inhuman. The audience members, who had all seemed like normal people earlier that night, loomed monstrous and bizarre. Their bodies swayed and leaped; raw, physical presence, the air wet and heavy, and as I tried to move out of the way of a gyrating couple, I slipped on the floor and fell against a pillar. I reached behind to steady myself and found my hand touching a naked thigh. Two eyes gazed at me over a bare shoulder. The chanters emerged from the shadows, and they, too, were naked. I ran my hands down my chest. My shirt was soaked through. The hair on the back of my hands was matted in strange patterns. I chanted along in a language that belonged only to me.

The spotlight shone down on the primordial couple. Her legs were wrapped around his waist and he was holding her aloft and thrusting, thrusting with complete abandon. Her head was spinning, and her long, black hair lashed out over the bodies around her, flinging little beads of sweat that were each for a moment caught in the violent light. And beyond them, just outside the penumbra that fell on the centre of the room, a familiar body was pressed up against another pillar, two familiar eyes burning with a spiritual ecstasy. I staggered into the darkness, through the corridors and hallways, until I could taste the cold night air on the fire escape. I looked out over the back alleys and quiet houses, each containing its own pitiless mysteries, and threw up.

XVIII

———————

I DO NOT know how long I spent leaning against the flaking metal railing of the fire escape, but it was enough time to void ·my stomach completely. I'd had the presence of mind to jam a cinder block between the door and the frame, and when I was feeling slightly less ill, I ventured back into the darkness. Things had more or less degenerated in the great hall. The music was still playing, but even in the state I was in, I could tell the orchestra was basically improvising on a few simple themes. The centre of the hall was filled with dancers in various states of undress. The bodies of the fucked and the stoned were lying about beneath the mezzanine.

My recorder was in the breast pocket of my jacket, and when I looked at the little screen I could see that it had been running for nearly four hours. The thought that I had put myself through this for a reason floated unhappily into my mind.

There was no sign of the naked couple, no sign of Theresa. The mechanical ziggurat was now lit in soft burgundy, and I could see hanging above it the cord from which the overseer had hung. The stage door beckoned in the wings. In the cinder block quiet of the hallway, voices echoed from the dressing rooms, and I followed them until I reached an open door. Inside, someone was talking loudly about loading times.

I peered around the corner and rapped gently on the metal frame. "Hello," I said, "I was just wondering —"

"Alexander! I was wondering where you'd gotten to." Theresa was sitting on Sean Porter's lap. The room was filled with people lounging around in housecoats. The principal dancers were stretched out on a couch, limbs entwined, a joint burning away on the lip of a beer can.

A diminutive man wrapped in a kimono looked questioningly at Sean. "Is this the journalist?" he asked.

"Yeah, this is Alex," said Sean. "Don't worry, he's going to be very discreet. Alex, you had some questions, right?"

Theresa was running her hands through his hair. She seemed very stoned.

"Yes, I do, thank you very much for accommodating. Are you the composer?" I asked, directing the question to the man in the kimono.

"'Composer' isn't exactly the right word. The music was created collaboratively. But I guess you could call me the dramaturge."

"And may I ask your name?"

"You can call me Petronius."

"I see. I wonder if you could tell me, in your own words, about the inspiration behind the, uh, piece."

Petronius cocked his head and looked over at Sean, who nodded. The story Petronius told was not that different from the one Theresa had given me earlier. The performance was meant to celebrate the libidinal and Bacchic, it was a broadside against the ossified forms of classical music, a hymn to the healing powers of eroticism, etc. I asked how the collaborative aspect had worked. Petronius gestured for the other performers to chime in.

"We're not a hierarchy," he said. "Everyone had a say in creating the music. All I did was establish the basic narrative arc."

The atmosphere of the room was relaxed and druggy, but the performers were surprisingly articulate, and I scribbled down their answers, asking for points of clarification on technical matters here and there. They seemed to enjoy talking about what they had created. I supposed they didn't often get a chance to. I tried to work the interview around to the key question about the fallout from their previous performance, but Petronius kept bringing it back to aesthetic and political ground, and eventually I had to ask the question point-blank:

"Do you think Fera Civitatem bears any responsibility for the safety of people who attend these events? Or for the damage to the theatres?"

The question was met with laughter, though Petronius seemed to find it irritating rather than funny.

"Why single us out? No one has to come — we're not forcing anyone to do drugs. You don't hold a bar accountable for the drunk who drives home from it."

"Well, actually, I think Ontario law does —"

"You care so much about Ontario law? These old theatres are sitting empty, and we're returning them to their rightful owners, the people who live in this city. They're all going to be torn down, anyway."

"So you're just speeding up the process?"

Petronius shrugged. "We didn't mean to start a fire. Someone threw a joint in a garbage bin. Happens all the time. And it didn't even do that much damage."

"Alexander is very worried about health and safety issues, and damage to heritage architecture," said Theresa, head resting on Sean's shoulder. "He thinks you're being irresponsible. I tried to explain that that's the point."

"If you need a quote for your story," Petronius said, "you can say that we unequivocally condemn capitalist property fetishism and the social fascism that drives art and artists into unsafe liminal spaces while profiting off the pharmaceutical industry."

"Got it. Okay, Sean, I wonder if you could fill me in on —"

"Actually, Alex," Sean said, caressing Theresa's left breast, "I think it would be better if you leave me out of this. People might get the wrong idea."

"And what idea is that?"

"I'm just a participant, man, I'm not involved in any of this."

"You look like you're involved."

"Just enjoying some time backstage. People in this city have a real stick up their ass about rule-breaking, and any association between me and Fera could do serious damage to the whole project. Did you have any other questions?"

"I guess not."

"We're all looking forward to reading your piece," Sean said. "Theresa, do you want to show Alex out?"

Theresa got up reluctantly and led me back down the hall. She was a little unsteady on her feet.

"Don't be a bitch about this, Alexander, okay?" she said when we got to the exit. "This is really special."

"I won't be a bitch."

"Wonderful." She cupped my cheek in her hand and kissed me. "I'll see you this week?"

"I don't know about that, Theresa."

"What, now that you've got the story, you're not interested?"

"I'm just not good at this sort of stuff."

"What sort of stuff?"

I gestured impotently toward the hall.

"You're disappointing me, Alexander."

"Yeah, I know."

"Call me if you change your mind."

I'm not sure how I found my way back to Queen West. The bars had closed, and my footsteps rang loud in the empty streets. I wouldn't change my mind about calling Theresa; the way Sean had told her to walk me out assured me of that. I might not have minded if it hadn't been Sean. But there was a grinding inevitability in me, a fateful tug toward candour, that most ineffectual of virtues. I could not believe in the city of pigs. I could not trust any fantasy that denied the endless sucking pull of power.

XIX

IN A NARROW office on the fourth floor of a renovated warehouse in Old Toronto, I sat waiting for a sign. According to the two clocks hanging on opposite walls, it was both 10:15 and 10:21. The brown door in front of me had the word *Editor* stuck to it in old plastic letters. I had given myself plenty of time to make it across town, but still ended up jogging the last few blocks. Sweat trickled down the inside of my collar. Under my blazer, my cheap cotton shirt was stuck to the skin of my back. It turned out that I need not have worried about being on time. When I'd knocked on the door, a dry voice had told me to sit tight for a couple of minutes.

"Alexander Otkazov? You can come in now."

On the far side of a desk covered in papers, books, and a massive stack of compact discs, Henry Zimmermann gestured for me to sit down. Behind him, a modest window looked out on the alley. Above the rooftops, the rust-coloured bulk of Scotiabank Tower loomed over the spire of St. James Cathedral.

"Have we met before?" he asked as he reached out to shake my hand.

"I believe so," I said. "At Sean Porter's ..."

"Yes, yes, I remember now. You were interested in freelancing. And now you want to work here. A bit of an escalation in your ambitions, eh?"

"I suppose so."

"And you've also sent in this pitch for a feature about Fera Civitatem."

"Yes."

"I'm going to be honest with you here, Alexander — we've had applicants with more robust portfolios. Many of them are regular contributors to the magazine. Though, of course, what you have written is decent enough."

"That's kind of you to say."

"A B.Mus. in performance from McGill, a national medal, a couple of grants, a concert series, then some independent teaching, and now ... you work at a restaurant. Is that correct?"

"It is."

"Certainly tells a story."

"I think you'll find it's all about how the story gets narrated ..."

"I wasn't unmoved by your cover letter. I'm a man who believes in the possibility of redemption. You make a strong enough case for your experience as a performer and as a journalist. But this is a job that requires what I like to call 'character.' A certain sensitivity. Flexibility, even. The capacity to weigh different obligations prudently. This is not a very big city, you understand, and one must be careful about how one deals with sensitive matters ... which is, of course, not to say that we don't value our editorial integrity very highly, and strive to present our readers with as candid a view of the latest classical music news as possible."

"Between my time as a concert pianist and my years writing —"

"Yes, yes, but what I'm interested in is your coverage of 'The City of Pigs.' From what I heard, it was a somewhat irregular performance. Boundaries were pushed. Shock was experienced. How do you intend to write it up?"

"I've actually already finished the piece."

"Really?"

"I emailed it to you last night."

"Ah, yes, well, I haven't quite had time, it's been a busy morning, you see, and my inbox ..."

"I did take the liberty of bringing a copy with me. I noticed that most of the features in the magazine tend to be between two and three thousand words, so I split the difference and aimed for two and a half thousand."

I handed Zimmermann a document from my bag and waited in silence as he scanned the first few lines.

He looked up at me over his spectacles. "You don't mind if I ..."

"Go ahead." Sunlight poured down the brick wall outside the window. It was a clear morning, unseasonably hot.

Zimmermann leaned back in his chair and held the typed pages up to the light, as if looking for a hidden message.

"It's fine," he said. "Strong lede, good mix of coverage and analysis. And the sensory details are especially vivid, which will be a nice change from our usual tone — which, I'm sure you know, runs rather more toward the prosaic and informative. No, don't worry, it's a good thing. Shows a degree of versatility and, uh, panache. Though of course we generally do have to be rather careful about word count. Some of the more exuberant flourishes might, as it were, have to go. My God, it does seem rather hedonistic, though, doesn't it? I mean, one grasps the allegory. And on a certain level, I suppose all the nudity serves a purpose. Don't misunderstand me, I'm not a *prude*, there's nothing *wrong* with a bit of titillation. But take this bit at the end here with the, ah, sex at the, um, the climax of the show. You've handled it with great sensitivity, but we might need to find more … elliptical language. You weren't able to get anyone on the record about whether or not it was simulated, eh? Aside from this quote about how they're 'celebrating the carnal foundation of all being,' which I think we can both agree doesn't shed much real light on the matter. No? I see. Obviously what they're doing isn't exactly kosher, but putting on a live sex show would make them guilty of a number of other, uh, violations. And if it wasn't real … what I'm saying is, we don't want to take any chances, legally speaking."

I waited for him to say something more, but he sat there silent, the pages still in his hand.

"Should I …" I began tentatively, gesturing for the door.

"No. I mean, yes, sure. I've got another interview at eleven, but they have not, to my knowledge, included a completely new piece of reportage in their application, so unless they're hiding something remarkable, it's probably going to be good news for you. But I'll be in touch either way."

He shook my hand, and I made my way down to the street. I had been feeling quite unwell, but the fresh air was reviving. The streets of the financial district were windy and cold, the plate glass reflecting an infinite sky. When I had passed through their valley of shadows, I was once again amid the comforting yellow- and red-brick shopfronts and pale-green parkettes. I decided to celebrate with dumplings. Waiting for the light to change in Chinatown, I noticed the high, bulky roof of a theatre rising behind the empty shopfront on the northeast corner, its former name — *The Oren* — fading away in black paint. It suddenly struck me that this must be the theatre where "The Garden of Earthly Delights" had been performed so many months before.

The light turned green, and as I drew closer, I saw that what had once been a Chinese grocery had a development sign in the window. The sun-blasted poster taped up behind the glass told me the whole corner block was to be turned into a condo tower. Bitterness washed over me. I walked around back to the alleyway, to see if I could find the legendary stage door Fera Civitatem had broken into after cracking the lock. There it was, set in a shallow brick alcove. The same kind of metal door I had walked through the week before. But when I approached it, I was surprised to find that no such lock existed. Indeed, there was no handle at all. It could be opened only from the inside. If they had broken in, it had been a much more sophisticated operation than the mythology suggested. I wondered if Petronius understood how Fera had been used, or was being used. Or did he really believe his own story? Perhaps he'd never finished *The Republic*, and didn't know that the city of pigs really was a rhetorical device, the impossible utopian society that had to give way to the enlightened despotism of the philosopher king. Something told me Sean Porter and Lionel Standish had read their Plato more carefully.

SECOND MOVEMENT

THE LOWER REGISTERS

I ARRIVED IN the city on a Tuesday afternoon, under low clouds. I walked out of the train station, and the statues in the park, the homeless people shuffling beneath the trees, the grey faces of the pedestrians seemed to belong to another time. My hotel was on top of the hill, across from the citadel, but I followed the station road twisting down to Bishop's Wharf. I'd seen the water from the window of the train as we came in along the port. Grey like the weather.

Everything on the waterfront was new and clean but the water itself. I smoked a cigarette and threw the butt into the filthy scrim licking the wooden piles. The smell of salt and kelp and dead things clung to the pier. I was completely alone.

On the far shore, the holding tanks and cooling towers of the derelict refinery lay flat against the horizon, the pilot flame of the flare stack extinguished. In between, the sleek back of a small island rising from the water. But it was the harbour I was interested in. For years it had been the place where Europeans stepped out of their histories to become happy, provincial Canadians. And now, below its surface, a machine was being built — the first in this country, the largest in the world. Yet there was no evidence of it at all.

It started to rain. I pulled my jacket closer and walked up the hill. My shoes kept slipping on the slick stones of the street. The lobby of the hotel was sepulchral, and a long, washed-out man stood behind the front desk. Pushing his glasses up his nose, he asked if he could help me, although he didn't look like he wanted to. I told him my name and he consulted his computer screen. He began flipping through a small box, looking for a plastic key card.

"Business," he said, and I realized he was asking why I had come.

"I suppose."

"You suppose."

"I'm writing a piece about the organ."

"Oh, that." He gave me a look. "What a typically stupid idea. This city is always coming up with these stupid ideas. Because of the money, I suppose. Or rather the lack of money. They keep thinking one of these big projects is going to bring in a bunch of business for the city. Never occurs to them to invest in something that might actually provide folks a steady job, but there's always a handout for some professor, some

halfwit with a plan that will 'really put Halifax on the map.'
You heard about the refinery? Turning it into a terminal for
cruise ships. Say it'll boost the local economy, bring in those
American dollars." He stared wetly over his glasses and paused,
rooting his tongue along his molars. "Tell me something: If you
were here on a five-star cruise liner in from Boston, would you
stay at my hotel?"

I tried to look sympathetic. He hadn't handed over my key
yet. "Perhaps with the organ, it will be different," I said.

The proprietor nodded. There was a twitch around his left
eye that made it look like he was winking. "Listen, I'm United
Church myself, so it's not like I'm against organs as such. Used
to love listening to my gran play the one they had up at St.
Matthew's. Beautiful sound, especially with those old hymns.
You know, 'Holy Holy Holy,' 'O God, Our Help In Ages Past.'
I get all choked up just thinking about it. They took it out
when the young minister decided to start playing everything on
his guitar. Saved him paying my gran, you see. No sense for the
tradition. I'm telling you this only so you know I'm what you
might call sympathetic to the organ, generally. What I don't
understand is, if they were going to build the biggest organ in
the world, why did they decide to put it at the bottom of the
harbour?"

II

THE ORIGINS OF hydroörganonology are contested. Print references to underwater organs are almost non-existent before the nineteenth century, but this has not stopped some of the more enthusiastic hydroörganonologists from arguing that they are nearly as old as their more famous terrestrial counterparts. Textual evidence suggests a hydroörganon may have been among the many pleasures Tiberius arranged to be built as part of his Villa Jovis on Capri, although the archaeological record is so scant (and the possibility so unlikely, given the villa's placement high on a rocky promontory) that most scholars dismiss it as being fanciful. A more substantive piece of evidence is the *San Marcos*, discovered just off the coast of Spain in 1977, which included several large pipes and a wind-chest dating from the fifteenth century. Given that the remains are a mere kilometre from the site of a galleon known to have been wrecked en route from Genoa, however, the argument that it is a primitive hydroörganon, and not simply the scattered parts of a conventional organ, rather strains credulity.

Most scholars agree that the first indisputable reference to an underwater organ came with the publication of Giovanni Bonavista's *Catalogue of Musical Instruments New and Proposed* in 1765, which includes schema for a rudimentary hydroörganon featuring ten pipes and a bellows operated through an ingenious series of hoses and manual pumps. Bonavista claimed that the hydroörganon was a completely novel instrument (and was, in fact, the first to use the term *hydroörganon* to describe a subaqueous organ), but this claim has been frequently debated. Skeptics point out that Bonavista was hardly scrupulous when it came to crediting his sources, and had a tendency to claim authorship for ideas for instruments that had venerable, if usually obscure, theoretical pedigrees.

It wasn't until later in the nineteenth century, following the spread of the Industrial Revolution across Europe, that speculative hydroörganonics really became a popular exercise for engineers and organ makers. No less an inventor than Isambard Kingdom Brunel came up with a design for a hydroörganon to be built off the coast of Cornwall, and Richard Strauss and Igor Stravinsky are both reputed to have written works for the theoretical instrument (autographs are yet to be found for either).

But it was after the Second World War that hydroörganonology really came into its own as a discipline. During the postwar construction boom, several of the more experimental architects placed miniature (non-functional) hydroörganons in artificial ponds, marine parks, waterfalls, etc., and John Cage's journals are filled with references to the instrument. It is rumoured that he made several attempts in the sixties and seventies to raise funds to build a test hydroörganon in the Hudson River, near Stony Point, and it has been argued (most notably by Dr. Susan Shaw, the maverick director of Winnipeg's new music festival during its turbulent and anarchic period in the late 1980s) that Cage's legendary *4'33"* was inspired by the paradoxical acoustical possibilities of an underwater organ. Shaw believed the famous four and a half minutes of silence were a tribute and gesture toward a future in which that silence could be filled by the deep tones of a hydroörganon. She even theorized that Cage had written a companion piece to *4'33"* consisting of a score exactly four minutes and thirty-three seconds in length to be played on a hydroörganon, once it had been invented.

But the beginning of modern hydroörganonology — hydroörganonology as a fully actualized musical discipline — is precisely datable.

On August 15, 1993, an unknown aquatic engineer/architect/amateur organist named Kenji Saito announced that he had completed his "Senritsu," the first full-scale, fully functional hydroörganon to be built in the modern era, on a promontory off the coast of Numazu in Japan's Suruga Bay. Overnight, hydroörganonology went from being an armchair science to a controversial new form of public art, one that united disciplines as diverse as acoustics, oceanography, architecture, and musicology.

Saito's masterpiece offered a concrete example of the challenges of practical hydroörganonics, and a new way of thinking about the musical (and musicological) possibilities of the instrument. The first public performance on the "Senritsu" featured a program built around Bach's *Clavier-Übung III*, with some of Saito's own improvisations thrown in to show the range of the instrument. A recording was made, but issues regarding ownership and copyright have kept it from public release. Those who have heard it note that it is vastly inferior to the experience of seeing the "Senritsu" in action.

But even at this, the first recorded performance of a hydroörganon, the audience was sharply divided as to the nature of what they had witnessed. Most found the music itself completely secondary to the spectacle of watching the air jet and bubble out of the great pipes, and acknowledged they were at best able to hear only a rich humming sound, with a few quavering variations as new pipes were opened. But others (a decided, though not insubstantial minority) claim to have heard a completely breathtaking range of tonal patterns. Not the music of a terrestrial organ, but a completely faithful transformation of it. Hatsuo Tanako famously described it as like "hearing Bach performed by whales." Konstantin Volkov, a professor of baroque music at the Moscow Conservatory who had been personally invited by Saito, likened the experience to hearing Shakespeare translated into Russian.

Over the course of the late summer and early autumn of 1993, Saito brought several diving groups down to view the hydroörganon, and word spread in avant-garde musical circles and among the more speculative branches of musicology of this massive organ built into a rock face at the bottom of a Japanese bay. The question of what the hydroörganon meant, having been completed at a time when the traditional pipe organ seemed little more than an anachronistic remainder from an era when people didn't have electricity and believed in God, quickly overshadowed the actual experience of listening to the performances themselves. At least, for all but those stubborn few who insisted they heard something remarkable when the pipes were opened. Musicians and theorists made the pilgrimage to Numazu because they felt it would be gauche to write about the "Senritsu" if they hadn't actually heard it. Some of them came away utterly changed; most of them managed to get something about it published in *Music Perception* or *Interface*.

As the winter of 1993–94 set in, Saito stopped bringing groups down to "Senritsu," citing the unpredictable weather conditions. He spent the winter in his cabin on the slopes of Mount Fuji, where he could see the restless waters and dream of his hydroörganon. It is generally agreed that it was during these months he wrote what would stand as his own most complete theoretical account of hydroörganonology: 深音, usually translated into English as *The Bass Note*.

Saito resumed his tours the next spring, to redoubled interest from both the local and international baroque and classical communities. He received letters from Arvo Pärt, Philip Glass, and Kaija Saariaho, and was interviewed by the BBC. It was an odd story, and people liked its oddness. This young Japanese Renaissance man, with a quasi-mystical theory of harmony and a deep love for the music of Johann Sebastian Bach, had created an instrument that the professional music world had always imagined to be nothing more than a curiosity. And he had made it beautiful — some even believed he had made it sing.

Kenji Saito's burgeoning career as the first professional hydroörganonist ended early in the morning on June 18, 1995, when his body was found floating off the coast of Nishiizu. He was wearing his wetsuit and his mask was off, although his oxygen tank was still at 30 percent. It was clear he had drowned. No one, however, was ever able to explain why.

III

THE BAR BELOW Argyle was not the kind I would have walked into if I weren't travelling with a per diem. Everything was old except for the servers, who were very young. I took off my jacket and ordered a dark beer at the bar. I asked the bartender what she thought of the organ, and she looked at me as though she wasn't sure what I was talking about.

"The organ being built in the harbour," I said.

She thought organs were supposed to be in churches. And who goes to church anymore, even in Halifax? I told her it wasn't strictly an ecclesiastical instrument. She shrugged and moved on to the next customer.

I pulled out my notebook and stared at the bullet points I'd scribbled down, necessary facts I might need to refer to in my interviews the next day. Zimmermann had not given me as much time as I would have liked to prepare (though all the time in the world might not have been sufficient), and I'd comforted myself with the thought that a long train ride would provide the perfect opportunity to get reacquainted with the particulars. But as soon as I had settled into my seat, I was overcome with a profound listlessness that didn't dissipate until some point in the middle of the night, long after I'd switched trains in Quebec City. It would have been much easier to fly, of course, but someone high up at VIA Rail was a sponsor, and my ticket had been practically free. All it cost was four days of my life.

In the morning I woke in an ill temper, my face plastered against the glass, and I spent the day with my laptop open, staring out at the brush flying past the window. Every time I summoned up the urge to start some preliminary writing, the memory of a photograph flitted across my mind, a memory that evoked related and unpleasant memories.

I'd first heard about hydroörganons in Montreal, amid the first tremors of the nervous breakdown that would euthanize my fledgling career. I was about to embark on a series of concerts that was meant to take me across the eastern part of the country. The program was heavy on the kind of material I played a lot of in those days — Cage's pieces for prepared piano, some Messiaen, a piece by Shlonsky — and I had been plagued with insomnia. I dealt with the insomnia by drinking, which made the insomnia worse, which made my playing worse, which made my drinking worse. Hoping it would bolster my confidence, my girlfriend, Sophie, threw a party the week before the first show. It was at this party, sitting on the fire escape of our apartment in the Latin Quarter, that Sophie's friend Jean-Sebastien showed me the photo of vast stainless-steel pipes glowing in the blue light of the Tyrrhenian Sea.

Jean-Sebastien had just returned from Italy, where Antonio Carpaccio, one of Saito's many imitators, had recently completed his "L'Imperatore" off the coast of Naples. I was looking for a quiet place to smoke until it was all over, which was how I found them together on the fire escape. Jean-Sebastien hadn't stopped talking about Italy since he'd arrived. This was tiresome, but not out of character. He was a few years older than us and worked full time as an organist. At the time, I assumed all the talk about Italy was something he needed to puff himself up: most professional organ work is lethally dull. But Sophie was quite taken with it, and kept asking him to tell her more about the hydroörganon concert he'd attended.

I was unaware that they were sleeping together. But while I watched Sophie's eyes as he described the mighty sound he'd heard emanating from the instrument, the unbelievable complexity of texture and intonation it was capable of, I could feel that the ability to play was not the only thing slipping out of my grasp. My suspicions were confirmed the next day, when I tried to ease the tension of a Sunday-morning hangover by poking fun at Jean-Sebastien's obscure pretensions. I could hardly blame her when she moved out a few weeks later. I would have broken up with myself, if such a thing were possible.

The tour began with a disastrous performance at St. Matthias and proceeded apace. By the time I reached Kingston, I could barely climb up to the stage. Fumbling through Cage's *Bacchanale*, I got stuck at the end of the A section. I repeated the final bars over and over again, overcome by dread and unable to move forward or stop. Eventually someone was kind enough to escort me offstage. It was the last time I played in public. The dates in Ottawa and Toronto were cancelled, and I returned to Montreal, my humiliation complete.

In the years that followed I would sometimes dream of blue sunlight playing over a set of glimmering pipes eight fathoms down. I would push my way through the cloying seaweed, trying to reach the masked hydroörganonist sitting in front of the manuals, but a crowd of spectators would pull me back. I started writing to keep the dream at bay. In time, I came to believe that writing about music was a higher calling. Of all the arts, the beauty of music is the most unreliable; one can experience it only in time. Words last forever.

I thought about all of this in a bar below Argyle Street, as I drank dark beer and watched the young servers bring plates of seafood to the old and wealthy. I wondered whether the bartender, if told about the instrument being constructed in her city's harbour, would agree that it was a monument to human vanity. But she didn't say anything more about it, and neither did I.

IV

SAITO'S TRAGIC DEATH, and the simultaneous publication
of the English edition of *The Bass Note*, provided the impetus
for the first academic conference dedicated to hydroörganonology. Held in Fuji in early 1996, it drew scholars from across
the wide range of disciplines connected theoretically to the
hydroörganon. By far the most widely attended panels were
led by musicologists eager to establish that their own theories
of the hydroörganon had the greatest explanatory power and
revolutionary potential.

The Bass Note was a fascinating document, but it did not
lay out any kind of coherent theoretical program. Saito had

seemed less interested in explaining what the hydroörganon meant than in exploring what it could do — specifically, what it could do to Western music. Saito's lens was highly idiosyncratic. Starting with Psalm 42:7 ("Deep calleth unto deep at the noise of thy waterspouts: all thy waves and thy billows are gone over me"), Saito, whose father had been a Presbyterian minister, set out in brief an interpretation of the entire baroque organ canon as an exploration of the idea of depth. Whereas traditional representations of Christian cosmology imagined the divine as being "above," Saito posited that organ music is at its most powerful, and at its most unique, in the lower registers. Saito's thesis, arrived at after a number of technical digressions on the nature of lower frequencies of sound, appeared to be that the divine is most present in the literal, sonic, geographic, and symbolic "depths." God is the throbbing hum of an inhumanly low frequency, a bass note that sustains the universe. This, Saito believed, was the true meaning of the old *musica universalis*. By placing an organ, the instrument most capable of rendering deep registers (and the Western instrument most closely associated with divinity), in the literal depths of the ocean, the hydroörganon became a nexus of spiritual power.

Hydroörganonologists who read *The Bass Note* fell in love with it immediately, both for its technicality and its outrageousness, long and durable academic careers having been forged on far less.

What quickly came to be considered the mainstream of hydroörganonological theory derived less from Saito's text itself (although it is generally — and, perhaps, carefully — acknowledged to be a classic of the field) than from the secondary work of James Whitney and Nicola Fanucci, both of whom argued that the hydroörganon represented the end and apotheosis of

Western music. In his book *Trans-Musical Expressionism and the Aural Aquatic: Critical Essays on Kenji Saito's "Senritsu,"* Whitney argued that in a world where most musicologists are still trapped in a logocentric obsession with sound as the essential basis for music, hydroörganonics heralded a rupture in its rejection of auralnormativity, one that liberated musicology from the heteropatriarchal colonialist logic of late capitalism. What could be more revolutionary in the history of Western music — he argued in the final, incendiary essay, "Subaqueous Rhapsody" — than an organ that didn't make any noise?

From a strictly musicological standpoint, Fanucci's thesis followed a similar trajectory. Starting with the argument that Saito had completed the long process of deconstruction that began nearly a century earlier with Arnold Schoenberg, she garnered significant praise among eco-critics for showing that hydroörganonics also operated as a kind of environmentalist guerrilla aesthetic. Acknowledging that the building of "Senritsu" had caused some environmental damage to its immediate location (in order to accommodate the massive wind trunk and the pumps bringing air down to fill it, a sizable portion of rock had been blasted away), Fanucci argued that "Senritsu" ultimately symbolized a more "harmonious" (readers were coyly asked to pardon the pun) relationship between humans and their natural environment. A side effect of having such a valuable tourist attraction in what was still a commercial harbour meant local governments had to be more thoughtful about how they disposed of industrial waste: with scores of scuba divers descending to witness concerts every day, an unprecedented degree of attention was now being paid to water quality and biodiversity in Suruga Bay.

Not everyone was equally taken with the novelty of "Senritsu," however. Johann Schröder argued that the principles underlying "Senritsu" were the same that had governed Ctesibius of Alexandria's third century BCE hydraulas, which had established the essential blueprint of all future organs and hydroörganons: air forced through pipes of varying lengths and sizes to create vibrations of specific pitches, which were manipulated by opening and closing pipes. While Schröder conceded there was a degree of novelty in Saito's idea of building a full-size functioning pipe organ underwater, he upbraided what he saw as an overly "fetishistic" tendency among the new stars of the hydroörganonics movement to paint the innovations of Saito and his followers as heralding a completely new era in the history of organ technology. What was really interesting about the hydroörganon, and about *The Bass Note*, Schröder argued, was Saito's relationship to the tradition. Rather than seeing him as a kind of radical deconstructionist, Schröder suggested that Saito resembled no one so much as old Bach himself, who had likewise seen very clear parallels between the formal structure of music and the structure of the cosmos.

Of course, there were also responses from more reactionary voices. Harold Dankworth-Jones, a research chair in musicology at UCLA, gave a withering denunciation of Seito's work at the Conference for Musical Aesthetics at Heidelberg in 1998. In his opening keynote, Dankworth-Jones suggested "Senritsu" had as much artistic merit as the London Eye and about the same function. An earlier generation of musicologists, he argued, would not have been fooled by this kind of stunt. But the rise of postmodern theory had had such a corrosive, degrading effect that the once fine minds in his own department were now more interested in pumps and bubbles than the hard historical and theoretical work required to grapple with the genius of the great composers. And as for the organists sucked in by this nonsense, well, what kind of commitment to craft could there be in playing a Bach chorale prelude, if no one could properly hear it? Where was the discipline required to master the old instruments and techniques, Dankworth-Jones wanted to know. At least Picasso could paint like a realist when he wanted to. If they were so impressed with gimmicks, what did the hydroörganonologists think of the "wave organ" in San Francisco? Was this, too, a bold new aesthetic movement?

The hydroörganonologists present did not take this well, and insisted they had as much in common with the "wave organ" as a Stradivarius did with a plastic guitar. Over the years, they would go to great lengths to distance what they believed was the purity of their own art from such vulgar popularizations as the cretinous "sea organ" of Zadar, with its inoffensive, repetitive harmonies and smug Croatian street vendors. Likewise, the family-friendly hydraulophones, with their cute watery burbling good only for playing irredeemably banal pieces like Pachelbel's "Canon in D," were mere circus games compared with the grandeur and might of the hydroörganon.

To everyone's surprise, after being little more than an academic curiosity during the first years of its official existence, the hydroörganon became a serious concern in the early years of the new millennium. Local and national governments began to take an interest in the economic possibilities of the hydroörganon. After his death, Saito's remarkable accomplishments and the tragic, made-for-television arc of his creative life began to attract media attention. Profiles followed in the *New Yorker, Der Spiegel*, and *National Geographic*. Television crews interviewed his artistic peers, his assistants, his bewildered parents. They interviewed Schröder and Fanucci, whose expensive words and Ivy League diction cast the enterprise in an excitingly intellectual light. Attempts were made (in vain) to unmask his mysterious financial backers. Famous organists agreed to give performances on "Senritsu," and tourists flocked to Suruga Bay to watch them.

There was still a clear divide, among those who witnessed performances on the hydroörganon, as to whether they were, in fact, listening to anything. Those who said they did hear music ("sonicists," they called themselves) claimed they had a more refined sensitivity. Those who didn't tended to assume that those who said they did were hopeless exaggerators and poseurs, the same kind of people who believed they could tell the difference between a Châteauneuf-du-Pape 2002 and a Châteauneuf-du-Pape 2006. But regardless of what came to be known as the "sound question," the "Senritsu" was such a fun thing to watch that spectators continued to don their wetsuits and descend for the daily performances. As for the musicologists, such questions generally didn't interest them; they settled on whatever accounts best suited the critical narrative they were trying to build around hydroörganonology, which tended to align nicely with whatever arguments they were making about other aspects of twentieth-century musicology.

Plenty of cities have made a tourist industry out of music. But whereas the restaurants and hotels of Salzburg have benefitted from the Mozart festivals, Numazu, the nearest town to "Senritsu," also raked in cash from the rental of scuba gear, the chartering of boats, and tours of the various sites associated with Saito's secretive life.

Other coastal cities realized that there was a substantial economic incentive for backing similar projects of their own. In the grand scheme of things, a working hydroörganon cost significantly less than a new concert hall, and provided a similar kind of high-culture prestige. The early 2000s were a feverish period of hydroörganon construction. Hydroörganons were built in San Francisco, Marseille, Seattle, and Naples. They became a symbol of status, a way of establishing a city's cultural, cosmopolitan bona fides. New pieces of music were written with the hydroörganon in mind, which dovetailed nicely with the development of popular electronic drone music. The "Senritsu" was even featured during a chase scene in a James Bond film, the air bubbles from its pipes providing a screen for Bond's escape after a particularly tense encounter with Yakuza assassins.

Construction tapered off after the recession of 2008. It was hard to justify spending money on something so frivolous when people were being asked to surrender their pensions for the sake of austerity. There was also the matter of the aging ideological combatants in the theoretical world of hydroörganonology, who could drum up little sympathy for the cultural wars of the nineties among the new generation of hydroörganonologists, all of whom were much more interested in critiquing the barriers facing upcoming women hydroörganonists and hydroörganonists of colour than in designing newer, larger, more creative hydroörganons.

And so it came as somewhat puzzling news when the Chebucto Project announced it would be building the world's largest hydroörganon in Halifax Harbour. Rumour had it that the same family of billionaires who controlled most of the oil and natural gas industry on the East Coast were behind the venture, but it proved impossible to either confirm or deny this. And hydroörganonologists have never been particularly zealous about following the money trail behind their favourite projects.

V

———

I WOKE UP the next morning bilious and grainy and hungover. Rain on the window. I was supposed to be meeting a man named John Philips at a café on the Dartmouth side of the harbour at 9:30. I didn't know what schedule the ferries ran on, or whether I should take the bus. The hotel's complimentary coffee tasted like tree bark. The shower never got warmer than tepid. I hadn't unpacked my clothes. I hadn't written my questions. I had only a general idea of what I wanted to know. Why build a hydroörganon in Halifax. Why build a hydroörganon now. Why make it the largest in the world. What was there to prove?

When I got to the café, I was fifteen minutes late and soaking wet. Philips had already had a coffee and a croissant. The café was famous for its croissants, he explained. I really had to have one. It was part of the experience. They were the best croissants in the Maritimes. I told him I'd eaten at my hotel. The water from my jacket dripped onto the floor below me.

Philips was the kind of Maritimer who, despite never having really spent any time on a boat or outside of the city, felt that being born in a certain proximity to the sea entitled him to pronouncements on the nautical life. He spoke about the beauty of the Atlantic, the tragedy of the fishery, the humble nobility of fishermen — all that *Lost Salt Gift of Blood* shit.

He seemed more in his native element when talking about the importance of Nova Scotia, the vibrant cultural scene. Halifax, he told me, was a "world city." Haligonians had music and the ocean in their blood. He himself was a great music lover. Listened to music all the time. Had I heard of Joel Plaskett? Great local musician. And did I know he lived just up the way? Also a great city for fiddle music, Halifax. If I couldn't get to a "genuine East Coast kitchen party," I should check out one of the excellent bars along Argyle Street. Had I heard about the first-rate nightlife in Halifax? People who visited Halifax loved to hear that wonderful, authentic, totally unique, world-famous East Coast fiddle music played at open-mic nights. People from all over the world came to hear it. Nova Scotia was like no other place on Earth, which was why it was the perfect place to build the largest organ — sorry, yes, hydroörganon — the world had ever seen. He was proud to represent the provincial government's interest in the project. "Music and the ocean: you won't find two more authentically Nova Scotia things in all your born days."

Something about the way he said this made me wonder if he used phrases like "all your born days" when talking to people who actually lived here. I asked whether he had any qualms about the fact that the organ was going to be under-water. Were Haligonians, with their famous love of music, going to be diving down to witness the dull heaving of the pipes, the careful finger-work of an organist they were barely able to hear?

Philips chuckled, a gurgling sound that started somewhere in his cheeks and ended in his nasal cavity. Had I heard of the legendary "Citibank Colossus" in Long Island Sound? Well, the "Chebucto" had fully double the footage of pipes, and three times the power — and people thought there was nothing hap-pening in Halifax!

He didn't answer my question about where the money was coming from.

"It's a private-public partnership," he said. "All the ne-cessary paperwork has been filed with the province and the Halifax Regional Municipality, and I'm sure if you file a re-quest for information, they would be happy to let you access it."

He asked whether I would have a chance to meet the archi-tect while I was in town. I told him we'd be speaking later that afternoon. She'd arranged for me to take a tour of the worksite. He laughed professionally.

"You're a lucky man, seeing our beauty without her clothes on." (I assumed he meant the organ.) "This is going to go down in history. Largest of its kind in the world. Make sure you men-tion that in your article."

I told him I would. He said it had been a pleasure.

John Philips walked out of the café, corduroy jacket creased around the oval of his shoulders, sweat glistening on the skin of his neck that bulged over his collar. His shoes were carefully polished, and his hair was arranged to minimize a growing bald spot. I wondered what he thought had happened during our conversation.

VI

———

THE WEATHER CLEARED up around noon, but the weak
sunlight only made the city look browner. I was standing on
the pier going through my notes when I noticed a tall, broad-
shouldered woman staring at me from a nearby bench. She had
short grey hair and the kind of advanced fibre shirt worn by
people who go hiking in the Himalayas. I realized she must be
Rebekah Schumacher, chief architect of the Chebucto Project.
She had recognized me before I recognized her.

"Mr. Otkazov?" she asked when I caught her eye.

"Yes."

"You're early."

"It's a nice day."

"Above the surface, yes. But the rain means more silt in the harbour. We can still go down this afternoon if you want to, but I'd advise waiting until tomorrow."

"I leave tomorrow night."

"We can do it in the morning. The weather is supposed to hold."

"Are you still free for an interview?"

"Yes. But I'd prefer not to speak in public."

"You understand that I need something from you on the record."

"Of course. I just don't like speaking in public."

Schumacher got up from the bench and started to walk away. Not knowing what else to do, I followed her.

Rebekah Schumacher. Before leaving for Halifax, I had spent nearly a week trying to trace the outline of her life. It wasn't only that she had zero social media presence, no webpage, an almost non-existent digital footprint; it was that the information that did exist was tantalizingly suggestive of a rich and productive life. Even after employing some of the more arcane journalistic tricks for digging up buried identities, I had been able to put together only a cursory biographical sketch.

Born in London in 1959 to a Jewish family from Odessa, Schumacher was accepted to study piano at the Royal College in 1976. She graduated with honours, having switched her specialty to organ, and seemed to have left London in 1980 after a brief stint at St. Martin-in-the-Fields. No record exists of where she went, or how she spent the following six years. She resurfaced in Tokyo, playing organ at an Episcopal church. She must have met Saito there at some point in the late eighties. He was known to have been working on his plans for "Senritsu" at that time, but it was not clear how exactly she was involved in the project. She did appear in a very peripheral way in some of the documentaries on the construction of the hydroörganon, and in photographs taken during that time. A tall woman with short black hair, smoking a cigarette outside Saito's cabin. Standing in the background while Saito pored over the blueprints. Sitting in the boat with two of his assistants, eating a sandwich. It was likely she had played the "Senritsu" at some point, and Saito must have seen something unusual in her, because the only people he invited to work with him were as mad as he was. She returned to the West shortly after his death, to study marine engineering at MIT.

In 1998 she came to the attention of academic musicologists after publishing her remarkable first monograph, *On the Ontology of Sound: Notes Toward a Hydroörganonology*. Noted for its lucid prose, *On the Ontology of Sound* was the first work of hydroörganononology to really wrestle with the implications of what was by then known as the "sound question" — i.e., how to understand the radically different experiences audience members had during concerts on the hydroörganon. Her monograph made the novel argument that, regardless of whether one heard or did not hear music, the hydroörganon provided a purer way of "listening to" and, therefore, a better way of understanding the works for organ by Johann Sebastian Bach and Dieterich Buxtehude. It was thoroughly savaged by her more militant peers, who saw in it a conservative and even theological sort of essentialism. Few scholars have picked up her line of reasoning since.

Schumacher landed a job as organist and choirmaster at St. Augustine's in New York City around the turn of the millennium, and remained there for several years. During this time she published a few minor pieces on hydroörganonology, including a controversially negative review of the "Citibank Colossus," then under construction a few dozen kilometres from her home on the Lower East Side. In 2008 she took a sabbatical and did not return. She was credited with having worked alongside Carpaccio on the "L'Imperatore" in an advisory capacity from 2007 to 2008, and after its unveiling was one of several resident hydroörganonists, a post she returned to intermittently over the next few years. In 2013, it was announced that she had been chosen to design and execute the building of the "Chebucto" after a rigorous international hiring process.

It was much harder to discover anything about Schumacher's personal life. Those she had worked with spoke of her in tones of awe rather than warmth. None of the team that had worked with Saito responded to my requests for information (not surprising, given the language barrier, the time elapsed, and the understandable wariness with which they treated media re quests, given how the story had been sensationalized over the years). Even Carpaccio, who had intentionally sought her out to work with him on the "L'Imperatore," had little to say: although generally a loquacious interview subject, he was coy when asked about Schumacher. She was "an artist whose work I respected," which is the kind of comment one public figure makes about another when they either have nothing to say or far too much. She was, so far as I was able to ascertain, unmarried. No children.

All of this left me with a notebook full of questions.

She brought me back to her car and drove us out of the city, toward the end of the peninsula. Pulled over halfway to Sambro Head, near a conservation area. "I like walking here," she said. "You can interview me while we walk."

As we made our way down a path toward the ocean, I asked her what had drawn her to hydroörganonology in the first place.

"I like the ocean. And I like the organ."

"Why did you apply to work on the 'Chebucto'?"

"I needed a job. I was tired of playing organs and hydroörganons for audiences who didn't or couldn't understand what they were hearing."

"Do you mean the people who don't hear the music, the non-sonicists?"

"Not just those people. Even the sonicists have failed to comprehend the real meaning of the instrument. They think it's just another type of organ."

"Isn't it?"

"No." Schumacher said this dismissively, and when I pushed her on it she became more dismissive still.

"What is your vision for the 'Chebucto'?" I asked, hoping that a more open-ended question would get me a more expansive answer.

"I'd like it to work. And I'd like it to play nicely."

"Anything else?"

"I'd like it to be played only by people who understand what they are doing."

"How would you define that?" Schumacher looked at me blankly, as if the answer was obvious.

"This is the third hydroörganon you have worked on," I said, starting to feel desperate. "How do you see your vision being different from Carpaccio's, say, or Saito's?"

"Kenji made 'Senritsu' because he believed in God. Carpaccio made 'L'Imperatore' because he believed in himself. But I only believe in the ocean."

"I'm not sure what that means."

"When one is in the ocean, there is always the possibility one is a few moments from death. It strips away one's illusions."

"Would it be fair to describe you as a nihilist, Ms. Schumacher?"

"No. As I said, I believe in the ocean. I subscribe to an ocean-based metaphysics. But those who have not spent as much time in the ocean as I wouldn't understand it. And I'm sure that isn't what your magazine wants to know, either."

"Okay, then, can I ask you about your relationship with Kenji Saito? Would it be fair to say he was a mentor to you?"

"We were lovers."

"Really?"

"No."

We were walking across the smooth rock of the shoreline. Schumacher was staring out at the Atlantic. There was no sign of the city we had so recently left. No houses. Just the grey waves of the harbour.

She stopped walking and removed her hands from her pockets, let the strong east wind raise her arms as if there were aerofoils. I think she wanted me to be quiet, share the moment with her. So I put my notebook in my breast pocket and let the cold blow over me.

"We liked to talk about music," she said eventually. "And about the ocean. I thought what he was doing was important. But misguided. Because he believed that God had created the ocean, and he believed that putting an organ in the ocean would bring him closer to God. I suppose you could say it did, if you have a certain sense of humour. What Kenji didn't understand was that the ocean is God. And the hydroörganon is our means of worship."

"In your monograph you say that only by playing the great baroque masterpieces underwater can we grasp their full symmetry and order, and the terror this order should inspire in us."

"I wrote that a long time ago."

"You've changed your mind, then?"

"My mind has been changed by the ocean."

"What do you mean?"

"I wouldn't say that now. I would say that once you have heard the *Leipzig Chorales* played on a hydroörganon as dusk is approaching and the water is growing dark around you, you understand that to be terrified of the ocean is to be terrified of death, and to be terrified of death is to be terrified of symmetry and order. To be terrified of the world. To be terrified of art. Which is good and right, because we should be terrified of these things. But there is something on the other side of terror, something that can be seen only if we let the terror pass through us and refuse to look away."

"Is that what you mean when you say audiences don't really understand the instrument?"

"You could take what I said to mean that, yes, I suppose."

"Do you ever worry that hydroörganonology is a passing fascination? That, years from now, divers will swim about their wreckage the way they now visit drowned cities?"

"I am going to answer your question, because you have come all the way to this provincial city to ask it. But I will not answer it on the record, for my hydroörganon is not yet finished. I would ask you not to mention it in your article."

"I understand."

"The greatest mistake Kenji made was telling the world about 'Senritsu.' It was his act of hubris. Just as the hydroörganon allows us to fully experience the reality of sound, playing the hydroörganon for no one but the ocean allows us to understand the ultimate truth about all human art. Nothing degrades a hydroörganon so much as the human eye. The hydroörganon should bring us closer to the ocean itself, and the closer we are to the ocean, the further we are from humanity. The day no one will pay to dive into the harbour to hear me play the 'Chebucto' is the day the construction will have finished, and the hydroörganon can begin its true work."

"Do you plan to stay here, then, once the project is over?"

"I think so. The ocean is everywhere, but here it feels very present. And there are so few people. Perhaps you will understand when we go down to see it tomorrow. Perhaps not."

With that, Schumacher began walking back to the car. Our interview was over.

VII

―――――――

PERHAPS I WOULD understand. Two days later, the words still bothered me, sitting silently in my Pullman seat as the train cut its way north. Had I understood anything I had seen or heard in my short time in that city? What, indeed, might it mean for me to have understood? I flipped through the pages of my notebook, and thought about what I would tell Zimmermann. I knew what kind of story he wanted me to bring back. But that was not the story I had found. Rebekah Schumacher was the real story, silence was the real story — silence, and the great envelope of money that made it possible. There was something heroically monstrous in Schumacher's dream, her single-minded desire to build an instrument that no one would ever hear. And she must have known with certainty that her dream would come true, that long after we were gone those great pipes would remain, a monument, a cenotaph.

Outside my window, the forest was endless. From time to time the darkness was punctuated by the baleful gleam of water slipping over river stones in moonlight. But this Tartarean landscape was only an illusion of light and shadow. The only mystery lay in perception.

When I had met Schumacher on the docks on the morning of our dive, she'd said nothing of our conversation the previous day. In her silence I read no discomfort, only the certainty of a person who speaks only when she wants to speak. We boarded the boat. She introduced me to the pilot, a small man named McLaughlin who opened his mouth only to spit over the gunnel. Schumacher gestured for me to change into the diving suit she had brought. I had been trained to do this back in Toronto (an expense Zimmermann agreed to only because the story demanded it), but I was clumsy with the apparatus, and Schumacher made little clicking noises with her tongue while she helped me attach the regulator valve. When the boat reached the harbour mouth, where the water was cleaner, she tapped me on the shoulder. She slipped off the side of the boat, and I followed her into the ocean. It was a sunny day and the light reached deep into the water. Below us, the seabed sloped into darkness.

We swam for a long time. Schumacher seemed always to know where we were. At certain points, she would point out things of particular interest — wrecked fishing boats, an old mine. And then we rounded an outcrop and I could see, glinting in the distance, a series of massive pipes rising from a rocky ledge.

As we drew closer, I became aware of the mind-beggaring scale on which the complex had been built, for *complex* is the only word that can describe the massed ranks of pipes, the flights stretching out like great silver wings on either side of the oblong stone pediment in front of the keyboard. The ledge on which this vast palace of metal had been built stood at a juncture where the gentle slope of rock and sand falling away to the ocean floor met the base of the headland rising sharply toward the surface. Out toward the eastern depths, one could make out the fish, the kelp, the chains of seaweed glowing in the heavy aqueous light of the sun. The rock of the headland encircled the hydroörganon's towering mass so that it seemed almost natural.

Schumacher swam down to a bank of levers below the bench and slid two of them into place. The hydroörganon shuddered to life with a low mechanical hum. She gestured for me to join her. I hovered in the water above, watching as she removed the flippers from her feet so she could manipulate the pedals. The keyboard had a full five manuals. She looked up at me and raised her shoulders, as if asking whether I was ready. I nodded. She slid a few stops out, placed her hands over the first and the fourth manual, and played a chord.

There was a rush of air from the pipes, and a jet of bubbles was expelled. Then the force of the air pushed me backward from the instrument, and I was left floating several metres in front of tenor pipes as thick as tree trunks, watching the air stream up toward the surface. There was a low rumble, one that grew and slackened in intensity. It was joined by a quavering and a quaking as Schumacher opened more stops. But that was it. I watched as her fingers danced between manuals, and I could see the machinery vibrating, the air pouring up toward the surface as new pipes opened. I could see the patterns in the bubbles and sense the hydroörganon's energetic pulse. Schumacher played on, and as I became accustomed to the instrument's power I began to notice the visual pattern of pipes opening and closing, the fountains of air developing a kind of rhythm as they exploded and were contained. But when I closed my eyes, there was only the rumble and the hum.

What had it been like for those who heard a melody, I wondered. What was it like for Schumacher, who remained at the bench, fingers flying over the keyboard, feet pumping the pedals. What must it have been like for Saito, during the lonely nights when he played for the ocean and for God.

Schumacher ended her performance with a flourish of her right hand. And I could see her shoulders shaking, as she rested her hands beside her on the bench; heaving, as if she were in the grip of a strong emotion. As if she were crying, perhaps. Or laughing.

The sunlight played across the silver of the pipes, and the green of the vegetation, and the brown of the stone, and fish began swimming back toward the hydroörganon, nosing about at the pipes, sliding silently, effortlessly, between the gaps. And to the east the ocean grew darker and darker until it defied comprehension.

THIRD MOVEMENT

THE LAUGH OF
MEPHISTOPHELES

THE DIABOLICAL WAS much on people's minds during the long, golden autumn of 2016. Washington, D.C., and Fifth Avenue were as far away as they'd ever been, but my evenings, like those of everyone I knew, were spent in a state of nervous agitation. I usually felt nothing for politics beyond a kind of infinite resignation. I was not used to being surprised — least of all by Americans. And yet the daily stream of headlines was also thrilling: whatever else you might say about the devil, it is impossible to deny his gifts as an entertainer. Recent events were cause for feelings of constriction and fear, but the sense of pressure and rising pitch suggested, if nothing else, that something was about to shatter.

At the office, too, there was a sense of unease, although I found it harder to put my finger on why. Zimmermann's moods had always followed a predictable series of ebbs and flows throughout the week, but they were more erratic now, prone to sudden modulation. He spent hours on the phone with his door closed. The number of lunch meetings he took increased. He arrived late, and stayed later. The cheerful five o'clock Friday drinks he was in the habit of sharing ceased altogether. I knew better than to ask if everything was okay.

Other things went on much as they had always done. I walked home from work through the West End under flurries of golden leaves, hymns rang out from the bells of the Portuguese church on Bathurst Street at six o'clock, an earthy smell of decay rose from the gutters, and on wet evenings you could hear the lichens and mosses spreading their delicate tendrils across the tree trunks in Trinity Bellwoods Park. In the restaurants along Ossington Avenue, young people hung their coats on hooks underneath the bar and drank overpriced lager, and the conversation always spun toward that most libidinally pleasurable of topics: What the fuck was going on?

In a perverse way, I welcomed the distraction. It provided cover for other, more private anxieties that confronted me when I climbed the stairs to my room and sat down at my desk at the end of the evening. The piles of books kept getting taller, the tabs in my browser multiplied, and my notes became ever more detailed and specific. When the streetcars cackled outside, I turned up the Wagner to drown them out. I heard eldritch messages in every rat's squeal and pigeon's cry. I began to fear that the patterns I was charting were meaningless emanations, ribs of sand along the shallows of a beach.

In bed I thought about the strange path I had taken. The lives of people around me, bewildering as they often were, seemed to follow certain trajectories, giving rise to meanings that were not so much metaphysical as dramatic. Their stories unfolded according to fateful logics, driven by certain essential virtues and vices. But my own experience seemed to be nothing more than a series of disconnected episodes, containing rises and falls that dissipated into tedium. The only real change I could perceive in my own life was the crass novelty of particulars, days that were differentiated only in the peculiarity of their annoyances. I sought relief from these thoughts in meditations on a simple cottage by the sea, and the old couple who lived there, and the son who had just come home, and the relentless wind blowing them down into the future.

||

_____

MY DISCONTENT HAD begun several months earlier. Spring had come late that year, and a dull chill hung over the city even in May. Sasha and I dug out the flower beds on the back roof while Ted brewed his beer for the summer. We listened to the same four records we had been listening to since February, and we complained about the same people we were always complaining about. Sasha wanted to get a dog. Ted had taken to calling himself a democratic socialist. I stayed up late looking at the cross-hatched streets of foreign cities on Google Maps and listening to whatever the Spotify algorithm offered up.

I had been at the magazine a year, and in that time had lost the desperation to please. I no longer felt gratitude when the biweekly direct deposits came through. The endless stream of new releases and new concerts and new names I had to familiarize myself with bored me. I spent hours on end scrolling through headlines and Tweets that had nothing to do with music, watching the lives of people unfold in distant cities, growing quietly enraged at candidates I was ineligible to vote for in a country where I would never live. Mesmerized by the grand politics of the wider world, I found it increasingly hard to summon any strong feelings about my own writing, or the snide responses it inspired from our tireless readers. Zimmermann believed that our role was to report the news, such as it was. Anything that carried a whiff of controversy was ruthlessly purged. By the time my articles made it online, they had nothing to do with me.

I told myself that this was simply a seasonal problem, that the protracted winter and the cold spring had undermined morale, that things would fall back in place when the weather turned. When Sev invited me to a party one Friday evening, I was happy to accept. The party was being hosted by the university music department. There is (or there should be) a certain sterility to parties organized by professors, especially when students are in attendance, so my expectations were low. I just needed to get out of the apartment. I picked up a bottle of Douro as a gift for the host and met Sev at his apartment after work. He buzzed me in and greeted me at the door wearing a pair of cotton briefs and an oxford shirt.

"You're overdressed," he said, handing me a glass of gin and closing the door behind me.

"I came from the office."

"You could take off the tie."

"Think how laid-back you'll seem in comparison. Can I smoke on the balcony?"

"Just don't use the planter as an ashtray this time."

Beyond the rooftops of the Annex, the sky hung in bands of purple and gold and red. The mechanical arms of the cranes rising above Bay and Bloor swung quietly through the evening air, watched over by the concrete shells of towers already nearing completion. To the north, a train glided east along the Dupont tracks, its noise drowned out by the traffic on St. George. I watched Sev through the glass door. He was trying to decide what to wear. He put on a pair of dark-blue jeans that hugged his shapely legs, then removed them and tried on a pair of chinos, then went back to the jeans. He slipped in and out of a series of seemingly identical jackets, trying them on unbuttoned and with his hands in his pockets, buttoned with his hands out of his pockets, unbuttoned with his hands out of his pockets, and finally the classically anxious buttoned-with-hands-in-pockets. He eventually settled on a Lincoln green blazer that looked marvellous against his brown skin, and left the buttons undone.

Like many beautiful men, Sev often seemed to be careless about his appearance. He wore nice clothing because he had grown up wearing nice clothing, and he bought linen and wool and silk because he liked how they felt against his skin. He probably didn't know what shade of green his blazer was, or the difference between merino wool and any other kind, and this only enhanced his charm. Things I had felt the need to learn, he had always taken for granted. There were rooms in his life I could never enter. Yet standing in the chilly air of his balcony as he moved through the soft light from his desktop lamp, rubbing the sleeve of a shirt between his fingers, I felt closer for the distance that lay between us.

The party, it turned out, was not so much a party as an event. The cavernous living room of Professor Dalrymple's Georgian home was packed, and a microphone and speaker had been set up at the front of the room beside a baby grand. A large, sweaty man in an ascot was already offering a few introductory comments.

"... just as we are grateful to the Great Lakes Opera Company for taking a chance on this remarkable new talent. We are sure to spur even more innovation and development in this next generation of composers, a generation that has already shown itself to be capable of creating stunning new operatic music, music that is not only sensitive and emotionally rich, but which is also in a certain unmistakable — I might even venture to say, characteristically Torontonian way — dynamic. So, without further ado, I'd like to introduce Charlene Williams, who will be saying a few words on behalf of the Jackson Institute."

The way people around us started to check their phones, I concluded Charlene Williams must be from the Canada Council. In blandly affirmative tones, she explained that we should all be extremely grateful to Senator Hamish Jackson for funding the Jackson Institute, which in turn funded the Jackson Fellows program, which in turn funded Susanna to return to the Faculty of Music to write the opera that was now, apparently, being produced by the Great Lakes Opera Company, which, in a happy coincidence, was also funded by Senator Jackson.

Senator Jackson, a stooped goblin with a face wrinkled by age and sin, sat in the front row, munching absent-mindedly on a handful of nuts. When he stood up to introduce the beneficiary of his largesse, everyone politely ignored the shells and half-chewed fragments spilling onto the floor.

"I first had the pleasure of meeting Ms. Susanna Pietrovalda three years ago," he said, mumbling and sucking at his dentures. "If I'm not mistaken, it was at a reception at the Lexington ..."

But I had no interest in the reception at the Lexington. I was frantically scouring the room. It seemed impossible that Susanna could be here, at this party. I had had no idea she was even in Toronto. But when she rose at the end of the Senator's speech and joined him at the front of the room, it was impossible to mistake her. The long plaits of ginger hair, the dusting of freckles across the bridge of her nose, the contained energy, the aloofness. In her severe black dress and high white collar, she looked almost like a priest.

"It is an honour to be here tonight with all of you. My thanks to Professor Dalrymple, Charlene, the Canada Council, the Jackson Institute, and, of course, Senator Jackson himself. One of our most famous novelists once wrote that all artists are mendicants, and it is as a humble mendicant that I thank you for your generous patronage. I'm never sure what to say in situations like this," polite laughter, demure smile, "so I'll just say that when I first conceived of *The Laugh of Mephistopheles*, I knew I wanted to do something out of the ordinary. But I could never have dreamed that I'd be lucky enough to have it premiere in an actual construction site! I don't want to give away too much about it yet, but let's just say we really are embarking on an experiment. Who knows whether it will succeed," more polite laughter, "but thanks to the support this production has received, I believe that even if it fails, it will at least fail interestingly. Until then, enjoy the champagne."

There was an explosion of grateful applause, and Susanna pulled a bottle of Prosecco out from behind the piano and popped the cork off in a flamboyant but practised way. I clapped along, unable to take my eyes off her as she and the senator toasted each other with generous coupes.

"What's all this about?" I asked Sev.

"Yeah, I should have mentioned — Professor Dalrymple said something about there being a big announcement. Good on Susanna, I guess," he said, then grabbed my elbow to guide me through the crowd, which was now breaking up into little clusters of conversation. "There's refreshments at the back."

"What a bizarre idea for an opera. You know, I wouldn't mind asking Susanna about the —"

"She's not going anywhere. And Dalrymple said something about prosciutto-wrapped asparagus."

We made our way to the refreshments table. Over the years, I had sampled a great number of snack platters at faculty events, and come to the conclusion that such platters basically served a ritual function, an offering to the hearth gods of etiquette. There needed to be food, and so there was food. Quality was completely beside the point. It seemed that Dalrymple understood this axiom perfectly: there was, indeed, prosciutto-wrapped asparagus — greyish squares of pork folded awkwardly around greasy hempen spears, stacked like fallen infantry between a pile of hardening cheese cubes and a tray of overripe grapes. The white wine tasted like cream soda, and the red wine tasted only of tannins. I left the bottle of Douro in my bag and nibbled at a piece of wet spanakopita, looking around to see if there was anyone I knew.

The crowd was mostly students and faculty types, but there were a few individuals whose clothes marked them out as professional administrators. Something about the jewellery and the shoes, a lack of proportion at once studied and self-consciously outré. Sev had struck up a conversation about departmental politics with another recent graduate. I couldn't be bothered to keep up with the specifics. Susanna was surrounded by a circle of women at the front of the room, her mouth barely opening when she laughed. A large man was making his way toward them. His tall, sway-bellied frame had the slightly obscene look of an athlete gone to seed, and his tailored wool blazer drew attention to rather than concealed this. He pushed confidently through the cluster of admirers and extended a large, thick-fingered hand to Susanna. With his other, he grabbed her upper arm and pulled her into the handshake. It was Lionel Standish.

A careful smile spread across Susanna's face as Standish loomed over her. He did not release her arm. The group of women discreetly shifted to the other side of the piano. I sidled through the crowd toward them until I stood at a respectful distance with my glass of wine, as though I were simply waiting for my turn to talk to her.

"… but this is magnificent news. Your last tour de force did not go unremarked upon, I assure you. There have been whispers in certain quarters, you know, whispers that portend a rosy future for this production. And, of course, for your career. Naturally, one is reticent about bringing such things up in this casual, and so to speak, informal setting," here he gave a throaty laugh, "but suffice it to say that we expect great things of you, and — well, see, the press is already sneaking in for the scoop! Susanna, do you know, ah, this young man?"

"I don't think so," she said, not really looking at me.

"Alexander Otkazov," I said, extending my hand, and looking into her eyes for any sign of recognition. Standish had, by now, let Susanna's go, and she gave mine a not-unfriendly shake. "I'm a staff writer at *Modern Classical*. We're very much looking forward to hearing more about this production."

She seemed to be on the verge of saying something when Standish continued.

"Mr. Otkazov has something of a fascination with stagings of an avant-garde persuasion. He wrote, if I'm not mistaken, the piece on Schumacher's wonderful organ that was of such great interest to our little musical establishment last fall."

"I heard about it."

"Would it be fair to say you have a similar interest in performing music in unconventional spaces?" I asked.

Standish had his arms crossed above the hump of his belly, grinning mysteriously.

"Not really," Susanna said.

"I see. Sorry if I was mistaken, but didn't you say your opera is set to premiere in a construction site? That would seem —"

"It's not some kind of gimmick. We thought very carefully about the setting. We mean to incorporate the acoustical properties of the space into the performance. It's not a site-specific composition, exactly, but it's site-informed."

"Right, and the piece itself is an adaptation of *Faust*?"

"Sort of."

"Susanna is going to stage the unstageable," said Standish, grasping Susanna's shoulder in a porcine hand. "She is basing her opera on the impenetrable second part of Goethe's immortal poem. A hymn to destruction and creativity!"

"Really?"

"We've chosen not to call it an adaptation," Susanna said irritably. "The libretto incorporates elements of the poem, but I want to stress that it's an original work."

I wasn't sure if she was bothered by my questions or by Standish's hand. Perhaps she saw them as being much the same thing.

"And who will be directing it?"

"I will. It was part of the terms of the agreement — I have complete creative control. It was very important to me that I be allowed to stage it as I have envisioned."

"When will rehearsals begin?"

"It's not up to us, but we're hoping to have things moving in the next few weeks? Perhaps Lionel can tell you when the rehearsal space will be ready. He keeps telling us it'll be soon." The way Susanna was smiling at Lionel made me glad she wasn't smiling at me.

"I'd very much be interested in dropping by when things get going," I said. "This is certainly the kind of thing we'd want to do a feature on ..."

"Well, I'm flattered by the interest, of course. And I'd be more than happy to arrange an interview. Maybe it would be best to set something up later this summer? Once Lionel has been able to sort things out?"

We shook hands and I made my way back to the refreshment table. It really didn't mean anything, I thought, that Susanna hadn't recognized me. Neither of us had changed at all.

III

IN SOME WAYS, I had always known Susanna. There must have been a time when I hadn't, deep in childhood, perhaps, on one of those summer days when the keys were perfectly responsive and the piano boomed and splashed exactly as I wanted it to. But becoming conscious of Susanna was like becoming conscious of the world. To remember the time before Susanna, I would have had to remember a time before I was myself.

We both grew up in a university town in the highlands beyond the Niagara escarpment, a cluster of stone churches and sculpture gardens surrounded by a rampart of strip malls and six-lane highways. Susanna lived in one of the residential neighbourhoods downtown, where the respectable yellow-brick homes were inhabited by tenured academics who dabbled in pottery and witchcraft. From an early age, she was understood to be a musical prodigy. Five or six at the time of her first violin recital, she left the audience amazed by her technical skill and the maturity of her phrasing. A local news feature quoted a professor at the School of Music as saying her performance convinced him of the truth of reincarnation. The piece was accompanied by an obnoxious photograph that showed her standing poised and serious in a dingy choir loft, the corners of her mouth pulled back in what I alone understood to be a smirk.

My own performances elicited rather less enthusiasm. My path to music was the grinding ordinary one. My father, coming as he had from a culture and family that took classical music seriously, enrolled me in piano lessons early on. I later came to understand this as an act of deep tenderness on his part, an attempt to say something for which he had no words, but at the time it felt like another mundane expectation. Classical music was everywhere in our home. Learning to play was like learning to read.

Susanna's parents had decided the best way to nurture her rare talent was through homeschooling, so she didn't attend any of the local elementary schools. But we were in a children's choir together, and as we grew older, we began to circle each other warily at recitals and concerts and festivals. She ascended through the Conservatory program quickly. If we hadn't lived in such a provincial place, I would perhaps have lost track of her as she ascended to a more advanced and competitive milieu. But in our provincial town, all the kids who were interested in that kind of thing were forced to interact with each

other. Whenever I played in public she was there, smiling and
ruthless. She must have been dimly aware of me, too, because
when I was ten or eleven, I was asked to accompany her in a
performance of Bach's first violin sonata. We spent a few tense
afternoons in her parents' solarium before I was politely told
they'd found someone more suitable.

I think my father was more offended than I was. He
viewed the country he had immigrated to as less artistically
developed than the one he had left, and he took the snub personally. His own father had been conductor of the Voronezh
State Symphony Orchestra for a brief period in the sixties, and
although my parents never spoke of it, I had a sense that my
father's melancholy, hanging in the air of our home like a cool
mist, had something to do with the fact that he had abandoned music for a more reliable career in chemical engineering.
It was precisely this practical background that had given him
the means to emigrate during those difficult years after '91,
and though he never achieved in Canada the kind of career
he might have had if things had gone differently back home,
he was able to find steady work in a lab. Combined with my
mother's income as a cleaner, we lived well enough. But it was
only in the evening, when he sat down in his chair in front of
the stereo system and put on one of the Brahms or Bruckner or
Shostakovich CDs he was always borrowing from the library,
that his melancholy seemed to retreat.

I had just started my first year of high school when he
died a statistically predictable death from lung cancer. I
played Rachmaninoff's *Nocturne No. 1* at his funeral, and
my mother looked down at the program dry-eyed while his
friends from the lab shuffled past the casket. On our way
home from the cemetery, she explained that we were still ten

years away from paying off the mortgage and I'd probably need to get a job. I didn't say anything. I'd always assumed we rented.

The bench of the ancient upright piano jammed up against the door to the kitchen was the only place I could really relax in the months that followed. School was dull and alienating; my weekends were spent amid the slapping meat and whirring blades of a deli counter. The friends I had were friends of convenience, people to eat lunch with so I didn't seem like an antisocial freak. Occasionally I would be invited over to someone's house to play video games, or we'd go to the movies at the cineplex on the edge of town. I never allowed a single one of my classmates to enter my home.

My mother had never been very sociable, and after my father's death, she retreated into the furthest reaches of her capacious soul. I had always thought of her as being the hardnosed and practical one. But in my father's absence, she adopted strange habits. She stopped eating meat, and began spending what little extra money she had on crystals from the bohemian shops on Wyndham Street. Middle-aged women came over for tea, their scarves smelling of incense, their bangled arms clattering every time they moved. At first I worried this was part of some misguided attempt to contact her husband in the afterlife, and that she'd end up getting fleeced by some hippy with a Ouija board. But I later came to suspect these inclinations had always been there, that her husband's softness and the upheavals that had driven them from their home had caused her to develop an impermeable crust to protect herself from the world. Freed from the ethereal weight of her husband's sadness, this crust had started to flake. I was meeting the woman my mother had always in some sense been.

Working twenty-four hours a week allowed me to contribute to the household without having to drop my piano lessons entirely. But Susanna easily outstripped me, and by tenth grade she was enrolled in an arts school in Toronto. Her performances back home became infrequent, and when she did play, it was often one of her own compositions (I was gratified to discover they were pleasant but dutiful, lacking in any kind of visceral emotion). In time, she won admission to the Boston Conservatory. I counted myself lucky to get into McGill.

Never having had much to say to one another, we lost touch. For years I didn't think about her at all. By the time I graduated, Montreal had become my entire world. And then one night in early 2014, after a night spent wandering in and out of Mile End bars, I opened YouTube and found myself watching a video for a new piece called *Quartet for Jawbones*, composed by a Brooklyn-based artist named Susanna Pietrovalda.

The *Quartet* is now so well known that it would be difficult to explain the impact it had on those of us who discovered it the way it was meant to be discovered, alone at night through YouTube's invisible algorithms. It seemed simple enough, at first: four scantily clad performers in a black cube singing a four-part harmony, accompanying themselves with a series of counter-rhythms created using their own bodies. But as the video went on, the physical percussion became more violent, the performers slapping their cheeks, chests, and thighs hard enough to leave red marks. This led to a distorting effect on the melodic lines, until by the end the pure harmony had degenerated into a series of fleshy hoots and grunts. It was like listening to a pack of wolves dismember an elk carcass — you really felt like something was happening.

The *Quartet* became a minor sensation. Reviewers described it as an organicist response to Xenakis's *Metastasis*, and Susanna as a Canadian Caroline Shaw, if Caroline Shaw had been raised by feral cats in a ravine behind a parking lot. The story behind the composition, when it came out, only made the piece more compelling. Apparently Susanna had been on the cusp of finishing her degree in performance when she suffered a catastrophic nervous breakdown and was found wandering in a park by the Charles River one morning, raving about intonation. She spent nearly a year in recovery before switching into the composition stream and completing her degree with honours, frightening the entire faculty with her caustic irreverence for the conventions to which she had previously been so committed. She relocated to New York, ostensibly to pursue an M.M. at The New School, but spent most of her days in a Brooklyn studio with a group of musicians, videographers, and modern dancers, dreaming up the horrifying sounds that would eventually become the *Quartet*. In interviews, Susanna was distant and cerebral. This endeared her to other female musicians and composers, who found her unapologetically intellectual approach refreshing, and she was soon garlanded with all the clichés of early success: she was a *wunderkind*, a phenomenon, the classical music voice of her generation.

I became obsessed with Susanna, for these reasons and for others. There was something symmetrical about the course our lives had taken: the year my father died, she was accepted into the Etobicoke School of Music; the year my own career was at its apogee, she had been at her nadir; when I was sitting alone and drunk in my apartment, unable to play a single note, her first serious composition went viral. She had pushed herself to the very limits of her creativity, hit a wall, and discovered something extraordinary on the other side of it. I had fled the first glimmerings of success, and in failure found the relief I had so long been looking for.

For months I puzzled over what I should do with this revelation. And then on a cold day in late autumn, I walked down to Central Station with my suitcase and wiped out the last vestiges of the person I had been when I arrived in Montreal so many years before. Or so I told myself at the time.

IV

———

IN JUNE THE weather turned, and suddenly every alley smelled of lilac. Bars opened their windows, and terraces spilled out onto the sidewalk. The garden on our back roof overflowed with tomato vines and little blue flowers, and a feeling of extroversion and goodwill descended on the city. My melancholy deepened. Sev would be leaving soon, and Sasha had just departed for a summer visiting family in Hong Kong. Ted and I barbecued sausages on the back roof after work as the evening light slid across the brick walls of the Gladstone Estates. Ted had become a political obsessive, and the conversation circled around primaries and superdelegates, the virtues of socialism and the betrayal of the working class by the liberal intelligentsia. I didn't mind listening. He knew a lot more about it than I did. Raccoons skittered above the rooftops and wobbled down drainpipes to their secret conclaves behind the dumpsters. I told him about Susanna, and he said heartwarmingly rude things about Canadians who come back to Toronto after living in New York.

I raised the possibility with Zimmermann of writing about the opera shortly after the announcement, hoping he wouldn't be interested, but he jumped on the idea immediately. He already knew about the project, but applauded this rare instance of initiative on my part anyway. I was directed to get in touch with the company to find out whether I could sit in on a rehearsal.

"It should be a real profile, Alexander, front-cover material: a young woman composer, already making waves, unusual staging, connections in New York. We need to showcase this kind of talent. Especially with all the, ah, gender stuff, sexism in classical music, that kind of thing. I don't need to tell you we've taken some criticism in the past. Try to be sensitive to the subject matter and the, you know, the political climate. People are just looking for reasons to get mad these days. Have you seen the comments on the website? The *bile* in there. You know, people used to have to pay for the postage if they wanted to abuse us like that. I sometimes wonder if setting up a website was a mistake ..."

I knew very well what I needed to say, but when I sat down to email the company, I found myself unable to type. As I pressed "send," I would have taken a step toward interviewing Susanna, which would lead to further steps, and before I knew it, I would be sitting down in front of her with my little notebook and my pen and my recorder, asking all kinds of asinine questions. And she would probably answer them very graciously. Then we'd contract a photographer to take some pictures, and the next thing I knew, I'd be back in that small city in the highlands, watching her smirking face stare back at me from a picture. But this time it would be a glossy magazine, and I'd be the one quoting some unctuous professor about how brilliant she was.

My paralysis was interrupted by Zimmermann bursting out of his office to ask if I knew where the 2013 tax return was. I didn't, so I spent the rest of the afternoon sifting through bankers boxes while he made phone call after phone call from behind a closed door. The email, once deferred, became even harder to write. Somehow the days filled up with other, more urgent business.

In the end, I didn't have to write it: a week later, the opera company emailed Zimmermann, asking whether we might be interested in doing a piece on their surprise season opener, a new opera called *The Laugh of Mephistopheles* by a promising young composer from Toronto. Zimmermann forwarded me the email without comment.

V

———◆———

SUSANNA AND I met at a café in the financial district. It was in an old building, with brass fixtures and an embossed tin ceiling and a clientele that wore wristwatches that would have paid my rent for a year — you could practically smell the money when you walked past. The coffee was roasted on-site, and the servers were all from Belgium. Susanna arrived precisely on time, or at least, I assume she did: I was five minutes late, my hands clammy and shirt spotted with sweat. She was making notes in a big binder and shooting off emails on her phone.

"So, where do you want to begin?" she said, putting her phone down on the table. "I have to be uptown by noon."

"Have rehearsals started?"

"They're under way, yes."

"Wonderful. I thought we could go over the inspiration behind the project. You mentioned earlier that the opera is an adaptation — sorry, not an adaptation, a ... version of the Faust story? Or it's based on the Faust story?"

"We're trying to avoid that kind of language. The opera is in conversation with Goethe's *Faust, Part Two*, which is not the story most people are familiar with. As I believe I mentioned, we've adapted sections of the poem in the libretto, but really we're trying to tap into the philosophical spirit of the story. Have you read *All That Is Solid Melts into Air*?"

"Marx?"

"Berman."

"I thought that was a Marx thing."

"It is, but ... that's not important. We're thinking of the Faust story as an epic about development, about modernity. The opera takes the Faustian theme and turns it into a meditation on globalization and capitalism and the fragmentation of the human condition. The librettist and I have been trying to push this idea to its very limit. That's why we decided not to have it staged in a regular theatre — we want our audience to be confronted with the forces of creative destruction embodied by the modern city in a more visceral way."

"That sounds pretty abstract."

"Music is an abstract medium."

"But opera is also dramatic."

"Right, and there's plenty of what you could call 'plot' in there, as well. But you asked me about the inspiration, and the inspiration is philosophical, so that's what I was trying to explain. I don't want audiences coming to this thinking they're going to see Faust singing love songs to Gretchen."

"I was going to ask about that, actually, because there have been so many versions of Faust over the years, you know, Gounod, Berlioz, Busoni ..."

"All of which basically follow the plot of *Faust, Part One*."

"... and I wanted to know how the story you're telling is different."

"Well, as I said, we're picking up the story where most adaptations leave it, after Gretchen's death. The second part of the poem is a lot denser, more classical than Romantic, and it's pretty heavy going, which is why people aren't as familiar with it. But it's a great narrative: basically Faust and Mephistopheles embark on a bunch of adventures, and Faust ends up as a kind of emperor figure, taming the sea, building new cities, bringing enlightenment to Germany. We're trying to channel that idea that the old world needs to be torn down before the new one can be born. To do that we're going back to the fundamentals of what opera is: sound, words, images, space, and time. *Faust, Part Two* is a bit of a maelstrom, and the music reflects that."

I jotted down a few notes. Susanna's tone was even and professional, but I could sense her impatience. I hoped my own wasn't apparent. The word *philosophical*, when used to describe a work of art, always made me want to spit.

"How do you see this piece in relation to *Quartet for Jawbones*? Both in terms of the music, and in terms of the use of visuals? Many critics felt that you were really breaking new ground there."

"Critics love saying that kind of thing. No offence."

"You don't think the critical reception of your first composition helped you land this commission?"

"Obviously, it did. But I'm not … I mean, that's neither here nor there. I'm not going to be grateful for the good press, because then I'd have to be resentful of the bad press. You can't worry about stuff like that if you want to keep moving. But to answer your question, I'd say that a lot of what I was working out in that piece, musically speaking, I worked out. I was thinking a lot about beauty and disgust — the co-constitutive relationship between beauty and disgust. And the relationship between sound and image. I learned a lot. I guess you could say I'm applying some of what I learned with this piece. If you wanted to."

"I was just pointing out that a lot of people seem to think you're doing something interesting and new. And they might be excited by the idea of what you could do with a bigger canvas."

She responded to my passive-aggressive flattery by looking at her watch. "What would you think, Alexander, if you went to a contemporary production and it opened with a baroque overture?"

"I'm very fond of baroque music."

"But it would be funny, right? It would be hard not to see a comic element in it. Someone writing a perfect baroque overture in the twenty-first century. Like, if you went to a new music festival and someone was doing a full concert of newly composed Gregorian chant, you'd think about it differently than if you went to a see a performance of actual Gregorian chant, right? You'd have to assume it was ironic, or that the person writing it was a little touched. Once these old forms have passed away, they can come back only as quotation, or homage, or a joke — not serious art."

"You can take inspiration from them, though. I mean, look at Schoenberg, Pärt, the Minimalists ..."

"Isn't that the problem, though? The best composers of the twentieth century pushed music to its limits, deconstructed every aspect of the tradition, decamped to West Africa and Bali and Tuva to steal from other people's traditions. They tried everything — serialism, aleatoricism, indeterminacy, jazz, overtone singing, electronics, electroacoustics, tintinnabuli, game pieces, transethnicism, noise, distortion, silence — I mean, there's nowhere left to go. Classical music is exhausted. Some of the minimalist stuff is recent enough that you can use it without seeming anachronistic, of course, but an honest composer will have to acknowledge that at this point, nothing is more derivative than an atonal piano piece that incorporates polyrhythms. It's all been done. Did you see the premier of Barbara Monk Feldman's *Pyramus and Thisbe* last year? What a gruesome spectacle. Just a bunch of corpses parading around on a stage. I'd never seen anything so soporific.

"I thought I could do something new with the *Quartet*. For a while, I thought I *had* done something new with it. But that's because I made the mistake of listening to the critics. When I got some distance from the piece, I realized nothing I'd written would have surprised an educated listener in 1975. And this isn't just a problem for music, either, right? Literature, painting, film — it's like all we can do anymore is regurgitate. Even politics. I mean, look at the election, for chrissakes, they're still relitigating the twentieth century. The people who get nostalgic about the fifties versus the people who get nostalgic about the sixties. The only really fresh thing about the *Quartet* was the visual aspect, and when you got right down to it, all we did is make a music video for a piece that got called classical music because it was written by someone who was recognized as a classical composer. It seemed novel only because that whole scene is forty years behind pop culture.

"I was living in Brooklyn at the time, right, and in Brooklyn there's no shortage of people trying to make a career out of weird pop art. And I met all these people who didn't know anything about contemporary classical music, who seemed to think I was just doing a sideways take on trance. So that's when it clicked: for five hundred years, the culture has been evolving through fragmentation. In the Middle Ages, everyone had the same ideas about music, whether they were a king or a peasant. Then things started to change, and a couple of centuries on, the peasants had their own music, the burghers had their own music, the aristocrats had their own music, the church had its own music, the enslaved had their own music.

"But now all those strands are coming back together and everything is, at least formally, less and less differentiated. When that sunk in, it became obvious that the way forward was not to try to create new sounds, but to dive into the maelstrom. Embrace everything. That's why we chose to take our inspiration from *Faust, Part Two*, and that's why we wanted to see it staged in Toronto rather than New York, in a construction site rather than a concert hall. And on that note," she said, checking her watch again, "I think I should be on my way."

I had barely registered any of this when she got up from the table. Not knowing what else to do, and feeling strangely formal all of a sudden, I got up, as well. She extended her hand, and I shook it weakly. Anticipating the question on my lips, she told me to read Goethe before I asked any more questions.

She paused at the door for a moment before leaving. "Do you get home much anymore?"

"Sorry?"

"My parents live here in Toronto now, and I haven't been back in years. Is your mother still there?"

"Yes."

"I hope she's doing well. Give my regards next time you see her. I always thought it was so sad, what happened to your father."

VI

———

I WALKED UP Yonge Street to the disreputable stretch of strips clubs, hookah bars, and army surplus stores between College and Bloor. Here the old spirit of the city had managed to hang on, improbably, amid the foundation pits and fluorescent pharmacies that pockmarked the rest of downtown. I was headed for Eliot's, a cramped, three-storey bookshop run by a dyspeptic Frenchman. I'd had a soft spot for his shop ever since I saw him turn down a box of Harry Potter books a suburban couple was trying to fob off on him for fifty dollars.

When I opened the door, he looked up from a paperback and nodded warily.

"Do you have Goethe's *Faust*?"

He blinked his rheumy red eyes and pointed up the stairs. Piles of Graham Greene novels were stacked on each step. I was about to ask if *Faust* would be lumped in with poetry or drama, but the way he returned to his paperback felt decisive.

I'd never been a dutiful reader. My father insisted I familiarize myself with all the old Russian stuff, so I'd had my fill of Dostoevsky and Turgenev and Tolstoy early on. It had left me with a strong conviction that no novel should be longer than two hundred pages. I had been turned off short fiction in high school; it was always so much work to get into a story, and once you found the rhythm of the thing, the main character would suddenly be reminded of their grandmother's tea kettle and it would be over. The only writer I never got tired of was Balzac — all that sex and scheming. I'd always gotten my intellectual stimulation from music. If I was going to spend the evening reading a book, I expected to be entertained.

In the cluttered stacks on the second floor, I eventually found an old two volume Penguin edition translated into what appeared to be doggerel. I brought it down to the counter.

The Frenchman checked the prices on the flyleaf. "Did you get an urge for edification?" he asked.

"Just some background reading."

"I assume you've already read the Marlowe," he said, flicking his tongue across his lips. "Are you planning on reading Mann, as well?"

"Mann?"

"*Doktor Faustus*," he said, as if explaining something to a small child.

"I wasn't planning —"

"To gain a full picture of the German psyche, they must be read side by side."

"I'm not really interested in the German psyche, per se, more just interested in the, uh, Faust legend itself. And the musical adaptations it's inspired."

"In that case, Mann is even more essential. He did, after all, base his Faust character on Arnold Schoenberg, much to the composer's chagrin."

"No, I knew that, I just ..."

"We have a copy upstairs."

I made my way back to the fiction section. There was nearly a full shelf of matching black hardcovers hanging perilously near a rafter. Mann had clearly had a lot of time on his hands. I paused in Renaissance Drama, wondering whether I would look stupid if I picked up the Marlowe, as well. I had a feeling the Frenchman approved of me (because of all the Balzac), and I was worried I would drop in his estimation were I to tacitly acknowledge that I hadn't thought to read it first.

He didn't say anything as he rang me through. But as he punched in the new books, I could see him shaking his head a little.

"There's a very good bit about Beethoven's Op. 111 in the Mann," he said, as I walked out the door. "I'm sure you'll appreciate it, if you know anything about music."

VII

———

OVER THAT SUMMER, I retreated from the world into the stained pages of my books and the depthless blue of my computer screen. The heat was cloying and heavy, the air sweet with rot. At night my room became so unbearable that I strung up a hammock on the back roof. Rats and raccoons foraged below me and the sky above glowed an apocalyptic orange. I sweated and yearned for a breeze from the lake.

On afternoons and evenings when I wasn't working, I took long, solitary walks to the deep ravines in the north and east of the city, up along the Don River and around the outcrops of Rosedale. The air was cooler in the creek bottoms that curled into Midtown and Forest Hill, where coyotes slept in their dens and the owls hunted at dusk. From time to time, I happened upon encampments where the outcasts of the twenty-first century had made homes for themselves in dells and under the shadow of bridges. I started to see the city differently. From below, it was more ephemeral, a dream of concrete and glass and steel hanging above the solid earth.

These walks often took me past the old Oren Theatre, demolished the year before, now replaced with four vast and trunkless legs of concrete. The construction site was obscured by a billboard advertising *The Oren — Condo Living for the Bohemian in You*. The logo of the Kilbride Development Corporation was blazoned across the bottom corner, with a QR that took you to their website. I visited it one day, over a bowl of noodles, curious about what kind of people made money off this sort of thing. The board of trustees was a gallery of white teeth and slaughterhouse smiles, credentials listed in bullet points below each pecunious face. When they weren't meddling in real estate, the trustees were bringing their corporate expertise to bear on universities, hospitals, media conglomerates, newspaper empires, life insurance companies, energy companies, the symphony, the ballet, the Commonwealth Games. It was a petri dish of influence, the great cousin-fucking conspiracy that had built this country and still profited off it 150 years later. And there, above them all, chairman of the board, was the distinguished mug of Lionel Standish (Great Lakes Opera Company, Enfield Energy, Princess Margaret Hospital, the Jackson Centre for the Humanities), leering out from the best of all possible worlds.

It was amazing, really, how easy it was to learn about the Kilbride Development Corporation's holdings. Everything was out in the open, every deal a matter of public record. They had properties across the city, and quite a bit of angry prose had been written about the quality of their construction — within three decades, apparently most of what they'd put up since the beginning of the millennium would be unfit for habitation. They were responsible, too, for the architectural style that had become typical of Toronto: bland high-rise towers that incorporated heritage facades in a gesture toward preservation. There was something sarcastic about the buildings showcased on their website, the way pillars of steel and glass rose out of brick warehouses and stone banks, as if the architect had made a show of obeying the letter of the law while violating its spirit. I could understand the impulse to tear Toronto down, house by house, and build a completely new city in its place, as the Soviets had tried to do in Moscow. And I could understand the desire to fix it in time, like Paris, maintaining the character of the nineteenth century into the twenty-first. But there was something craven about a city caught between revolution and reaction, unable to dream a future for its citizens and unwilling to shake off its provincial slumbers, gears spinning on without plan or direction save for the mindless imperative of money.

As I hunched over my desk at night, the first small insights into Susanna's project glimmered from the pages in front of me. I passed from Marlowe to Goethe, and from Goethe to Mann, from Mann to Bulgakov, and the rest of that great river of literature flowing from the Faustian spigot. At first I simply wanted to know more about the books that had inspired the music, but the further I descended into the chthonic depths, the more I saw the endless stream of adaptations in a psychological light, as an obsessive return to a traumatic event still in the process of unfolding. At the end of *Faust, Part Two*, the hero dies and is taken up to heaven, his restless striving rewarded, his contract with Mephistopheles broken by divine grace. But this is an ending, not a conclusion: Mephistopheles still tends the infernal machinery. As Mann and Bulgakov understood very well, every generation gives birth to Fausts of its own. The epic of development doesn't conclude, because it cannot conclude: its trajectory is apocalyptic. Susanna, I suspected, understood this. Whether Lionel Standish understood this, as well, I could only guess.

VIII

———

MY INVITATION TO sit in on a rehearsal came at the end of August. They were now only a few weeks from opening night, and Susanna felt the production was at a point where it could be seen by an outsider. I was well gone in my research by this time, and spent my waking hours carrying on a long internal debate with Susanna. I had begun to see menacing symmetries between the world and the books stacked up on my desk. The buried rivers jetting from pipes set deep in the walls of ravines, the packs of wild animals descending on the city at night, the sinister police stations with their dark windows and subterranean gates, the jagged shards of glass plunging through the gothic facades of museums, the nineteenth-century buildings torched by developers, the condominiums spreading like metastasizing tumours, the brick dust piling up outside construction sites, the stench of the sewers, the piledrivers' rhythm, the homeless legions: somewhere in the city a great engine was purring, and I had finally learned its name.

Because of the unusual nature of the performance venue, the musicians and crew had spent the summer preparing in an alternate practice space. I was surprised to discover, after Susanna sent me the address, that it was a Victorian corner block only a few streets from my apartment. I would have completely missed the small door leading to the interior of the building had Susanna not told me to look for it. Inside, a wide staircase led up to a landing dappled in soft pink and green light shining through the stained-glass windows above. The landing led into a rather handsome vestibule, with a coat room and an old ticket window. Farther inside I could hear the cheerful, discordant sound of musicians warming up.

The hall I walked into was oddly familiar. A mezzanine hung in a great semicircle above a central hall with a raised stage at the far end, where Susanna was talking to a group of people lounging around in street clothes. The polished floorboards creaked beneath my feet and I realized that I had been here before, not so long ago. With the curtains pulled back on the windows high above, I could see how ordinary and rundown it was. Just another abandoned theatre. The musicians all seemed very relaxed, which I found annoying: four weeks out from the premiere of a supposed masterpiece, people should be threatening to cave each other's heads in. It occurred to me that I could work this observation into a lede, and I had just pulled out my notebook and started jotting something down about the general ambience when a hand clapped down on my shoulder.

"Good evening, Alexander." It was Lionel Standish. "Susanna told me you'd be joining us for tonight's rehearsal. I must say how pleased I am that the magazine has taken an interest in this story. So much going on this season, and here you are doing a cover feature!"

"Hello, yes, happy to be here," I said. "Very much looking forward to —"

"I assure you the experience you have in store will not disappoint. I usually keep my distance from productions the company puts on, of course; no one wants a board member breathing down their neck when they're practising their scales. But I've taken a special interest in Ms. Pietrovalda, and wanted to ensure everything was to her satisfaction, and now I just can't keep away. She's doing such marvellous things with the story."

"Yeah, I've been reading a lot over the summer, you know, Goethe and all that, and the whole Faust thing really does seem to be an, uh, apposite text, especially with everything that's happening this year, you know, the —"

"Ah yes, the epic of development! It's a shame, isn't it, that most people know only the first part of the poem. We're all such incurable romantics — we can relate to the love story, Faust's betrayal of Gretchen, seduction and remorse and so on. It's so beautifully done, so quotable ... *'Nun gut, wer bist Du denn? Ein Teil von jener Kraft, die stets das Böse will und stets das Gute schafft.'* If you read only the first part, though, you miss the whole thrust of the narrative. Gretchen is betrayed to destroy all the old pieties that made her betrayal necessary. Which I think you'll agree —"

"Actually, pardon me for interrupting, but can I ask if you were involved in acquiring the opera?"

"Well, I wouldn't want to take all the credit. But when I found out Susanna was taking on the challenge, I knew we needed to have it premiere in Toronto. A story of destruction and rebirth for a city that only recently began to wake from its pious slumbers. And what better place to stage it than a building that is, like Toronto itself, yet to be completed?"

"Yes, it's such a clever idea. And you know, while I have you here, could I ask a couple of further questions? Because from what I understand, the building it's being performed in is one of yours — I mean, it's a Kilbride property, right? Perhaps you could tell me a little about how this unique arrangement came about?"

"Quite simple, really. I approached the board of trustees about the possibility of using one of our projects currently under development, and they agreed. There were some concerns about safety that needed to be ironed out, of course, but nothing too extraordinary. Senator Jackson was a great help on that front. Journalists love to criticize the real-estate industry in this city, but I think you'll find that most of us are happy to support a good cause. Between you and me, and strictly off the record, the heritage preservation crowd and the whole tenants' rights movement have done more than anyone else to make this city 'unaffordable.' A lack of vision, you see. They can't accept that the city has to shed its old skin to grow. No one in their right mind would take living above an old shopfront with a bunch of roommates over a brand-new condo, but people are so attached to what already exists."

"Well, as you mentioned, there is that affordability question. I mean, what does a condo go for these days — three-quarters of a million?"

Lionel laughed and rocked back on his heels. "Three-quarters of a million isn't so much money. Anyone who really wants to live here will find a way. I have very little sympathy for the defeatist attitude. Of course, there are always those who can't make it work, and there always have been. But why let those with no stake determine the city's future?"

"Chinatown Fruit and Vegetable, for example."

"Yes, that's a perfect example," Standish said, squinting, his feet coming to rest firmly on the ground. "A single grocery store, on a street with dozens of them. And we're turning it into three hundred new units of housing."

"How many do you think you'll be able to build here?"

"Pardon me?"

"You recently purchased this building, as well, right?"

Lionel frowned and crossed his arms above the bulge of his stomach. He looked studious, but not, as I had hoped, surprised. "The Kilbride Development Corporation did, that's correct. Though this hasn't yet been publicized. How did you find out?"

"Well, you're using the space for the rehearsal. And the bar downstairs has been closed for months. And there was a Fera Civitatem concert here. Though that one didn't work out quite as well, did it? The building didn't sell until almost a year later."

"You have missed your calling, Mr. Otkazov! You should be at one of the newspapers. In fact, if you ever want to make the move, I can put in a good word for you. Not that I imagine Mr. Zimmermann would want to lose you, with the magazine going through such difficulties. You both have my deepest sympathies on that score. Believe me when I say how much *Modern Classical*'s … troubles … have been weighing on my mind. We're all trying to do our part to ensure it remains the vital organ it has always been."

"You know," I said, impressed by how effortlessly his flattery had shaded into a threat, "this hall feels so different in the daylight. The last time I was here, I was sure I'd entered one of the circles of hell, and now it just seems like an old church."

Standish laughed with what sounded like genuine delight: "'The mind is its own place, and in itself can make a heaven of hell, a hell of heaven.' Why don't we find out what our dear Ms. Pietrovalda has in store for us this evening?"

Susanna and the singers had concluded the pre-rehearsal meeting, and greeted us with professional warmth. She explained that they were still clarifying some of the blocking for the scene to be rehearsed that evening. It was a big set piece (which was why she'd invited me to join them), and it required a bit of complicated choreography. We took our seats in a row of chairs that had been put out in the middle of the hall, and Susanna directed for the curtains to be lowered. The dimmer went up and a pool of white light fell on centre stage.

An older man was seated on a throne. The violins struck a high note that lingered in the air for a measure. Just as the sound began to fade away, the trombones gave a low growl and started into a slow, staccato progression that was, after several repetitions, joined by a bit of sustained and ominous bowing from the strings. Out of the darkness on either side of the throne stepped a woman and a man. They began to list items and amounts into the seated man's ears in time with the trombones, and at the highest point in the melodic sequence, they turned to the audience and sang the word *owed*. They were joined by a second couple who began listing other items, and by a third and fourth couple, until a crowd had gathered around the seated man. With each new couple, the texture of the music became denser with the addition of woodwinds, trumpets, and finally, a pipe organ.

It was all getting a bit unbearable, when the seated man rose to his feet. Everything cut out but the organ, which settled on a dissonant, throaty chord. He began to sing in a beautifully resonant heldenbaritone about sorrow and financial ruin. He ended his little recitative by asking where his fool had got to, at which point there was a sharp, sudden glissando on the strings and a second spotlight came on above the stage, illuminating a woman hanging from a large hoop suspended above. The violins and the rest of the string section launched into a lush and raunchy cabaret tune as the woman began doing acrobatic tricks and singing in a husky contralto about what a downer accountants can be.

As she sang, the old man joined in with a series of questions: who was she, how had she gotten in, what had she done with his real fool, etc. The hoop slowly lowered as her routine went on, and when it was only a couple of metres from the stage, she jumped down and concluded by suggesting that his accountants had gotten him into this mess, but she could get him out of it. This moved into a back-and-forth where she explained that she knew a man of science who could put his financial troubles to rest, responding to his dignified phrasing with an ironic rendition of the same melody.

By this point it was obvious that the contralto was Mephistopheles, and that this was the famous scene in which Mephistopheles convinces the Emperor to adopt paper money. She beckoned a tall, bearded man from the wings (Faust, presumably), and at the Emperor's prodding, Faust and Mephistopheles entered into a comic duet, a kind of mock-Socratic dialogue about how money has no value on its own but exists as a social relation. Musically, it was clever in an understated way. Faust sang in a timeless lyric tenor, the

Emperor's bombastic lines were straight out of Britten, and Mephistopheles shifted seamlessly between styles without ever seeming to affect them — an extraordinarily difficult trick to pull off.

Mephistopheles launched into an aria about the hidden treasures that lie beneath the earth and the false piety of commodity fetishism, and flitted about the stage pulling banknotes out of what seemed to be thin air; in asides, the Emperor expressed his skepticism and Faust allayed his fears. The obvious cracks between the different styles of singing were papered over somewhat by the driving minimalism of the orchestral accompaniment, but I found myself wondering how long this kind of thing could be sustained for. The climax came when Mephistopheles, having gathered an armful of bills, threw them in a shower over the Emperor. The accountants, who had been growing more and more animated, rushed forward to gather them up in a frenzy. Faust declared that the Emperor's troubles were over.

"So you can offer wealth," the Emperor said, "but what of love?"

The minimalist theme slowed, the underlying polyrhythm morphing into steady 6/8 time. Heavy, opulent strings swept in and projectors snapped on around the hall, casting videos onto the ceiling and stage area. The images were repetitive, consisting at first of natural motifs (flowers opening, tides washing in and receding, murmurations of starlings, etc.). The clips were at speed with the music, which had developed into a kind of late-Romantic tone poem reminiscent of early Strauss or Mahler, and as the piece went on, the pastoralism of its opening gained momentum and colour, with the bassoons performing pleasing little runs that were mirrored by

the flutes. The visual motifs began to change: here and there
a paddlewheel appeared, or a spinning loom, or a coil of rope
falling loop on loop. A violin began to play a yearning solo,
and the image of a beautiful woman flashed across the screens,
at first so quickly it was hard to register anything about her
appearance, but then with greater and greater regularity until,
as the solo reached its emotional climax, her haughty face was
everywhere. As the final gentle notes of the poem faded away,
we were left facing her in silence. The room released a sigh. The
scene was over.

When the lights went up, Susanna began issuing instructions. She felt the transition from Mephistopheles's aria to the
tone poem had been too abrupt, and asked that it be taken
again. The singers reassembled in their places and picked up
from the part where the accountants rushed forward to gather
the money. The transition was rehearsed three more times.
Susanna still didn't seem quite satisfied, but to give the singers
a break, she moved on to some notes for the first violinist, a
very tall, very thin man whose shaggy hair made him look like
a toilet brush.

Susanna had perfect command of the room, and it seemed
obvious that the relaxed atmosphere I noted at the beginning
was a function of the confidence the performers had in her
judgment. It was also, perhaps, owing to the fact that she talked
about the score with cool detachment. When the conductor
suggested that a certain passage was dragging the momentum,
she asked whether he thought it should be cut. He said it might
work better as a cadenza, and the first violinist agreed. Susanna
seemed perfectly satisfied with this. But on other matters she
stood firm, giving long and often highly technical explanations
of why it needed to be exactly as written.

The evening was well advanced when the rehearsal finally wrapped up and Susanna led me over to a quiet corner so we could commence the interview. I started with some general questions about why she had chosen to cast Mephistopheles as a woman, where the idea to incorporate tone poems and projections had come from, and so forth — straightforward questions that would give Susanna a chance to offer up the kinds of quotes a profile is built around. As I'd expected, she was reluctant to provide the type of soundbites I was looking for, so I made a few banal statements for her to agree with (which, of course, she didn't), and in rejecting what I'd put forward she provided the kind of lines I was looking for in the first place, but with a more combative and sardonic edge. This was all part of the game, as she and I both understood very well.

What I really wanted to get to, of course, was the rather odd mishmash of musical styles. Clearly this was what she wanted to talk about, too, because she started speaking more slowly, pausing to find the precise words.

"You may recall from our previous conversation that I have been thinking a lot about where classical music can go after the deconstruction it underwent in the twentieth century."

"Right."

"This is my answer."

"If you could expand on that a little, I'd be grateful."

"You can't have someone just get up and sing a Romantic aria out of Verdi and expect it to be taken seriously. But if you have someone singing a Romantic aria right after someone does a burlesque show, then a point is being made."

"So the fact that the Emperor, and Faust, and Mephistopheles are all singing in these very different styles is a kind of collage?"

"That's not the word I'd use."

"Because ..."

"A collage exists in space. Music exists in time. So to have something come after something else and before something different entirely is an unfolding experience — it suggests a narrative of its own, a parallel narrative to the actual text. Extending that idea, I've tried to view the score horizontally and vertically, with the conjunction of different textures and styles within a single piece working not to create a Hegelian synthesis — you know, classical plus blues equals jazz, or something like that — but to create the sense of multiple contradictory syntheses being made and undone at once. Isn't that the modern condition, the ineluctable sense of forward motion coupled with the anxiety that progress may not necessarily be progressive?"

"There's a lot to unpack there."

"I've been thinking about it for a long time."

I tried to get her to be a little more specific, to bring her ideas down to the level of the scene they had just rehearsed, but whenever it seemed like she was about to say something concrete, she retreated back to thinner, more abstract air. I suspected this was not an accident. She had obviously thought through the meaning of every note — she just didn't want to have that meaning pinned down onto the page. Eventually I gave up, and the interview moved on to the kinds of boring practical questions that are needed to fill in the background of a profile. I thought I knew the answers to some of them already. But Susanna's life, as narrated by Susanna, was less dramatic than I had imagined; or perhaps it was just that she'd got her story down pat after all these years of telling it.

"I do have one more question," I said, as Susanna got up to leave, "and sorry if it's a kind of obvious one, but why

The Laugh of Mephistopheles? What's laughter got to do with it?"

"I think it will make sense in the context of the whole performance."

"I mean, I get that he's, or in this case, she's, a witty character, but based on what I've seen this evening, I don't get the sense that she's *funny*, exactly ..."

"Laughter isn't just about humour — there's all kinds of laughter. I've always thought it's a bit like music that way."

"Is it because Mephistopheles gets the last laugh?"

Susanna looked at me, puzzled. "This isn't a joke, Alexander. If you need me to clarify any points — technical points, I mean — send me an email. I really do need to be going."

IX

———

AFTER MANY AGONIZING hours spent typing and deleting and rearranging the material I'd gathered, I sent Zimmermann the final draft of the feature. He called me into his office the next morning and asked me what all the stuff about modernity and construction sites was doing in there, and where I had gotten the mistaken impression that our readers would want to know so much about the history of the Faust legend.

"Why do you torment me like this, Alexander? This is a thousand words over. We're going to press on Friday, so please, please, for the love of whatever you *do* take seriously, get me something I can actually print by the end of the day."

I sat down at my desk, deleted five paragraphs, added a few clichés about young geniuses, and emailed it back to him. It was a relief, really, to have permission to stop caring.

We walked to the subway together that evening. He generally got over his irritation with me quite quickly, but this was not the case today.

"Why do I have to keep explaining these things to you? I could understand, during the first few issues ... there's a learning curve, of course, for all of us, I try not to be unfair about that ... but it's been a year and a half, you know, and you're the only staff writer. I rely on you to get things done right the first time. I can't always be looking over your shoulder. In my day we were expected to turn out pieces like that all the time — sometimes you even had to dictate it over the phone. Do the interview, get the quotes, organize the story, turn it in by four o'clock. We're not trying to reinvent the wheel. I don't know what's so hard to understand."

"I just thought that given the nature of the piece, some background might be helpful. So people have a sense for what she's trying to do. To make it interesting."

"But it's already interesting. It's a young composer, first opera, big grant, performed in a construction site ... it writes itself. Get out of the way and let the story be the story. I sometimes think you might have been happier in a graduate program."

"I don't really have an academic mind."

"An academic mind ... no, I don't suppose you do. But do you have a journalistic mind? I wonder. I'm being candid with you, Alexander, because you're young, and you've still got time to find your way. No, look, I'm not firing you — good God, what kind of a person would fire someone while waiting for a street light? Very unprofessional, not to mention dangerous, I mean, they could push you into traffic, for one thing, or start crying ... all I meant was that you should take some time, think about what it is you want to do. Obviously, I want to see you succeed, I just hope you can knuckle down a bit, start getting it right the first time. Hold deadlines in greater respect. Well, here we are. Are you walking? Very good, very healthy. One wants to fill one's lungs and stretch one's legs on such a fine day. Who knows how many more we'll have like it."

X

THE LAUGH OF MEPHISTOPHELES premiered at the beginning of October. Susanna emailed me a pair of complimentary tickets, and expressed pro forma gratitude for the glowing profile, adding that she wished I'd been able to see the whole performance before writing my piece as it would have helped me avoid certain lacunae in the reportage. Zimmermann laughed sourly when I forwarded him the email, and told me I should go along and write a few column inches about it as a follow-up. At that point, music was not the foremost topic on anyone's mind. The carnival south of the border was coming to an end, and people were expending quite a bit of energy assuring each other and themselves that the election would turn out in the boring obvious way. I felt slightly bad that Susanna's big moment was to be so spectacularly overshadowed by the infamous real-estate developer's fall.

I invited Sev to come along as my guest. He had been disappointed by my piece, and told me as much the day it came out. He agreed to come along to see, as he put it, "just how much polishing you gave that turd."

We made our way through the evening mist to the place where the performance was being held. The steam from the sewer grates smelled of sulphur and gasoline, and the tower looked like a glass cenotaph. Inside, the raw concrete was festooned in electrical wires and shining ductwork. A freight elevator took us up through the skyscraper's bones. We exited into a cavern lit by soft golden LEDs. Above us an observation deck looked over the hall, and outside the glass windows, the lights of the financial district blinked through the murk.

Between two massive columns a stage had been erected, and around it large white screens were suspended from cables that disappeared into the vault above us. The audience seemed cowed by the space, their conversations hushed and echoing.

"All this concrete is going to be hell for the acoustics," Sev said as we found our seats. "Fucking stupid idea, if you ask me."

He was right, of course: when the LEDs dimmed and the overture began, it was like listening to an iPhone amplified through a tin can. The noise from different sections of the orchestra reflected off the angular surfaces and created dissonances where there were supposed to be harmonies. It took some time to realize that even in Roy Thomson Hall, the overture would have put one's teeth on edge. As Susanna had suggested, the composition was an unhealthy mix of different influences and eras, a wailing electric guitar quoting a Bach prelude while the horns tried to resurrect Wagner's ghost. A certain harmonic logic was present, but it was hard to follow through the bewildering cacophony.

"I hate you," Sev whispered quietly.

When the overture came crashing to an end, Faust emerged onstage, surrounded by screens filled with Arcadian images. His voice, which had been so clear and moving in the concert hall, seemed scooped out and shallow in this inhospitable environment. His solid bel canto aria, which would, in another context, have been unremarkable but well delivered, was stripped of anything resembling character. I had just about come to the conclusion that the entire thing was an irredeemable disaster when Mephistopheles arrived on the scene. With a sense of incipient horror, I began to realize that Susanna had foreseen the effect the concrete box would have on the music and had, in fact, taken it into account: what the voice of her principal character lost in richness, it gained in dramatic energy — the acoustic problems amplified her irreverence and playfulness, made them seem less stagy. Where the Emperor and Faust, both played by singers who had been trained to dominate the space they were in, seemed reedy and inconsequential, Mephistopheles, whose parts never stayed in one style for very long, seemed even more colourful and lively. It was the kind of calculated nastiness only a great artist could achieve.

Despite Susanna's protestations to the contrary, it became clear as the show went on that the opera hewed quite closely to the emotional structure (if not the actual lines) of *Faust, Part Two*. After Mephistopheles dazzles the Emperor with his economic innovations, she and Faust embark on a quest to bring back Helen of Troy. They travel to Classical Greece, where Faust ignores the Emperor's bidding and decides to keep Helen for himself. They have a son, Euphorion, who pulls an Icarus and flies too close to the sun. Helen vanishes into smoke, and Faust, standing alone on a mountain outcrop, forsakes his idylls and decides to remake the world. In an aria that could have been tremendous in a more agreeable room, he declares his intent to wrest his new kingdom from the seas. Against a background of devilish trombones and sainted violins, he declares his credo:

> *So realm and rule to me will fall;*
> *The glory's nought, the deed is all!*

The lights came up for the intermission. I looked around in hopes that the construction firm responsible for the building had had the installation of plumbing at the top of their work order.

"There are some porta potties at the back, if that's what you're worried about," Sev said. "I made sure, just in case I needed somewhere to be violently sick."

I found my place in line, and tried to judge what others thought of the performance so far. There was quite a bit of complaining about the sound quality, and the portable toilets, and the temperature. The ancient Russian women ubiquitous at opera performances everywhere, who had sensibly chosen to bring their furs, were making a loud fuss (in Russian, of course) about the inclusion of electric guitar. Lionel Standish was hanging around by a column off to one side, drinking from a champagne flute with a woman I recognized to be his wife. When I got out of the toilet, I found that Sev had joined them.

"Ah, Mr. Otkazov," Standish said as I approached them. "We were all talking about your magnificent piece of reportage, the acuteness of the observation, the density of detail ..."

"My husband is just trying to embarrass you," said Mrs. Standish. "We were talking about politics. Though it was a very fine piece of writing. Margaret," she added, extending her hand.

"Alexander," I said, shaking it and looking into her eyes, which were large and brown and surrounded by very fine, expressive wrinkles.

"I know."

Margaret was significantly younger than her husband, perhaps in her early forties, and had a green pashmina draped over her shoulder. Except for a few streaks of silver, her hair was very black, and piled messily on top of her head, which made her seem taller than she actually was.

"You're not a Muslim, are you?" Standish asked Sev, going back to the topic they had presumably been on before I arrived. "I can't imagine it will be easy for those of the faith should things not go well for the Democrats in the coming weeks. But one must admit that the choices our American friends have been presented with are hardly ideal ..."

"My family is pretty secular," Sev said, with more grace than could reasonably be expected, "though my mother's people are more Catholic than you'd want them to be."

"Ah, yes, I always forget that you are the product of an interfaith marriage. How fortunate we are to be living in such enlightened times —"

"Lionel, don't you think it would be more interesting to hear what Sev has to say about all this?" Margaret said gently.

"Yes, yes, that's very right. It's always good to hear a younger person's perspective on such matters. They say your generation is firmly in the leftist camp?"

"My opinion can be summed up pretty easily," said Sev. "A plague on both their houses."

"Well put! Very well put indeed. I must say I agree, though of course my wife chides me about my flippancy toward politics — and rightly so, rightly so — but do you not feel, even against your own better instincts, that there would be something satisfying should Mr. Trump carry the day? The agent of chaos, the reality star from Queens raising his shining middle finger to the United States of America? I mean, if we *must* choose between a steroidal superego and an untrammelled id, isn't there some part of you that is rooting for the id?"

"Lionel, how much champagne have you had? The bell is about to go off — we should be getting back to our seats."

"*In vino veritas,* my love. But yes, we should perhaps prepare our hearts for what will doubtlessly be a remarkable second half. I hope you will both take my comments in the spirit of playfulness in which they were intended."

"Always good to talk to you, Sev," Margaret said, "and nice meeting you, Alexander."

A flashing light above the stage indicated the end of the intermission. Margaret walked away, Lionel's hand resting at the curve of her waist. The back of her dress was scooped low, and her shoulder blades rose like headlands under her skin.

"I can't quite seem to figure out what that guy's deal is," I said, as we settled into our seats. "I mean, the way he talks ..."

"That's what happens when you've had more money than God your entire life and no one can afford to tell you you're full of shit. I can't imagine how Margaret puts up with him."

"Yeah, she seems nice."

"She's a fucking saint."

Orange light flooded the room, and the kettledrums began a chugging rhythm accented on the offbeats by high sforzandos from strings. The screens flashed with archival footage of miners and earthworks and spoil tips. The low hum of trombones and bassoons built slowly to a crescendo and then dropped away, returning again a measure later. An electric guitar joined in with a wash of distorted chords that were just recognizable as a quote from *Night on Bald Mountain*. The pace picked up, and one of the trumpets launched into a rousing solo that was answered by a full-throated response from the string section. The projected images evolved in loops, the hardscrabble labourers giving way to blast furnaces, steel mills, and great mounds of slag rising up along the shores of a sterile ocean. The brassy individualism of the horn was answered by a wall of furious sound, but as the interplay went on, the strings became increasingly subdued, and the trumpet cheekier and more triumphant.

A mournful blast on the organ signalled a change of mood, and the music shifted into a mournful and elegiac passage that rounded out the exuberant fury of the tone poem's opening movement. This in turn led into a jazzy passage in which the trumpet reappeared, cockier this time and with a buzzing mute in its bell. The strings backed the trumpet up, giving the kind of colour that, on a Count Basie record, would have been provided by a horn section. But where the sound of the trumpet called out for the recognizable harmonic structures of swing or ragtime, we were given a discomfiting kind of twelve-tone pastiche — Berg, but with a smoother rhythm. On the screens above, two young workers were lying in a hole, shovelfuls of dust pouring over them.

Spotlights fell on six singers wearing coveralls. They were joined by a chain each was carrying over the left shoulder. The basses plucked out a progression that sounded very similar to the "Song of the Volga Boatmen," and each singer in turn sang a brief lied about their distant homes. One came from a mountain village, one was a priest's son, one was from the "far east," one had impregnated another man's wife, the last had been a soldier in the Emperor's wars: all had been gone a long time. When the stories were finished, they joined together into an optimistic chorale expressing hope that their work would not be in vain.

Faust bounded onto the stage with Mephistopheles in tow, and began peppering the first worker with questions about how the project was coming along. Lack of food, lack of supplies, the enormity of the task — all these things had stood in their way. But the foreman reassured Faust and Mephistopheles that they would soon be finished. After the labourers had left the stage, Faust began a powerful aria about how much better it was to put one's energy toward raising cities and making the earth productive than to indulge in feeble pursuits like sex and drinking. As in the first act, the dignity of the piece was undercut somewhat by the deadening, distorting concrete, but when Mephistopheles joined in and transformed the piece into a combative duet by arguing that it was all very much the same to her, the humour came through even more incisively.

The debate ended inconclusively, and the scene shifted to Faust's study, late at night. Moons and stars were projected onto the screens above, and the organ played a plaintive canon as Faust expressed regret that his work was coming to an end. His reverie was interrupted by a church bell. Faust was surprised: he thought he had rid his territory of such outdated superstitions. But Mephistopheles coyly slid onstage to explain, to a lilting maritime folk melody, that nearby there was one family still holding out against his advances. The screens lit up with a video reel of a young man returning home with a pack over his shoulder and being greeted by his aged parents. The couple lived in a cottage by the sea and had a small chapel on their land, and the three went there together to pray. Faust demanded that Mephistopheles serve them their eviction papers; this last territory would be his, as well.

Mephistopheles winked knowingly at the audience and beckoned to the wings as Faust retired to bed. The labourers stepped onstage and sang a sinister motet as the screens above showed the property being torched and the couple and their son burned alive. When the steeple collapsed and the flames licked up around blackened corpses and a crucifix turned to ash, the soot-stained faces of the workers broke into smiles, and the motet shifted from A Minor to C Major. The orchestra joined in with a glorious chord that heralded a triumphant violin chaconne.

Around us the flames gave way to long, heroic shots of architectural confections, gleaming glass pyramids, impossibly graceful marble towers, sun-kissed concrete arches, skyscrapers made of steel as fine as spun sugar. Mephistopheles led Faust back onstage and told him that his work was completed, but Faust kept asking about the old couple. Where had they gone? Mephistopheles told him not to worry, that they were beyond care, and that he should rest now that his vision had been realized. But Faust protested, until the labourers produced three skulls. Overcome with emotion, Faust collapsed onto the stage, dead, and was carried off by the workers.

Mephistopheles, in a way that for the first time seemed completely unaffected, sang an aria of understated simplicity over a cadenza of quavering horns about the emptiness of human life. Only she, who had seen everything repeat itself a thousand times already, could appreciate the gift of destruction. Out of the ashes of the old world, the new would be born. But (as the orchestra fell from zeal to melancholy) she acknowledged her one regret:

How shall this riddle run?
As good as if things never had begun,
Yet circle back, existence to possess:
I'd rather have Eternal Emptiness.

And then, as Mephistopheles's last notes fell into silence, a great Gloria rang out from around the room. The orchestra came to life with a cacophony of wailing and bowing and a high, pure note on the strings. On the screens above, the image of Faust appeared, raised aloft amid the sun-struck clouds. The hidden voices of the choir sang the final words:

Saved is our friend in peace,
Preserved from evil scheming:
For he whose strivings never cease
Is ours for the redeeming.

The chorus was repeated in a round for a long time, reaching new heights of noise and jubilation as the orchestra seemed to fall to pieces, each instrument outdoing the others in vigour until it reached a crest of pure sound and slowly began to fade away, and the image of Faust grew indistinct, and the stage darkened, the last lights fading slowly to nothing as a lone bassoon was left playing in the night. The screens rolled slowly up into the girders, revealing the city stretched out before us. The mist had cleared. Ten thousand golden windows shone down Yonge Street to the lake, which lay like a rich black smudge between the lights of the city and the glow of the sky. The bassoon played on and on until it was silenced, as I'd known it would be, by the pealing laughter of Mephistopheles.

XI

––––––––––––

"WELL, THAT WAS certainly something," I said, once we'd gotten down to the street.

"Something awful."

"You think so?"

"Come on, man. What was it, a quote book of the last four hundred years of music? Tonal chaos. Metrical chaos. The fucking acoustics. People are going to go nuts for this."

"The idea —"

"I know, I know. It was a clever idea, clever staging, clever casting, the whole thing was so fucking *clever*. Am I the only person in this city tired of cleverness? Tired of ideas?"

"But there was an attempt at transcendence. You've got to credit her for that. I mean, the ending ... it wasn't just ugliness. There was real beauty there. And it was brave! Would you have preferred she played it safe?"

"I mean, I'd rather be appalled than bored. But are those really the only two options? It's just the same thing I hate about everything these days — like, the grasping, the desperation to be intelligent. Not everything needs to mean something, you know? Some things can just be nice."

"This country has seen quite enough niceness."

I left Sev at the entrance to the subway and told him I was taking the train home. Instead I walked the length of Bloor Street, back to the West End. There was a rudeness and good humour to Bloor Street on a Saturday night; so much of the old city remained in the grubby used bookstores and late-night cafés, the Korean and Ethiopian restaurants, the New Age shops and dive bars. So much vitality. Faust was coming for them, too, of course. The old department store with the gaudy lights and preposterous signage was closing; the theatre impresario's village was slated for destruction. Condo towers on the westward march. Perhaps Susanna would be on the march, too. Her opera, whatever Sev believed, was a work of genius — of cruel genius, the very best kind. She had listened to what the bricks of every city from Austen to Edmonton were saying, had heard the boundless, Mephistophelean laughter of money, and she had found it a very good joke.

FOURTH MOVEMENT

THE QUEEN
OF THE NIGHT

I

—————————————

I FELL IN love on the coldest day of a mild winter, sitting
beneath coloured lamps at a bar named for a city on the other
side of the world. I suppose it must be true that every time you
fall in love is different, because I had never experienced a love
so thoroughly tinged with hatred until that night in January
when Margaret Standish took the stage to sing *"Non mi dir."*

It was the first Friday of the year. The bar was filled with
people looking for an excuse to drink with strangers after the
holidays. My own Christmas had been lonely and unremarkable, an excuse to sleep late and watch television shows I forgot
as soon as they were over. The brief holiday ended with a visit

up to my mother's for New Year's Eve. We ate vegetarian versions of all the salads I remembered from childhood and she gave me a bottle of cedar oil, to keep me healthy through the winter. Sev had just returned from the West Coast, looking cheerful and rested after two weeks at the family home on Salt Spring Island. He was dying to be out in the city. Because I had missed him more than I'd thought I would, I agreed to get out of bed and meet him at Union Station. We walked the three blocks to the bar in air so cold it left a crust on the nostrils.

Every month the Amsterdam Bicycle Club hosted a classical cabaret, and Sev and I had been coming long enough to have developed a familiarity with the other regulars. It was nice to be able to smile and nod at people without having to speak to them. Sev was the only person whose conversation I really desired. He would be leaving again soon, singing the part of Don Bartolo at some production in New Jersey, and I could sense that a part of him was already saying goodbye to Toronto. He had left many places behind, and it was inevitable that this city, too, would recede into his magnificent past. And I would still be here, sitting at the same tables, listening to the same music, talking to people I liked less than him.

A bald man in a grey waistcoat took the stage and wished us all a happy new year, and thanked us for making it out on this cold night, and assured us we would not regret our decision before launching into a long series of thank-yous to various corporate and governmental funding bodies. I had nearly finished my drink by the time he invited the first performer onto the stage, a graduate student who set the tone for the evening with a sexless rendition of "*Habanera.*"

I had been to enough of these performances to know what kind of repertoire to expect. Arias from a half-dozen major operas, some musical theatre stuff. The selections themselves were rarely surprising: the same arias could have been sung in the same bar a hundred years ago and no one would have raised an eyebrow. The quality varied, as was to be expected, but even the better singers struggled to do anything with the words. Love and dishonour and betrayal and vengeance had outlived their time. We were nostalgic for these anachronisms in the same way we missed mechanical clocks and letter writing. No one wanted to live in that world anymore. The performers were priests of a dying religion, going through a liturgy they no longer believed in for a congregation that showed up out of habit.

The event was reaching its dreary conclusion when the bald man jumped back onstage to announce the final singer. She was, he told us, a beloved member of the classical music community, a mentor for young musicians, a performer whose appearances were made only more precious by their rarity, etc. We were asked to put our hands together for Margaret Standish. The room erupted in applause, and I sat up a little straighter in my chair.

I could see only her back as she made her way to the stage, but I recognized the coils of black hair piled atop her head, and the way she walked, like a ship under sail. The hum of conversation rose and fell as she took the stage and the accompanist laid down an arpeggio, but it died away when she began to sing. Her voice was tentative at first, giving each phrase a dramatic charge. You could hear the pauses and cracks as she sang *"Ah no mio bene!"* The silence in the room was anxious, each listener willing her to make it to the next note. This uncertainty lingered during the first heartbreaking phrases of the aria, the delicacy and weakness accentuated by the rolling accompaniment from the piano, which filled out the famous lullaby of the strings. And then came the gentle, yearning leap to the B-flat, which she handled so effortlessly the fragile opening bars suddenly seemed coy. In the next repetition of the main theme, the full power of her voice rose out of her chest, and I realized the hesitancy had been a trick. She'd known what she was doing all along.

Margaret did not sing like an actress. There was no gesturing, no attempt to draw us into the reality of the story. There was the voice and the piano, the libretto reduced to pure sound, the meaning of the words obvious in the way every single note contained the paradox of love deferred, every cadence a reminder that the aria would end. In those moments, no sadder thing was imaginable. She fell from the high notes in the runs toward the end with a sense of regret, as if they were friends she would never see again. The formulaic musical cliché that brought the aria to a close, too, was transformed from a triumphant resolution to an anxious question. The last chords resolved into a reverent silence, and it seemed for a moment that the darkened pub had grown holier, purged and sanctified by her voice.

Applause ruined the moment, and Margaret smiled and bobbed her head in a few gracious nods before stepping back down into the crowded barroom. She reached her table, and the leonine head of her husband rose to plant a kiss on her cheek.

"I hate to agree with the MC," said Sev, "but that was actually worth coming out for."

I nodded. I could see Margaret's shoulders through the crowd, and the wisps of hair falling on the nape of her neck.

"You want another drink?" Sev asked. "Yeah, of course you do. We can go over and say hello after. It's too bad Lionel's here. He's probably trying to show everyone what a supportive husband he is."

I was not at all sure I wanted to say hello. I never knew how to congratulate people on a good performance. Bad performances were easy — you just had to lie through your teeth and say "that was beautiful!" If you said that after someone did well, though, they'd think you'd thought it was bad, so you had to find something clever to say about why you liked it, which made you seem like a show-off. I preferred not to say anything at all, to let the performance be what it had been and get on with the drinking. And yet there were those little wisps of hair, the dusting of freckles on her neck. I felt compelled to get as close to those freckles as possible.

"Can you take this gin and tonic?" Sev asked on his return. "Margaret loves gin and tonics."

The Standishes were holding court over a long table. Their presence made it a zone unto itself, invisibly cut off from the rest of the room. But Sev never doubted his right to be in the centre of things, and he was quickly slapping people on the back and shaking hands and making jokes about how Lionel needed to let his wife get out more.

I offered Margaret the gin and tonic. "Sev thought you'd want to refresh yourself," I said. She smiled, and I could see that etched beyond the corners of her mouth was a pair of parenthetical curves that gave her a quizzical and oddly girlish look.

"Thank you. I don't know how Sev remembers what everyone likes to drink. He must have been a waiter in another life." She caught Sev's eye and raised her glass, which he acknowledged by inclining his head. She seemed aloof from the conversation, perched at the end of the table with one leg crossed over the other. Lionel started going on about some matter of

Toronto theatre lore, and she gestured for Sev and me to pull up chairs beside her.

"It's not fair that we never get to see you in a real production," said Sev. "You humiliate all of us as soon as you get on a stage, and then you retreat to your mansion and leave us wondering when we'll get to hear you again."

"I'm too old for schedules. The only people I want to sing for are the crows in my backyard. They're the perfect audience. Very understanding when you can't hit a high note."

"You did great. The way you handled those runs at the end — heartbreaking."

"Thank you. What did you think, Alexander? I recall you had some harsh words for the poor girl who sang that piece at the Four Seasons Centre last year."

"I thought it was very, uh, beautiful."

"Oh dear."

"I mean, what you did at the beginning was brilliant. You had the entire room in the palm of your hand."

"Alexander is probably not the best person to ask," Sev interjected. "He hates Mozart."

Margaret's eyebrows arched in surprise. "Really?"

"It's not that I hate him," I said, trying to affect nonchalance. "I just find it's all a bit breezy, you know? He's too charming."

"You don't want to be charmed?"

"I don't want to be manipulated."

"But all music is manipulative, isn't it? I mean, if you don't want to be manipulated into feeling something, why not just stay home and read the score?"

"It's not about being manipulated into feeling something, exactly, it's just that I like music that has a more intellectual side — I mean, I feel things when I listen to Bach, for example, but it feels more honest, like he isn't trying to seduce me into going along with something ..."

"That's a little obvious, don't you think, Bach versus Mozart? Do you really think one is more 'honest' than the other?"

Sev hid his smirk behind his drink, and my ears grew warm. The foolishness I felt had less to do with the argument than with my irritation at having believed I was entering one kind of conversation and finding myself in another. I began to say something trite about how the multivocal complexity of Bach's *Mass in B Minor* represented a fundamentally different, and much richer, musical philosophy than what could be found in most of Mozart's work, when Lionel, having finished his story, broke in to ask what honesty had to do with anything.

"Alexander was just explaining why Mozart is inferior to Bach," Margaret said, grinning slightly.

"Alexander is right! You can't argue it isn't *nice*, but it is also — I think we can agree — a little excessive. Are we not sometimes inclined to agree with the Emperor: 'Too many notes'?"

"'Just as many as necessary,'" said Margaret. This made everyone laugh, and soon Lionel was going on about what was, in his view, the lamentable unassailability of certain composers' reputations.

Margaret looked at me out of the corner of her eye as she sipped her drink. The smile on her face was victorious, as if she could see that her husband's support for my views was making me reconsider them. A strand of hair had fallen loose from the mass atop her head, and I was so close I could have tucked it behind her ear if I reached out my hand. But this was impossible, so I asked whether she would be singing again soon. She gave a sad little laugh and told me she performed only when people asked her to. It was an enigmatic answer and, I think she knew, an unsatisfying one, but she did not let the moment linger. She asked a question about writing, and I began to realize that what I had taken to be bluntness was actually a kind of deadpan humour.

Margaret had a disarming way of speaking. It was clear from the stories she told that she had lived in many places, among many different kinds of people, and knew a great deal about the world, but she was invitingly blithe about it all. She assumed I knew everything she did, and that knowing these things didn't make either of us special. This was more than a lack of pretension (although later I came to understand that she was a thoroughly unpretentious woman): it was a sense that there was no difference between talking about architecture and talking about the weather, that we were all living in the same world and any curious person would have something to say about it. She was entirely comfortable disagreeing with me, and in one or two instances told me flat out that I was wrong. But there was no sense of point-scoring in this. If I mentioned people or ideas she wasn't familiar with, instead of nodding along and pretending she knew what I was referencing (as I would have), she asked me to explain. It was intoxicating.

Around midnight, things began to disintegrate. Sev and I got our coats and walked out into the night to find a dusting of fine snow had fallen. The tire tracks made dark lines on the street, and I lingered in the shelter of the portico, clicking my lighter, trying to get it to spark in the wind. Sev hummed a tune on the sidewalk. I had just gotten the flame to catch when the door swung open. Margaret walked out in a camel-hair coat with Lionel following behind her, and when she saw me in that compromising position, she grinned.

"A smoker!"

"We all need our little vices." I coughed as the first delicious cloud left my lungs.

"You realize those things are highly addictive."

"Someone should have told me."

"Lionel, you don't mind if I ..." She looked at her husband questioningly. He shrugged his shoulders in exasperation and muttered something about how she was supposed to have quit. "Alexander, may I have one of yours? I've been trying to kick this nasty habit, but on nights like this, you can kick only so hard."

I proffered my pack as she reached her fingers out toward me. I moved in close to light it. It took a moment for the flame to catch. I watched its reflection flicker in her dark eyes.

"You know, Alexander, our conversation tonight made me think — I have these tickets to *The Magic Flute* for later this month, and Lionel can't make it. Can I convince you to open your mind?"

Lionel had moved ostentatiously away to escape the tobacco smoke and appeared to be dialing a cab. He guffawed when he heard Margaret's question. "Better you than me, Mr. Otkazov!"

I nodded, and she nodded, and I gave her my number while we waited for the taxi. Lionel helped her into the car, and waved at Sev and me before closing the door.

The night was black above us and the moon hung on the lip of the sky as we walked toward the subway station.

"You're a real nitwit, Alex," said Sev. "A real fucking nitwit."

||

———

IN TORONTO, JANUARY is the most intimate month. Under a blanket of darkness and lake snow, the warmest bodies are those of your friends, and we gathered like moths around the flickering tea lights in the Dundas Street bars. But that January was not like the previous two. The upcoming inauguration in the United States had created a sense of foreboding, as if we were all perched on the rotten seat of a latrine, waiting to tumble into 250 years' worth of shit. For most of us, this manifested in a good deal of hand-wringing. For Sasha, it had a galvanizing effect. She started attending meetings at some kind of activist group, and spent a lot of time researching refugee resettlement and labour organizing. She had gotten it into her head that unions were the only meaningful way to fight back. Ted was full throated in his agreement. It made me — and Sev, too, I think — feel a little useless. In theory, I was fully in favour of "burning it all down," as people liked to say. But I couldn't quite bridge the distance between the metaphor and reality. Arsonists don't tend to leave things better than they found them.

The anger took on a more personal edge toward the end of the month, when we received word that our landlord, an old Portuguese man who had been living in the Azores for the past fifteen years, had died. He had been more than happy to leave us be as long as he received his monthly bank transfer; it was unlikely that his son would be so sanguine. According to Ted, there hadn't been a rent increase in at least a decade, and we were sitting on prime real estate.

"I guarantee the mother*fucker* is going to send us an email next month saying that his 'daughter' needs to 'move in,' and by summer this place is going to be rented out for twenty-five hundred a month," said Sasha, spitting slightly and then wiping her mouth down with her sleeve. "We'll all be paying twice as much for basement apartments north of Dupont."

"We've got the lease through to the end of August," said Ted. "We have our rights."

"Possession is nine-tenths of the law."

"Know any good lawyers?"

It turned out Sasha did know some good lawyers. This was why she was so pessimistic.

"What I don't understand," I said, slowly, aware that I was heading into treacherous territory without a headlamp, "is why prices keep going up when you can't walk four blocks without coming across a construction site. A few months ago I was talking to a guy who's involved in real estate, and he said the key was to keep building more units. So if they keep building more condo towers, right, why do rents keep going up?"

"You poor sweet child," Sasha said, grabbing my arm affectionately. "Half those condos are empty. You think people are buying up those units because they want to live in a concrete box in the sky? The Canadian real-estate market is one of the best investments in the world. Imagine the ROI — half a million today, and in ten years you can probably double your money. You can't get that from an indexed mutual fund. I was talking to Ghassan," Ghassan had come up quite a bit lately; I gathered he was someone she'd met at her activist group, "and he said the only way to deal with the underlying problem is to stop viewing housing as a way of generating returns. It's the speculation that's killing everything. Who was this person you were talking to, anyway? They sound even more naive than you."

"It was, uh, Lionel Standish."

"Fuck me. Well, yeah, of course Lionel would say that. He's making money hand over fist off the international market. You're not hanging out with those fuckers, are you? Him and Sean Porter?"

"No, no, of course not. Just a professional conversation. He was explaining why it was a good thing that his company was redeveloping the old Oren Theatre."

Sasha shook her head and ordered another drink. Her disdain for Lionel made me very happy.

"Those guys ... sorry, I know you have to maintain a 'professional relationship' or whatever you want to call it with them, but Sean and Lionel are the most nauseating double act in Canada."

"You told me about Sean, but I didn't know Lionel —"

"Oh, he's not as bad as Sean. Or he's bad in a different way, I guess, would be a better way to put it. Sev knows what I'm talking about. How would you characterize their relationship, Sev? Pimp and john?"

Sev was clearly uncomfortable, but he was as drunk as the rest of us, and raised a finger in the air and thought for a moment.

"Not so much pimp and john as Master and Margherita. Sean works the black magic so Lionel can enjoy his illusions."

"And what about Margaret?"

There was a pause — Sev was clearly trying to remember another character from Bulgakov — but Sasha, unburdened by the constraints of literary allusion, supplied the answer:

"Margaret is the indulgence that's going to get Lionel into heaven."

III

ON THE NIGHT of the concert, Margaret was waiting for me at the Four Seasons Centre, on the broad wooden steps that looked out from behind the glass walls over University Avenue. She was still wearing her coat, and her hair was done up with chopsticks. She smiled warmly and asked how my weekend had been as she led me to our seats. I lied and told her I'd spent it working. The seats were better than any I'd ever had, in the third row from the orchestra pit. You could practically smell the rosin. We didn't have much time to talk before the curtain went up and we settled into the frictionless camaraderie of the audience.

I had seen the opera several times before, and didn't find
the staging particularly innovative. The conceit, established
during the overture, was that we were watching a village production of a play, which was actually *The Magic Flute* (the
Bergman reference was, presumably, lost only on the most
senile among us). The tenor playing Tamino was offensively
bland, but Papageno was full of energy, and Pamina gave a fine
showing, as well. When the Queen of the Night made her entrance and began "*O zittre nicht*," I winced pre-emptively. But
she gave a good account of herself, and the coloratura flowed
far more naturally than I could have hoped. As the plot moved
into the absurd masonic territory it is so famous for, I found
myself wondering whether contemporary audiences had also
found it impenetrably stupid, or whether they'd simply gotten
into the tunes. The tunes, were, after all, very memorable. And
the director seemed to understand that Papageno was often
the only thing keeping it from collapsing under the weight of
its own cleverness. Still, it did not quite merit the four curtain calls it received, or the hoots and whistles the audience
showered onto the stage when it was over.

"How did you find the second act?" I asked as we made our
way down the main staircase.

"The important question," Margaret said over her shoulder
as we slipped between the old men in their bowties, the ladies
in their pearls, "is what you thought of it."

"More reactionary than I remembered."

Outside it was snowing, and the traffic rushing past on
University had churned up a brown film of slush in the ruts of
the avenue.

"But I'd be interested in talking more about this," I said, "and
to hear your thoughts on the production more generally —"

"I love it when it snows like this," Margaret said, looking over at the grounds of Osgoode Hall. Beyond the wrought-iron fence, the front lawn was a dazzling white. "Even at this time of year. I never get tired of it."

"It's very poetic."

"Oh, I don't think it's poetic at all. I just like how it looks. Compositionally. The white and the black and the grey. Do you have any cigarettes?"

"I thought you were trying to quit."

"I've quit many times." She laughed. "I consider myself an expert on quitting — you're not nearly old enough to understand."

I reached into my jacket pocket and offered her a Camel. She used her own lighter, and when she exhaled, she did it slowly, letting the smoke slip gently over her lips and out the corners of her mouth. She smoked like someone who understood it was a suggestive vice.

"Shall we walk?"

We headed west on Queen, and for nearly a block Margaret was silent. I tried to steal unobtrusive glances at her. Over her simple dress, she was wearing her camel-hair coat. It was the kind of coat that clearly went better with other items in her wardrobe. Her sensible heels didn't give her any trouble when it came to navigating the slippery pavements, but she still reached for my arm when we stepped out into an intersection.

"I suppose in a sense it is reactionary," Margaret finally said. "But I choose to read it differently. That's the thing about Mozart: his music is so often at odds with the text, it leaves so much room for interpretation. Taken one way, of course, it *is* a story about hidden wisdom and the men who protect it from jealous bitches who don't know their place. But taken another, it's about the Queen of the Night, who just wants to get her daughter back. It's very fashionable these days to reduce everything to a basic moral point, but I just don't think *The Magic Flute* has a single moral point. That's why I like it. When you get right down to it, that's why I like music. Meaning is so much harder to pin down than with literature or painting."

"But music does have a meaning."

"Yes ... in a sense. But it's kind of secondary, isn't it? To the experience? When I still performed, it was never the meaning I was after. It was transcendence, or — no, that's not quite the right word ... it was a primal feeling, something pre-verbal. I was trying to get at things that existed before we had words for them."

"Did you find them?"

"I'd like to think I did, for a while."

"And then?"

Margaret laughed. It was not a mirthless laugh, but it created a distance between us. Or reminded me that distance existed.

"That is a story for another night."

"Can I ask you a question about something unrelated to *The Magic Flute*?"

Margaret nodded. We were standing at the corner of Bathurst. The ragged community gathered outside the shelter across the street had broken into song or an argument, I wasn't sure which.

"Why did you marry Lionel?"

"That's all tied up in another story, I'm afraid. A rather personal one."

"I'm sorry for prying."

"No, don't be sorry. It's a natural question to ask. We're in many ways very different from each other, and you're not the first person to have noticed that."

"Then can I ask you how you feel about what he does?"

"Sure, I guess. It's not a very interesting answer. I don't really know much about how the real-estate industry works — I just know he got started in his father's company. But that isn't what he really cares about. He's got a poet's soul. He really does love music: it's not an act or an affectation or anything like that. And he's got a great sense for it, too, even if he can't play much. Maybe in another life, he'd have been an impresario."

"Why didn't he do that? I mean, with his family money, you'd think ..."

"His father wanted him to stay in the real-estate business. It's not all privilege, being born into that kind of family. He never liked it much, but after the old man died, he entered into a merger with Kilbride. He's been a lot happier since then. It's given him a chance to focus on philanthropy. Which I think is close enough to being an impresario, for him, at this point in his life."

"His philanthropy certainly seems to go hand in hand with his business."

"Well, that's the nature of philanthropy, isn't it? No company is going to support something at odds with its economic interests. But real estate isn't like, I don't know, weapons manufacturing. Building things is a pretty respectable way of making a living."

"I suppose."

"Which isn't to say the city doesn't have problems, of course, but they're growing pains. This was never meant to be the great Canadian city — it was only with separatism and the language laws that business really started moving to Toronto. I'm not sure people of your generation understand how quickly things have changed. You know, they used to call this place the Methodist Rome; you couldn't buy a bottle of whiskey without filling out a form. I think that's why Lionel is so eager for change. He's old enough not to be nostalgic about the past. You must be sympathetic with that point of view, as an avant-gardist."

"I suppose I am. It's just that I'm probably going to be evicted this summer."

"Well, Lionel isn't evicting you."

"That's true."

Margaret was silent for a while, and I couldn't tell whether or not I had offended her. She stopped in front of the Trinity Bellwoods gate.

"Do you have another cigarette?" she asked.

I gave her the pack and opened my coat to block the wind while she sparked the lighter. She moved into the hollow of my arm as the flame sputtered to life. Once she had the cigarette lit, she moved the hand holding it up to my mouth, and placed it between my lips. I could feel the moisture of her saliva on the filter, and I wondered how Margaret could do this so naturally.

She lit the second one for herself. "Let's walk through the park. It's so peaceful at night, at this time of year."

"Now it's my turn to ask a question," she said as we walked between the pools of sodium light. "Why did you agree to come out tonight? Was it to ask questions about Lionel?"

She said this in the same warm and chatty tone she'd said everything else. I looked at her, trying to find some clue to her intentions, but the cheerful smile betrayed nothing.

"I was interested in learning more about you. Lionel is part of that."

This made her laugh, and I must have looked bewildered because she put her hand over her mouth and tightened her grip on my arm.

"I assumed you and Sev were a couple."

"What?"

"Come on! You two are very close. It's a natural thing to think."

"I, uh, don't think I'm Sev's type, exactly, he prefers —"

"Is he your type?"

"You know, I've never really thought about it. I've never had sex with a man. I mean, he is very beautiful."

"Beautiful, talented, charming, doesn't give a shit what people think. A true aristocrat."

When we got to the street, she checked her phone and asked if I'd wait while she got an Uber. I felt a damp heat inside my chest at the thought of her driving away into the night and leaving me alone on the corner.

"I'd like to see you again," I said, when the car was only a few blocks away.

"Why?"

"I think we have a lot to talk about."

"Really?" Margaret looked at me as if she expected me to say something else, but my mouth was terribly dry. "I have a feeling we'll see each other soon," she said as she climbed into the back seat of a black SUV, the phantom of a smile on her lips. "You have my phone number, after all."

IV

I AWOKE TO find Toronto shining under a layer of frost. The tree branches clattered in the wind on Gladstone Avenue as I walked down to the streetcar stop, and even the mass of people packed tightly into the central aisle seemed less gloomy and withdrawn than usual. By the back doors, I could see an elderly woman gazing out the window in silent delight, hands folded in her lap. I thought of Margaret drinking in the beauty of the day, looking out her window at the Don Valley shimmering with the movement of a hundred thousand ice-clad boughs.

I got off the streetcar at the Armoury and walked down the salty pavements of George Street. I hadn't slept much.

Normally I would have been red-eyed and irritable, and I attributed the buoyant feeling inside me to the sharpness of the air, the clouds of smoke drifting gently over the old warehouses. The lightness stayed with me through the day. Even Zimmermann's moodiness couldn't dispel it.

I had been assigned a story for our website about a young piano prodigy we'd covered many times before. He was putting on a concert of Strauss, Schumann, and Scriabin in a couple of weeks, and I was supposed to turn the marketing babble into a news story. I finished the piece in the midafternoon doldrums, and spent the last hour of the day badgering the Toronto Symphony Orchestra for a press image. As Zimmermann locked up, I tried to find an innocent way of asking him what he knew about the Standishes' relationship. But he was in no mood for questions, and as we walked down to the street, all he could talk about was the upcoming tax season.

"You should become an accountant, Alexander," he said, making his way around a pile of excrement on the sidewalk. "You're still young, it's not too late for you. Accountancy is a very good career path. Recession-proof. Though you'd probably need to be a little more punctual. And you'd have to become more, ah, sensitive to the distinction between opinion and fact. Actually, perhaps accountancy isn't the best route. Maybe law? I imagine Toronto is a good place to be a lawyer. So many sanctimonious hypocrites. And you have the right mentality for it, you know — you're always quibbling with even the smallest edits."

V

—

ALL THROUGH THE following week, the temperature hovered around zero. The city was lashed by sleet and cold rain. Pedestrians cut narrow tracks in the brown slush on the sidewalks, and passing cars threw up sheets of dirty water where the drains were backed up. I left my apartment only to go to work and spent as much time as possible curled up in bed, trying to decide whether to text Margaret. I could feel a familiar tickle of shame, an early warning that I was emerging from another long sexual hibernation. It had been two years since Theresa. It was surprising, given how close we lived to each other, that I hadn't run into her. But perhaps Sean had changed his ways. Perhaps she was ensconced in some dingy wing of his house in Forest Hill. Perhaps I was the only person in this city too miserable and craven to have a good time and damn the consequences.

On Saturday morning, I woke to the sound of rain on the window. I lay beneath the covers and thought about the day ahead. Greasy eggs and burned toast and sludgy coffee, a few hours struggling through Murakami and Ozawa's book for a belated review, a bit of listless masturbation, a dinner of pierogies and sausage, a bottle of wine, another conversation about American politics with Ted, *Barton Fink*, a Thomas Mann story, and back to bed again. It almost made me wish I still had my keyboard.

I reached for my phone and, without really thinking about it, sent Margaret a text — *I hope you had a good week, isn't the weather bad, are you interested in getting a drink soon.* Or something to that effect. I put my phone down and had a long shower. I wanted to stay in that shower forever, to join the patches of mould and learn their secret fungal languages and compose primitive mycelium tunes to play on my hyphae. By the time I got out, I was feeling much better, and put on Khachaturian's "Sonata." The rain, the darkness — the mood seemed right for some Armenian piano gymnastics. Apparently, Sasha disagreed, because she started banging on the wall of her room. I turned it down and made breakfast.

I had almost succeeded in forgetting that I had texted Margaret at all, but shortly after noon, a blue light started blinking on my phone and my heart rate went up. I put the phone in a cupboard and discovered that we were running low on bread. The light was still blinking when I returned. I thought about erections and male potency and willed myself to adopt the callous attitude of a Rastignac.

The message, of course, was perfectly polite and friendly. Yes, she would like to get a drink. Would Friday be convenient? Could I suggest a place?

I put the phone in my pocket and went back to bed. Rejection would have been far more comforting.

VI

WE MET AT the Wallflower, which I suggested in spite of the name. They never played loud music, and it had the ambience of a British colonel's living room. I arrived early and made small talk at the bar while a guy with cartoon animals running up and down his arms poured my beer. I pulled out my copy of *Cousin Bette* and read the same paragraph over and over until I felt someone sit down next to me.

"So?" Margaret said. Her teeth, when she smiled, were very white. I had never seen her hair down before.

"It's good to see you."

"It's good to see you, too, Alexander. Was there something particular you wanted to talk to me about?"

I wondered if her directness had something to do with money, or whether it was age. I hoped it was age. It was nice to think that when you got to a certain point in life, you lost the need to hem.

"Yes, actually. It's a bit of a personal question ..."

Margaret gave a full-bodied laugh. "Personal questions are the best kind. I was worried you wanted to talk about Mozart again."

"Why did you stop singing?"

"Why did you stop playing the piano?" She saw the blush rise to my skin, and took pity on me. "I'm sorry, that's not very fair. You asked first. Though I do expect you to tell me your story if I tell you mine."

"You might find mine a bit disappointing."

"Maybe, maybe not. It all depends on how you tell it. In my experience, people often fall back on clichés when talking about their lives because it's easier than trying to really think about who you are and why you've done what you've done. Clichés sidestep the whole problem. But they do tend to flatten things out. You're a journalist, though, so you probably know exactly what I'm talking about. Anyway, I don't do that, so if you're serious, you're in for a long one."

"I like long stories."

"Good. I haven't even started my drink yet, right? What's the rush?"

She took a long sip and fell silent for a moment, her head leaning to one side as if she was trying to remember the words to a song.

"So, I don't know how much you know about my life, but basically I got into the music thing early, my parents were very supportive, and I ended up being accepted into a good program in England. Everything was going very well — I did all the things you're supposed to do, and after I graduated, I got work right away. My parents were able to support me in between roles, which helped. I made my name, so to speak, playing a few popular roles — Donna Anna, of course, but also Violetta and Blonde and Zerlina. A lot of Mozart, which won't come as a surprise. It was an exciting time. This was back in the late nineties, and London was a pretty cool place to live, and it was so easy to get to Milan and Salzburg and Paris and all the other places you want to be if you're serious about a career in opera. If I didn't have a role to prepare for, I was auditioning. I got turned down a lot, but I was up for the same parts as Netrebko and Dessay. I convinced myself that if I just worked hard enough, I'd be able to beat them one day.

"The big problem was my range. I could handle the Es and Fs well enough, and could even push myself to a G, but I just couldn't consistently go further than that — I might be able to make my way through 'Der Hölle Rache' on a really good day, but I couldn't do it effortlessly. I couldn't play the Queen of the Night. Now, of course, I look back at that time and wonder why it mattered so much. I mean, who cares, really? But I was competitive, I was getting tired of singing things that were comfortable, and I was twenty-eight. So I got a new voice coach, someone with a reputation for pushing singers to their absolute limits. I worked at it day and night.

"Over time I started to notice myself getting tired more easily, even with parts I'd sung many times. It got so bad my agent told me she wouldn't help me find any more work until

I'd agreed to take a vacation. She said I needed to get out of my head for a bit, drink some wine, eat some good food, fall in love — whatever I needed to do to relax and give my voice a rest.

"I probably would have just found a new agent, but I was starting to get kind of worried. And it had been years since I'd really taken any time off, so I rented a little place in Tuscany and flew south to spend the spring recuperating. It was awful, Alexander. The cottage was on the edge of a village, and even in Italy most villages are pretty much the same as villages anywhere. The little houses, the grapevines, the view from the hills — I was so fucking bored. There was just no reason to get out of bed. By the second or third week, it had gotten *gruesome*. I moved into an apartment in Florence so I could at least spend my time doing something fun. Florence isn't a big city, but as far as music went, there was plenty to take in. I'd go to the Goldoni or the Comunale or just hang out in a little church while someone played organ.

"Anyway, one night I found myself at a little restaurant in Oltrarno after seeing some Verdi production, and I was enjoying a quiet dinner and a glass of wine when a large party showed up and began ordering all kinds of food and drink before they'd even been seated. The proprietor clearly knew them well and was happy to transform the entire dining room, which had until then been quite empty, into a banquet hall for these people. My Italian was not particularly strong, but you pick up a lot when you've spent years singing Italian opera, and I understood enough to know that they were music people. I found myself listening in to their conversation. This being Italy, it wasn't very hard to join in, especially after the wine started flowing. They had just been to a performance by a well-known tenor, and seemed sharply divided on the question of whether or not he was in decline. Many points were made for and against, most of which I did not really catch, but the debate eventually spun out, as such debates often do, to the question of great singers of the past, their voices, their failings, their triumphs, whether or not the press was fair to them, and so on. I ended up talking to an older woman named Raffaella, a real matriarch, who just sat back and made these witty little comments whenever one of the men started taking himself too seriously. This was more than fifteen years ago, but I still remember what she looked like. She had enormous jowls and almost no forehead and one of those big peasant noses. I was in love with her.

"Anyway, we began talking. She started asking all these questions about who I was and where I was from and what I was doing. It was kind of rude, really, but I didn't mind. It was like she wanted me to prove that I had the right to be sitting next to her. In the end, I just kept talking and talking and talking, and told her all about my voice and my problems and the fact that I didn't have a clue what I was going to do with myself if I couldn't expand my range. She just kept looking at me with this stony expression. I felt like I needed to justify it all, you know? Why I was wasting a whole season of my peak performing years in the Italian countryside.

"When I finally stopped talking, she waved another woman over and they started speaking very quickly, too quickly for me to follow. Then Raffaella turned to me and asked what I was doing the next day, and I told her I wasn't doing anything, and she said to meet them on one of the piazzas and they'd bring me to a doctor who could help me. It all sounded a bit weird, but Raffaella made me promise I'd come along. What else was

I going to do? I showed up the next day, and Raffaella explained that my voice was in danger, and they were going to bring me to a man who had an experimental clinic outside the city. From what I gathered, this guy, Dr. Carpenteri, had been doing a bunch of historical research into voice damage, and a lot of singers with my kind of trouble were starting to seek him out.

"We drove out of the city in Raffaella's old car. The roads weren't too good, and more than once I was convinced that I'd gotten caught up in a sex-trafficking ring or something, and I was going to end up with a bag over my head in some pervert's dungeon. After a few hours of climbing up into the hills, we stopped at this old stone building looking out over the valley. It was beautiful, a former palazzo or monastery or something. There were all these colonnaded walkways and little rooms off the main courtyard with a fountain in the middle. A young woman was sitting behind a desk in the vestibule to the main building, and Raffaella explained that I was an Englishwoman who wanted to meet with Dr. Carpenteri.

"Clearly, Raffaella had some pull there, because we were ushered onto a balcony and a pitcher of water was brought for us. I tried to get Raffaella to tell me more about Dr. Carpenteri, but all she'd say was that he did things in the old way, and that if I wanted to keep singing without tearing my vocal cords apart, he could help. She started telling me all these sad stories about sopranos who had gotten cocky and not listened to their bodies. It was interesting, because you heard these stories all the time, people were always whispering about, you know, so-and-so had to drop out of a production at the last minute because she got sick, or someone keeps having to get surgery and it's ruining their career. The fact that Raffaella was talking about it so candidly, as if it was a problem that could be fixed if people would just learn better technique, was refreshing. When I'd first arrived in Italy and I was spending all my time alone … your mind goes to bad places, right? You start to think, what if it's me everyone will be talking about this fall. I hadn't dared to sing a scale in weeks.

"When he finally came out, Dr. Carpenteri was not what I'd imagined. He was a huge man, six and a half feet tall at least, and bald as a stone. He looked like a boxer. But he had this gentle way about him, and he didn't start talking about my voice at all until he'd kissed Raffaella's cheeks and asked about her husband and poured himself a glass of water. I felt at first like I was just an accessory. They clearly knew each other well, and chatted about all kinds of things while I just sat there in the sun, wondering if I should have brought a hat.

"Eventually he turned to me and asked what the problem was, and I told him I was trying to expand my range. He wanted to know why, which made me feel a little foolish. I mean, I didn't want to come across as some unreasonable brat obsessed with success at all costs. But since I'd been dragged all the way up there, I was curious to hear what he had to say. So I asked if he was a fan of Mozart, and they both started laughing as if it was a huge joke. Apparently, Dr. Carpenteri had been a singer himself, so he knew all about the professional aspect of my dilemma.

"He asked me to sing a few scales. I felt like someone was pouring sand down my throat, but as I warmed up he began making these little 'tutting' noises, as if I was doing everything wrong. Raffaella was shaking her head. Dr. Carpenteri then asked me to sing an aria, any aria, and I gave him '*Batti, batti, o bel Masetto.*' I didn't make it more than a few bars. The look on his face told me everything I needed to know. He took me into his office and told me to lie down on the exam table. He started shining a light down my throat and asked me to sing different notes. He jotted a few things down on a piece of paper, then told me to sit up.

"'Signorina,' he said, 'You are defying God. Either accept your natural range, or make the most of the few performances you have left.'

"You can't imagine how it felt in that moment. I mean, just a day before, I'd been on a rest-cure, regaining my strength before having another go. And then all of a sudden I was in this old monastery and a man who looked like a builder was telling me my entire career was in danger. I was insulted. If I was actually in trouble, someone would have told me, right? Why should I trust this Italian? As far as I knew, he wasn't even a real doctor. I got only more suspicious as he showed Raffaella and I around his facility. He had all these theories about the human voice, about the natural limits that are built in at birth, and he kept talking about the wisdom of the tradition. According to him, none of the old opera singers had ever suffered from the modern problems that ended careers. He blamed the twentieth century, the desire to make everything bigger and bigger. Raffaella seemed to agree with him completely, and kept inserting these snide remarks about Wagner and Americanism. His entire practice was based on returning to a more natural and organic way of singing — a less bombastic, less virtuosic way, but one that would keep me performing into my eighties.

"At the end of the tour, Dr. Carpenteri brought us back to the balcony and poured us amaro and outlined the kind of treatment he could offer. He would slowly reteach me how to sing, starting with the fundamentals, and by the end of his course my voice would be much more resilient. I asked him whether I'd be able to extend my range, as well, and he shook his head. 'The vocal cord is a muscle,' he said. 'You can strengthen the muscle, but you cannot transform it. Your vocal cords will never be those of Lily Pons.'

"I told him I'd have to think about it, and Raffaella drove me back down into the city. She told me about all the people Dr. Carpenteri was trying to help, and how the greatest sopranos are not those who sing the highest, but those who sing the longest. I maintained a facade of agreeability — what else could I do? — and in the morning I booked a flight back to London.

"You can probably guess where this story is going, can't you? I threw myself back into my training. My coach assured me that the Italians are prone to eccentricity and had fallen behind the latest science. I was singing Donna Anna at an English National Opera production that fall, and as I got back into practice, my voice felt stronger than ever. But it was the last role I ever performed professionally. By the end of the run, I needed drugs to make it through to curtain call. I returned to Canada that winter. My father found a doctor who specialized in problems related to vocal performance, and I flew down to the States for surgery. The surgeon told me it was one of the most extreme cases of vocal lesions he'd ever seen. The good news was I'd be able to sing again, if I was careful and didn't push myself too far. No one needed to tell me what the bad news was."

Margaret sat back in her chair. We had both finished our drinks, and the flame from the tea light between us was floating in transparent wax.

"I'm sorry," I said.

Margaret shrugged. "I'm telling it to you because you asked, but I'm also telling you because you used to perform, which means you probably understand. If I could do it all over again, I'm not sure I would have made a wiser decision."

"So then what happened?"

"What do you mean? That's the story of why I stopped singing. That's how it ends."

"But what came next?"

"Well, after I recovered, I was a bit of a mess, as you can imagine. I moped around a lot. My parents were very supportive, but they didn't have any better ideas of what I should be doing. So I moved back to Toronto permanently, realized music was the only thing I was really interested in, and started getting involved in the community. Fundraising, that kind of thing. Not that I was very good at it. But then I met Lionel, and he was this kind of model for what it meant to love art without being an artist. It was weird, at first, him being so much older than me, but I felt like I'd lived through a lot in my twenties. I mean, I *had* lived through a lot. I wasn't in the same place, mentally, as people my own age. They were entering the most productive stage in their careers. We saw each other for a while, and then he proposed, and it seemed like I'd been given another shot at life. He was the one who got me singing again, in a way that was safe, that wouldn't do any more damage. He was very solicitous about my well-being. I think he's probably the first man who really was. He wanted me to be happy."

"Are you happy?"

"As much as anyone is. I think that to really take pleasure in music, I needed to give up on making a life out of it. The endless struggle to find meaning, to create meaning, to *communicate* can be so destructive. Everything becomes an idea, or a struggle between ideas. Don't you find it exhausting, Alexander? As a critic? The need to weigh music down with so much ideological significance, when it should provide a very pure kind of joy?"

"I don't know," I said honestly. "I have a hard time enjoying things for their own sake. The nice things are all tied up with the nasty things, and I suppose the real pleasure I get out of art is the pleasure of the struggle."

Margaret nodded thoughtfully but didn't say anything more, so I asked if she wanted another drink. At the bar, watching the bartender pull the tap down, I imagined the flesh of Margaret's vocal cords, their quivering, yonic shape, the scars that had healed over. I had been wrong, when she sang *"Non mi dir."* It hadn't been an act.

"Anyway," she said when I got back to the table. "I've told my story, now it's time to tell yours."

VII

━━━◆━━━

AT HALF PAST TWO, the tea light was dead and the bartender was wiping down the table next to ours and it was clear we needed to leave. I watched Margaret put on her coat and felt a tremor in my viscera, a loosening in my lower abdomen, a sick wet heat. It was a relief to get outside. The cold made it easier to breathe. In her heeled boots, Margaret's eyes were nearly level with mine. She seemed to be suffering none of my physical distress.

"So," she said, again.

"Do you want to come home with me?" I asked, fists clenched in my pockets.

"What do you mean — you want me to walk you home?"

"You know what I mean."

Margaret was smiling, but not like she had been inside. It was a tantalizing smile, a deep lake on a moonless night.

"I can't go home with you, Alexander. I'm married."

"Does that matter so much?"

"I think it matters a little bit."

"Why?"

She didn't answer, but the smile lingered. As soon as the question had left my mouth, my pulse slowed and the heat inside me began to dissipate. The humiliation had been in the words themselves.

"We've only seen each other a few times. I don't really know you. I have a lot to lose."

She was standing quite close to me, close enough that even in the soft glow from the bar window, I could see the fine wrinkles around her eyes. She had tied her scarf loosely around her neck, and her coat was not fully done up. I pulled her lapels closed and slid the buttons into place while she stood there with her arms at her sides.

"It's very cold," I said. Her face was turned toward me, and her eyes were watching mine. My fingers lingered on the last button. I could feel the warmth rising from inside her coat, and she was very still. I hugged her and felt her hands on my back. My lips found her cheek, just a brush, a suggestion.

And she whispered in my ear: "You'll have to do better than that."

So I did.

I don't know how exactly we ended up speeding through the city in a taxi, but I remember the light from the street lamps streaking across the window, and I remember her lacing her fingers into mine. We didn't speak until we reached a small hotel on the other side of the Humber River. I paid the driver and Margaret rang the bell at the front desk. I offered my card, nervous that it might be declined. The night clerk hardly glanced at us as he handed over the key. I must have looked very serious as we made our way down the hall, because Margaret erupted into a fit of giggles when we got to the door of our room.

"Have you never done this before?" she asked as I slid the key card through the lock.

"Never in the middle of the night," I said as we walked into the dark room, which smelled of cigarettes and bleach.

"I'm a little offended he didn't offer us an hourly rate. It's three o'clock in the morning!"

The door closed behind us and we were alone. She stood between the chipped desk and the queen bed, her hands in the pockets of her coat. There was still laughter in her face, and I was grateful for this because it made it easier to cross the distance between us and reach out my hand and touch the delta of freckled skin below her collarbone. Her heart was beating slower than mine, and her mouth was slightly open. I slid the coat from her shoulders. One by one, I eased the buttons of her shirt from their cotton holes, and when she was naked, I told her to lie on the bed. She slipped onto the coverlet and lay on her side, propping her head up in her hand and brushing her hair back from her temple. Blue veins climbing her legs, her breasts and slightly rounded stomach hanging gently toward the mattress. Margaret's body was the map of a city that already had a history. As I ran a finger along the rough skin of her instep, she rubbed her knees together and gave a little laugh.

"You know, this won't work if I'm the only one without any clothes on," she said, and sat up to undo my belt buckle. When she was finished, and her eyes were watching me the way mine had watched her, she sighed.

"My God, you're young. None of this has caught up with you yet, has it?"

I didn't let her say anything else. I had seen the clock by the bed. The night was already coming to an end.

VIII

———————

ALL THROUGH THAT spring and summer, Margaret and I
spent our Sunday afternoons lying naked in hotel rooms across
the Greater Toronto Area. She would text me on Saturday to
tell me where to meet her, usually in one of the grocery store
parking lots by the train tracks. I would arrive at two o'clock
and look for the heavy black 7-Series. The door was always unlocked, and Margaret was always lying back in her seat, listening to the radio. We were careful not to do anything that might
draw attention to ourselves until we were out of the West End.

At first, we stuck to smaller places on the far side of the
Humber — the Kingsway near Old Mill, the Halton Arms

in Mimico. But as the days grew longer and the smell of fresh dirt and vetiver filled the air, we drove north, past the freeway that marked the border of the city and into the hills and rolling fields beyond. We became familiar with the motels strung along the 400, the small, independent establishments that had managed to hang on past all reason in the small towns up toward the lake. We avoided bed and breakfasts, Airbnbs, anyplace where the shortness of our stays would be remarked on. To me, each of these motels, with their identical beds and rough sheets and sad television sets, was a luxury. I had not travelled much; the experience of throwing open the door to a room that was mine for a few hours and that I would never see again was still novel. I loved the bad paint jobs, the old ashtrays, the ratty curtains, the squeaking headboards, the slivers of soap sealed in their plastic wrappers, the phone on the nightstand, the smell of old tobacco, the linoleum in the bathrooms, the Gideon's Bibles, the little fridges with their lonely bottle of water.

Margaret loved these motels, too, though I think she found them quainter than I did. There was something Bonnie and Clyde about the whole thing for her, the fantasy of the open road, the motorcycles revving outside the window. As soon as the door closed behind us, she would kick off her shoes and do a little dance in her stockings, throwing her arms above her head and making temptress eyes at me until I came over and pulled the dress over her head and buried my face in her neck. She liked to strip the sheets off the bed before pushing me down onto my back and trying to pin me. She made love playfully, teasingly, as if we were both children at the back of a garden. When we were finished, she would open the window while I disabled the fire alarm so we could smoke in bed. At a quarter to six, she would hop into the shower and wash herself with soap she'd brought from home, and we would be on our way.

Lionel spent his Sundays playing squash or golfing before dining out, and although no questions would have been asked if she got home after him, Margaret hated rushing and wanted to make sure she had time to settle in before he arrived. Or so I assumed — after the parameters of our arrangement were established, she never talked about them. This suited me. My already unhealthy dislike of Lionel had hardened into a concentrated loathing, and the very thought of Margaret brushing her teeth and washing off her makeup and getting into bed with him at the end of the day sent me into sinister reveries. I did not know how Margaret felt about betraying her husband, and chose to believe that in some small way, she shared my disgust. Later it was clear that her habit of mentioning him only obliquely, and my willingness never to probe this aspect of her life, was what made those glorious afternoons possible.

In late May, the Standishes flew down to visit Margaret's parents in South Carolina for the long weekend. They had been away for Easter the month before, and I was resigned to the idea that holidays would interrupt our Sunday ritual. Nothing was explicitly stated: I learned what to expect by following Margaret's lead. So it came as a surprise when she called me the following Thursday evening and asked if I could meet her outside the Distillery after work the next day. She was "alone for the weekend." I was to bring an overnight bag.

We took the highway east out of the city, heading toward Montreal. I asked where we were going, but she just smiled and kept driving. The sun fell low in the sky behind us, and in the endless dusk of early summer, we listened to Prokofiev and talked about his sad compromised life, his retreat into irony, the fundamental uselessness of art in politically fanatical times. Night had fallen by the time we reached Belleville, and the water of the bay reflected the muted glow of the marina as we crossed into Prince Edward County. The highway behind us, the car's headlights cast a witchy glow on the narrow road. Low-hanging branches whispered against the windows. Margaret turned down a gravel track and stopped in front of a darkened lodge. The air was filled with lake smell and pine resin.

"Come with me," she said.

I followed her down flagstone steps into the darkness by the shore. Margaret stepped out on the dock and slipped out of her pants. Against the moonless water, her legs and buttocks were alabaster white, and her blouse flapped around her in the spring breeze. She turned to look at me, and I could see she was laughing. She undid the buttons and let her blouse blow like a flag of surrender back to shore before diving into the waves. I waited to see if she was all right. After a long moment, I saw her head emerge and her neck whip about to free the hair and water from her eyes. She set out in long, confident strokes. When I crashed through the surface, the cold shock made my arms spasm. My feet flailed about for purchase, but there wasn't any. I looked around to see if I could catch sight of Margaret. Her head was bobbing in the waves farther out from shore, and I swam toward her. She wrapped her arms around my neck and kissed me. It was a deep kiss, a kiss that contained all kinds of unsayable words, and when we were back on the dock, teeth chattering and fingers barely able to gather up our clothes, it seemed to me that something had shifted.

The lodge belonged to Margaret's parents. Long before The County had become a destination for wine snobs and realtors, she had boated along the shorelines and played on the beaches. Margaret asked me to split some wood for a fire, which I didn't know how to do. I hadn't spent much time outdoors; on the handful of occasions I had been invited to someone's cottage, the main goal had been to do heroic quantities of drugs in a private and hospitable setting. So Margaret taught me how to swing the axe and use a maul and coax a fire out of newspaper and kindling, and how to feed in the logs so they wouldn't smother the coals. We drank her father's Scotch and lay naked on his fur rug. I realized it was the first time she had brought me into a space that was truly hers.

The next morning I woke early, unused to the sunlight and fresh air. I put coffee on and wandered around the lodge. It was an A-frame, a large, open space facing the lake with a mezzanine leading to the second-floor rooms. In a small nook off the kitchen there was a piano covered in an old blanket. I pulled it off, sat down at the bench, and opened the fallboard. The instrument was old, and the key lips were chipped from long use. I played a tentative B-flat Major. The tuning was out, but not by much. I hadn't laid my hands on a piano since Montreal, and my fingers hesitated before the old habit took hold. I felt out the first prelude from the *Well-Tempered Clavier*. It came slowly, but it came. The tripping little notes filled the room and I played on through the first couple of preludes and fugues. I stopped when I felt a hand on my shoulder.

"It needs to be tuned up," I said. "And it should probably have been stored away from the window. It's amazing it's in such good shape, you know, the cold, the humidity ... it's not good for the instrument."

Margaret laughed and asked me to play a C Major scale. She sang along, and gestured for me to continue so she could warm up. I ran back down to Middle C, and then stepped up with a D Major. We continued slowly pushing upward while she found her voice. I kept it within a reasonable range. Margaret was gentle with herself at first, but as she felt the muscles begin to stretch, she went higher. I stopped playing and let her push on, tightening and relaxing by going up and then down again until she hung on the high B-flat and slowly fell away.

"God, that feels good," she said, shooing me off the bench and opening it up so she could rifle through the sheet music. "What about this?"

She was holding up the music for Korngold's "*Glück, das mir verblieb.*" I nodded and put the sheets on the stand. I played through the first chords and let Margaret find the note. I was grateful the piano part was so undemanding. Margaret's voice started out a bit hoarse, but when she slipped up to the high notes, it was perfect. I had always found the song a bit too delicate and pretty, almost like a pop ballad, but the roughness of the old piano tarnished the tinkling high notes, and the scars in Margaret's voice gave it a sense of weariness.

We sat with the final notes, my fingers splayed on the keys, her hands clutched over her stomach. Outside the window, the waves rolled out toward the horizon, lost in the ambivalent morning haze.

IX

EVEN BEFORE MARGARET tactfully brought up the issue at the end of our first night together, I understood that this was not like any relationship I had had before. As long as what existed between us stayed between us, it would not, in a sense, be real. And if it wasn't real, it could go on forever. I wanted this very much, and so I carried on as if nothing had changed. This was easy to do. Nothing really had changed. Except for a few hours on Sunday, I continued to live exactly what I'd lived before.

This mostly worked. It was only after I got back from Margaret's cottage that Sev started to suspect something was going on. He was back in Toronto for a couple of months between singing engagements, and he'd been trying to get in touch with me. The texts hadn't gone through because I didn't have reception. I tried to come up with some kind of believable, in-character excuse about having not paid my phone bill, but I'd already told Sasha and Ted that I was visiting my mother that weekend. Sev, concerned that my failure to respond to his invitation to get "drunk as lords" meant I had fallen off a bridge, texted Sasha, who told him I was away for the weekend. Caught in this rather obvious lie, I told him I'd just needed to get away from it all for a while and had holed up in Niagara Falls and turned off my phone.

I was not a very good liar, and Sev had a prosecutor's nose for fabulation and a reporter's curiosity about the lives of his friends. After our third pitcher of beer at the Bedford Academy, he got me to admit that I was, in a manner of speaking, seeing someone.

"I can't tell you who it is, Sev," I said peevishly. "So let's just move on to something else. I don't give you the third degree about who you're sleeping with. I don't have the time, for one thing."

"You just did, you dumbfuck."

"What are you talking about? I never pry —"

"I mean you just told me who you're fucking."

"No, I didn't."

Sev stared at me steadily over the rim of his pint glass until I looked away. He finished his beer and ordered another pitcher. I tried to tell him I didn't want any more, but he waved my protestations away.

"Since you're obviously trying to be a real gentleman about this, I won't make you say her name. But you know she's done this before, right? Gone behind her husband's back? I mean, they're both very discreet, but it isn't a huge secret. Not that it's surprising, anyway. I only say this because I know how you are about women."

"What the fuck does that mean?"

"How many people have you slept with since you moved here?"

"Two."

"Exactly. If you were out there every weekend, playing the field, it would be another thing. I just want to make sure you aren't getting the wrong idea about this."

I was now, of course, very grateful that Sev had ordered another pitcher. Margaret had never said anything about her previous affairs, but she hadn't needed to. It was obvious she'd done all this before. This didn't particularly bother me. It simply reaffirmed that she was restless and unhappy in her marriage.

"I appreciate your concern," I told Sev when our glasses were full again. "And obviously I understand that getting involved in someone else's marriage is not something you do lightly, hence my unwillingness to be open about it, but —"

"Getting involved in someone else's marriage? See, that's what I'm talking about — you're *not* involved in their marriage. You're having fun with someone else's wife. Big difference."

"Well, I think I'm a little involved."

"Alex, we're friends, right? But you're being pretty dense. If you leave this bar tonight having gotten one thing through your head, I hope it's this: these two people, whose names I'm not going to say because *Toronto is a village* —" he paused for a moment to let these words linger, "— have been through stuff you'll never be able to imagine. She's not leaving him, and he's not leaving her. Do whatever you want, but understand that."

"Yeah, I understand."

"Good. Now that we've got that out of the way, congratulations. The sex must be insane."

We tottered out into the June night sometime after two. I walked Sev to his apartment, full of warm feelings for humankind. Sev started telling me a very long joke about a moth having an existential crisis. He'd picked it up from an aging comedian who still commanded something of a cult following. It was his favourite joke. I already knew the punchline: the moth goes to a podiatrist's office, the podiatrist asks what's wrong, and the moth shares his woes. The podiatrist asks why the moth has come to see him and not a therapist, and the moths says it's because the light was on. I was drunk enough to be happy to hear him tell it again.

After he delivered the punchline, he stopped in the middle of the sidewalk and put a hand on my shoulder. "You get it?"

"It's because he's a moth."

"No, I mean do you *get* it?"

"Yeah, I get it, Sev. It's a good joke."

"We're all the moth, Alex. I'm the moth, you're the moth ..."

"That's very deep."

"... but Margaret's especially the moth. Margaret's the mothiest of all the moths."

"I don't know what that means."

"You will."

Sev clapped on the shoulder and we stumbled on to his building, with a brief detour so he could be sick in someone's geraniums. He hugged me good night when we got to his door, and I leaned against a lamppost and waited for a cab to come by. I was waiting a long time.

X

I HAD A week off from work in August, and spent much of July thinking about what to do. I should have been thinking about where I was going to move. As expected, we'd received a notice on the first day of July explaining that our lease would not be renewed. I'd need to find a new place to live by September 1. But during those long, hot days, September 1 seemed a long way off. And I told myself that it would be easier to find something appropriate closer to the move-in date, during the student rush at the beginning of the semester.

Holidays were a delicate matter at the magazine, and Zimmermann usually manoeuvred to have me out of the office during the slowest time of the summer. This had never been a problem, before, because I was so bad with money I could never afford to take a proper vacation. I gathered from certain vague hints Margaret had dropped that Lionel would be in Scotland for part of the month, and wanted to ensure that my time away from the office coincided with his time out of the country. Unfortunately, this was not something I could bring up with her: everything we had done together had the flavour of spontaneity — the Sunday afternoons, our visit to her parents' cottage in May, a second weekend away in early July: none of this had been confirmed until the day before. The assumption that I would always be free (although not unfounded) was beginning to wear, and I felt that we had grown close enough that it would make sense to at least talk about the possibility of making plans.

I broached the topic while we were lying in bed in a motel outside Newmarket. It was ferociously hot, and the air conditioner was broken. Perspiration was streaming down Margaret's face, and I licked a drop of sweat off her nose.

"I'm taking a week off next month," I said. "I was thinking of going up to Tobermory."

"The peninsula is gorgeous this time of year. But it's probably booked up already, no?"

I hadn't thought about this. I lay back on my pillow and hoped Margaret would pick up the thought, but she didn't.

"I was wondering if you wanted to do something," I finally said. "If you can get away for a couple of days."

She turned to me and propped her head up on her hand. I had worried she would become cold, but she seemed as friendly as she always was. I took this as a good sign.

"I don't know what my plans are next month. Lionel wants me to go to Scotland with him. I don't know if I'll be around," she said.

"Let's say you are."

"I'm not sure a hypothetical is that interesting, do you? I'm sure we'll be able to see each other as we normally do."

"Well, that's the thing, isn't it? If I've got a bit of time, doesn't it make sense to try to spend a bit more of it together?"

She leaned over and kissed me on the lips, and ran her fingers through the sweat that was collecting in the cavity of my sternum. She drew her face away, and I could tell from how she was looking at me that she had something to say, and was trying to find a way to say it diplomatically.

"Alexander, I'm having a lot of fun with you. And I appreciate how good you've been about this whole situation. And I would like to get away with you for another weekend before the summer is over. But it's ... important for you to remember that I'm also dealing with constraints."

"No, of course, I understand that. It's just the way things have been going, I mean, I keep my Sundays open, I wait for a text on Saturday, I never know ... you see how this is from my perspective, right?"

Margaret lay back in the bed and sighed, and before she started to speak, I already knew what was coming. She apologized, and acknowledged, and thanked me, and expressed her respect, her gratitude, her affection, and said a number of very flattering things, and then began to playfully kiss my arms, my chest, my stomach, and her lips went farther and farther down, and I was left with no doubt that things would continue just as they had in the past.

XI

ON THE LAST day of August, I packed up my bag, shook hands with Ted, and walked up to Sev's apartment in the Annex. I hadn't been able to find a place. Rents had gone up even in the short time since I arrived in the city, and I was blindsided by the amount I'd need to pay even for a bachelor. Sev had landed a supporting role in a production of *Arabella* in New York, and was out of the city for the fall. He'd handed the keys over before he left and reminded me not to ash any cigarettes into his plants. It was a temporary solution in every sense of the word.

Sasha invited me to a Labour Day barbecue at her new place in Parkdale. She had moved in with Ghassan and another of her new activist friends. I was morose, and spent the evening on the balcony chain-smoking and working my way through a six-pack of watery lager. I gathered that Sasha and Ghassan were an item. He seemed good for her: calm and witty, less pugilistic but perfectly capable of holding his own. There was a good deal of talk about alt-right goons, and that Umberto Eco essay on fascism. I asked Ghassan about who he thought the Democrats should nominate to beat Trump in 2020, but he just laughed and said something about being more focused on matters close to home. There was to be a provincial and a municipal election in the coming year; Ghassan believed the Left had a real shot at unseating the perennially corrupt Liberals if they ran as unabashed social democrats.

"I've never been very interested in politics," I said, sensing he might try to rope me into campaigning for someone. "My family's from Russia, so ..."

"Hey, man, I get it. My family's from Lebanon. But we can't count on things getting better if we don't get active, right? There are people to blame for all the fucked-up shit going on right now. Real people, living in this city. We have to take the fight to them."

In Ghassan's moist brown eyes, I saw what had attracted Sasha. He was not a fanatic, but he was a believer, someone who had surveyed the world and concluded the current state of affairs just wouldn't do. Someone who put up with the hysterics, and the virtue theatre, and the slogans that didn't rhyme properly, and the near certainty of failure because the alternative was worse: lassitude, passivity, all good instincts stunted and warped by the effort of not living in alignment with one's perception of reality. Walking this path, one had to make sure that certain things were never seen or never comprehended, neurotically repeating a story about why things were the way they were and could not ever be otherwise. Ghassan, on a basic level, was too emotionally healthy not to be a socialist.

At the end of the evening, Sasha walked me down and we shared a joint on the front step. I congratulated her on her good fortune.

"I like Ghassan," I said. "You seem a lot happier."

"Oh, Ghassan is great. But he's not why I'm happy. I mean, he is, partially, but it's more than that. I just felt like I was floating for so long, you know? Like I had all these feelings and there was so much shit I just hated. And it was easy to think it was all inside me, like it was my fault for not getting with the program. Sean would always tell me that the world wasn't going to change, so I needed to change myself. But that's not how *he* lives — he's got his fingers in everything, he's like that pig from *Animal Farm*, what was that pig's name? Napoleon. He's like Napoleon, he's figured out how to make everything flow toward him, money, drugs, pussy, houses — well, obviously houses can't flow, but you get the picture. And I don't want to be like Sean, but guys like Sean always make it a choice between being their accomplices or being their victims. These past few months, actually getting involved politically, it's been like falling to Earth. Figuring out how to hate things productively."

"There are people like Sean everywhere. Especially in activism."

Sasha waved away my words, coughing as she exhaled. "I know that — of course I know that. I've already met some of them. But you can't float forever, Alex. You've got to decide what you're doing and who you're doing it with. At some point, everyone's got to decide."

XII

IN THE END, Margaret and I did leave the city together one last time. She took me back to her parents' cottage early in September, when the lake is at its warmest and the fields are full of corn. I think Margaret could tell something had changed as soon as I got in her car. We ended up stuck in traffic on the expressway out of the city. She started telling me about the Bloor Viaduct. She'd been rereading a book about its construction, a novel by a Canadian writer she admired. She was surprised, going through the story again, by how colossal this novelist made it seem.

"I mean, look at it," she said as the traffic inched forward. "As bridges go, it isn't that impressive. I guess people do die falling off it, but it's hardly majestic."

"Do people die there?"

"Oh yeah, people used to commit suicide by jumping off all the time. It's why they put the nets in."

"Imagine committing suicide where a bunch of other people have already committed suicide."

"Well, Toronto doesn't offer many poetic places to kill yourself."

"Trying to do it in a poetic way seems very middlebrow. I always thought Tchaikovsky had the right idea."

"Intentionally contracting cholera?"

"Yeah. Very subtle. Leaves things open ended."

The sun was already low in the horizon by the time we reached the open highway, and it was quite late when we got to the cottage. Even with the wind from the lake, it was stiflingly hot. We went for a long swim in the moonlight and lay on the dock. Whenever I spent a night outside of the city, I was always surprised by the number of stars. There were the points of the major constellations, which I half remembered from childhood, and the dimmer stars whose names are known only to astronomers, and then the arc of little points that always slipped into a haze if I tried to focus on them too closely.

"I get the sense that you aren't completely happy," Margaret said, reaching over to rest her hand on my leg. "I didn't want to bring it up in the car, but I thought it might be better to clear the air tonight, rather than letting it hang over the weekend."

"I think it's just the heat."

"Are you sure? I was thinking, in Scotland, about how things are going between us, and I realized I've been a little unfair. I don't want to be condescending when I say this, but I forget how young you are, sometimes. I forget that it's not the same for you. It's just that you seemed so sure you wanted this, in the beginning, and I assumed you knew what you were getting into."

Margaret's tone was even, sympathetic. I think I could have kept it in if she hadn't mentioned that thing about Scotland, if she hadn't been gentle about it. Tenderness brought the bile up. I understood, even as I started to respond, that I was being childish.

"It's nice that you think about me when we aren't together. I just don't understand how that works. I mean, I think about you all the time — every day I'm thinking about you. But you've got this life with ... Lionel ... and you've got this — I don't want to say 'life,' but I don't know what else to call it — with me, and I can't shake the feeling that deep down you must despise one of us. And I really, really want to believe it's him."

"I don't despise Lionel. I don't despise you, either. I've got to say it's a little surprising that you'd suggest it. Isn't your generation supposed to be a lot more open minded about this stuff? You give me things that Lionel can't give me, and Lionel gives me things you can't give me."

"A house, for example."

Margaret reached for a towel and wrapped it around her shoulders. Her skin had been dried by the night air, but the patch of hair between her legs was still damp from the lake.

"If we're going to have this conversation, let's have it inside."

I followed her like a whipped dog. She didn't say anything as she got dressed, but she poured us a couple of drinks while I buttoned up my shirt. The lodge smelled strongly of cedar and heat radiated off the walls.

"I can understand how you feel," she said as she sat down on the couch. "I know from your perspective, my marriage must look a certain way. I know how Lionel comes across. He probably seems like an old man who hasn't evolved with the times. But he has been kinder to me than anyone else I know. When I married him, I understood that some aspects of our life together would be difficult, but I signed up for that difficulty. I am going to take care of him when he gets sick, I'm going to make sure his medicine is in order, I'm going to watch him die, I am going to mourn at his funeral, and I'll be there when they shovel the dirt onto his coffin. And I'll miss him until it's my turn to go. Do you know how good it feels to have that certainty?"

"I'm sure it feels very good, and I'm sure it feels even better when you get to do it all in Rosedale. That's why you're here with me, right? Because it feels so good?"

"I will talk about this with you, Alexander, because I'm fond of you and you deserve to be able to express your feelings. But let's be very clear: I had plenty of money before I married Lionel, and if Lionel kicked me out tomorrow, I'd still have plenty of money. Which you'd have noticed if you'd been paying attention. You think he's been paying for our motels? Looking over the Visa bills?"

Margaret said all of this without a hint of malice, sitting against the arm of the couch with her feet stretched out toward me. Occasionally, a drop of water would fall from the mass of black hair piled atop her head, leaving little damp spots on her white dress. Her nipples were dark through the linen. I could feel the coarse texture of the fur rug between my toes, the blood pumping through my limbs.

"Does he know about us?"

Margaret cocked her head and smiled. She seemed happy I'd asked the question.

"I don't know. He probably suspects something is going on — he's very sensitive about me. Picks up on little things. Does he know it's you? I doubt it."

"So how does that work? He doesn't care that you're involved with other people? You've agreed to have an enlightened open marriage?"

"Nothing so formal. And I don't know if he doesn't care. But when you've been married for a long time, you realize the value of silence. Or rather, if you stay married for a long time, it's because you've realized the value of silence. When we first got together, I assumed I was the only one, but after a couple of years, I started to notice things. Innocuous things, mostly — the occasional lie, late nights at work, sudden business trips. I knew he spent a lot of time around younger women, I mean, it's how he met me. He was never indiscreet, there was never any hard evidence, and whenever I needed him, he was there. It was hard, at first, and once or twice I started to think about confronting him about it, you know, having it out, making a big scene. Eventually I did. He came home one night smelling of another woman's perfume, and I forced him to tell me who it was — a Polish girl on tour with a choir. Twenty years old. I swear, I could have killed him. I could have driven a kitchen knife into his throat.

"He was very contrite, said all the usual things men say in that situation. He loved me, it meant nothing. Just clichés. And I knew it was more than that. There were rumours, people would drop little hints. He spent a lot of time with that awful Sean Porter, he was taking Sean under his wing — he's the one who got Sean his place on the Great Lakes Opera Company board. You must know about Sean; even I'd heard enough to know what he got up to with his girls. Lionel knew I couldn't stand any of that, so when they were going out together, he'd say it was something else. And then I'd find out that they'd had dinner with the latest pair of young dancers or singers or whatever, in from nowhere hoping to get their big break. This is going to sound terrible, Alexander, but I was always so relieved I never had to meet any of these girls. They just seemed to fade away and be replaced by new ones every couple of months. If they hadn't, I think I really would have left. It was exhausting, the worst two years of my life. I did end up talking to a lawyer about divorce, and when I told Lionel, he was so, so scared. It was almost childish terror. He was desperate for me to stay, said all the same things he always said, but this time he *meant* it, et cetera. And I did leave for a while — I went to California and had an affair of my own. But I missed Lionel, and I missed Toronto, and I started to realize that what I was really afraid of was getting old, of turning fifty and having my husband leave me for the younger model. It slowly dawned on me that despite his behaviour, Lionel had been serious about our marriage. He wanted me as a partner. He couldn't live without adultery, but he also couldn't live without me. So I went home and decided that there were certain things I just wasn't going to notice anymore.

"The thing is that when you're married to someone, you see all the worst parts of them. You see them in a way they'll never see themselves — not just the vices, but all the unconscious urges and physical tics and repetitive patterns and self-deceptions. The way their idea of themselves is different from who they really are. I mean, you literally see them as objects, as bodies snuffling about and making noises and telling the same stories over and over again. If you start bringing all of these things up, there's no end to it. And they see all the worst parts of you: the pettiness, the inconsistency, the little fantasies you make up to stay sane. Everyone says they want to be seen, but actually being seen, being confronted by all that stuff — it's horrible. To have someone know every disgusting detail about you. That's why fights between husbands and wives are so nasty. But if you're both still there at the end of the fight, and neither of you wants to shut it down for good, all that viciousness makes you stronger. Because if they've seen all that shit and they still love you ...

"Of course, if you're constantly clawing away at each other, you never have the time to heal, and that's where the silence comes in. You realize they'll never see themselves as you see them and you start thinking in terms of what things you should point out and what you should learn to live with.

"It's strange, because at first the silence feels incredibly lonely. You thought you would keep growing closer and closer until the boundaries disappeared. But the boundaries are part of being a person, and you realize there are better and worse kinds of loneliness. Or at least, you do if you're self-aware. Plenty of people persist in the delusion that the loneliness can be overcome if they just find the right person. Or they decide that the narcotic of lust is all they want."

"Is that what we're indulging in now, the narcotic of lust?"

"Narcotics have their place."

"What if I want more than that?"

"Then you should find someone who can give it to you."

XIII

AS MARGARET DRIFTED off to sleep, I understood that something had ended. There was, perhaps, a future in which the woman who was nestled into my armpit would keep returning to it, enjoying what was there to be enjoyed and continuing with the life she had chosen for herself as long as we both were willing. Accepting this reality with grace, I, too, could live a full life. I would get better at my job, start making a real effort, keep the magazine going when Zimmermann retired. Over time, Margaret and I would see each other less frequently, eventually I'd fall in love with someone else, but the memory of those Sunday afternoons would bring us closer together. She was a generous person, she would quietly help me where she could, and I would be part of a community again, go to dinner with Sev when he came back to visit, become a person who knew people. If I was careful with my money, maybe I could even buy a condo. My mother would come to visit, and she'd talk about how my father would have been proud. I'd go running along the lakeshore, I'd get a cat, I'd cut back on the drinking, I'd learn to cook proper dinners, I'd have a piano again, I'd become one of the old men in the bookshops along College Street talking about how I'd just gotten back from Bayreuth and how bad the new production of *Siegfried* was.

This future could begin the very next morning. Over breakfast, I'd be very candid and serious and thank Margaret for her generosity, for all that she'd taught me about life. And she would joke about how she was saving me so much time with her wisdom, how she wished one of her lovers had explained to her how everything worked. And I'd smile and tell her *I'd* explain how everything worked, and I'd chase her into the living room and lay her down on the bearskin rug, and I'd run my tongue up her leg and make her come until she was a giggling mess, and we'd spend the afternoon out on the lake, looking down through the clear brown water to the slippery boulders trailing down toward the drop-off, where the walleye and pickerel flickered in and out of their secret grottoes, and Margaret would recite dirty limericks, and I'd teach her about the secrets of Russian numerology, and when the mosquitoes came out I'd accompany her on the piano as she sang "*Non mi dir*," and we'd grill filet mignon on the barbecue, and we'd drink the rest of her father's Scotch, and she'd climb on top of me and I would disappear inside the warmest cunt in the world, and later, as the fluttering moths beat themselves against the screen, trying to leave the darkness for a place of warmth and safety and light, I'd ask her how exactly a person could experience the pure joy of music when they were being driven out of their home, and she'd tell me that all things work for the best in the best of all possible worlds.

I laid my hand to rest on Margaret's thigh, and she shifted toward me, sweaty and warm beneath the sheet. I tried to imagine her, young, singing "*Der Hölle Rache*," still-supple vocal cords straining for the high notes the Queen of the Night sang as she placed the assassin's knife into Pamina's hand. Had Margaret, in those moments, really felt hell's vengeance boiling in her heart? The desire to maim, to kill, to fuck and betray and destroy, to pull the temple down on top of every soul who had witnessed your humiliation? Approached a certain way, music gave us room to hold this desire, to look at it, to feel it, to move through it, and then to let it pass. But letting it pass would mean forgetting the spite in Sasha's voice when she talked about Sean, and his friends, and what they had done to her. If music was more than pretty sounds, if it *meant* something, reducing it to aesthetic coordinates could only domesticate and diminish it, render it safe for consumption, rob it of its essential violence. I did not want to be purged by my fever, as Fera Civitatem had said in its manifesto, or to retreat into the icy calm of the ocean and of God, or to make peace with the Mephisthophelean city by the lake. I wanted music to cut me open. I wanted to stay in the wound, to feel its pain every morning, to sink into the unhealing gash every night. To know and honour, as Sasha did, the cleansing rage of the Queen of the Night.

XIV

I WAS GIVEN what I already knew would be my final assignment shortly the week after I returned from that final abortive
weekend at Margaret's cottage.

"It's the opening of an arts space in some new condo building. Just a short news piece, you know the kind of thing:
'Toronto Developer Creates Space for Music to Grow' or something like that. Should be easy to get some quotes — you know
Lionel Standish, right? Just remember he's a donor. A crucial
donor, I might add, a man who has been most generous with
his money and —"

"Yeah, don't worry about it."

I walked along the lakeshore that evening, going far out of my way to follow the path through the overdeveloped board-walks and breweries, out past the rotting concrete stacks of the granaries on the quay, the baseball diamonds, the corridor be-tween the freeway and the abandoned theme park. The water-front trail was filled with joggers and dog walkers and cyclists enjoying the last of the summer heat, and far ahead I could see the towers of Mississauga rising in the distant blue.

I sat down to rest at Sunnyside Beach. A woman was play-ing with her dog in the shallows. She threw a stick out into the water, and the dog raced to catch it. But the stick landed beyond a wave and the dog lost sight of it. He gazed around, confused, tongue lolling over his long white teeth, until his eyes latched onto a large chunk of wood bobbing in the surf. He ran out and tried to fasten his jaws around it, but it was too large, and it floated away on a swell. He tried again, canines scrabbling against the rounded surface, but it evaded him no matter how wide he opened his mouth or how much purchase he tried to get on the rough bark. The owner kept calling out, trying to get the dog's attention. She pointed to a spot in front of her, where the stick was rising and falling a few feet from the shore. But dogs don't understand pointing, and he just stared dejectedly at his master's finger.

XV

———

THE OPENING GALA took place on a Saturday night. The address had been included in the press release, but I didn't really need it. I had passed the building many times while it was under construction. At sixty storeys, it wasn't the tallest new building, but it was tall enough. The architect, in a fit of whimsy, had added a number of colourful spots of cladding up the sides, which made it look syphilitic. The Chinese grocery, of course, was gone, as was the brick hump of the old theatre, but there was an entrance on the south side that had *OREN THEATRE* spelled out above in round showbusiness bulbs. I showed the doorman my card and he waved me on in.

The foyer was shining. The patterned tile on the floor matched the red of the cladding. A helpful poster explained that the "New Oren" featured a large convention space, a screen and projection room for movie showings, and a fully operational stage for theatre and community events. A crowd of people were standing around the entrance. I slipped through them to the auditorium itself.

The architects had done the best they could, given that the space was essentially a concrete box. Vast panels of wood and wire mesh covered the walls to soften the harsh angles, and the seats rose in a gentle sweep that was steep enough to ensure that each audience member would get a clear view without causing an acoustical imbalance. A balcony hung out over the first dozen rows. In a wistful gesture toward continuity, the shell of the stage had been designed using materials from the original, deconstructed to suggest a connection with the past without disrupting the modern sensibility.

A little bell went off and I shuffled into a comfortable chair in the middle third of the room, flipped open my notepad, and turned on my recorder. All I needed was three decent quotes, then a quick word or two from the main players, and I could leave.

The program, of course, was not designed with brevity in mind, and we had to sit through a series of boilerplate speeches from the MP, the MPP, the city council member, selected corporate types (including a sick-making turn by Sean Porter in his capacity as board member for the Great Lakes Opera Company), and the head architect. We were assured that this mixed-use building (in which opening bids for a one-room condo hovered around the $800,000 mark) was a triumph of public–private partnership, a testament to what could be accomplished when heritage preservation came together with smart urban design, a sign of the bright and vibrant future that lay ahead.

When it was all over, we were invited to a reception at the Ishpadina Cocktail Lounge on the second floor, which we were told had been named in honour of the First Peoples of the Land. I tucked my notepad back into my pocket and made my way up to the lounge, which was pleasant enough if you liked driftwood. A couple of servers were making their way around with trays of Prosecco. I helped myself to a glass and slipped a dollar onto the spot I'd taken it from. The server winked at me, and I felt slightly less shitty. I recognized a few people from the audience, incorrigible members of the arts scene who would have gone to this kind of event on a Tuesday morning at 9:00 a.m. if it meant they could be seen at it. I gazed out one of the floor-to-ceiling windows and looked down at the intersection. Night was falling, and the glass reflected the crowd milling inside. I watched the door, waiting for one of the people I needed to walk through.

My stomach clenched when Margaret appeared. She caught my eye and gave a cautious little nod. Lionel was behind her, his hand on the small of her back. Sean was following close behind. I drained my champagne and made my way over to them.

"Hello, Lionel — I wonder if I could have a couple of words."

"Of course! Always happy to." He shook my hand, and Sean shook my hand, and Margaret said a neutral hello.

"What does the opening of this new theatre mean for opera in Toronto? And what can you tell me about the arrangement between Kilbride and the Great Lakes Opera Company?" I asked, notepad in hand.

"Much is said about the tension between development and culture in this city, and too often the conversation assumes an adversarial relationship between these two laudable goals. I hope the New Oren will stand as a testament to the fact that development can serve culture, and culture development."

I nodded along as I wrote this down, and re-worded the second part of my question to make it seem like I was following up on what he'd said.

"Oh, the arrangement? Well, perhaps Sean could speak to that — it was, in many ways, his idea."

"Wonderful. Actually, Sean, I have a couple of other things to ask you, as well. Is there a more private place we could speak?"

"Of course. And we can have a proper drink while we're at it."

Sean led me to the elevators, chatting amiably about how the Great Lakes Opera Company planned to use the new space. While his back was to me, I clicked on my digital recorder and put it in my jacket pocket. We rode up to the top floor, and I followed Sean into a corner suite with the company logo on the door. The illuminated corridor of Spadina stretched down to the waterfront. The city had fallen into twilight.

"So, what do you want to know," said Sean, pulling out a bottle of tequila and pouring us each a glass. "I get the sense your question was about more than just the rental agreement."

"Have you kept up with Theresa?"

He looked puzzled. "No, not really. Great girl, don't get me wrong, but she just didn't vibe with the lifestyle. Which is fine. To each his own. You seemed pretty smitten with her, though."

"I suppose I was."

"Pussy was probably a lot tighter than Margaret's. Cheers," he said, bumping his glass against mine and drinking down the tequila.

I put mine on the table. "Pardon me?"

"Take the joke, man. Is that what you wanted to talk about? Now that you've dumped Margaret, you're getting nostalgic? You know, Theresa was really upset after that, she said you made her feel used. Women aren't property, Alex — you can't still be on that monogamy shit. It's 2017. Let people live their lives."

"It's not the monogamy I care about, people can do what they want, it's —"

"Yeah, yeah, sure. No one can admit to being a prude anymore. They have to make up new words for 'possessive.' What's your word? You 'demisexual,' or 'greysexual' or something?"

"No, I just don't think it's all that enlightened to manipulate young girls into fucking your friends."

"Is it manipulative to convince them they'll be happier letting go of their hang-ups, to expand their sexual horizons? I've never forced a woman to do anything she didn't agree to. All my hookups have been consensual, man. No one's suggested otherwise. You're the one who changes your mind in the middle of things, switches the rules as soon as you start getting feelings. That's the real manipulative shit."

"I think Sasha would disagree."

"Sasha? Sasha Leung? Man, she loved what we did together. Just between us, as men of the world, she was practically begging for it, a real firecracker. I was the one who had to kick *her* out — she would have stayed with me forever if I'd let her."

"She's not begging anymore."

"It was what it was, man. Is it my fault if she got bitter? She consented when it mattered."

"So you say. But I actually didn't come up to talk about that. I wanted to ask about the relationship between the Great Lakes Opera Company and Fera Civitatem and the Kilbride Development Corporation. It seems to me that Great Lakes has been funding Fera to incentivize property owners to sell. Can you confirm that?"

Sean shook his head and drank the tequila he'd poured for me. He seemed to be enjoying himself. "Dude, you have really gotten lost in your own head. I mean, off the record, it's true, but who the fuck cares?"

"It seems like a pretty grimy thing to do."

"Do you have any idea how real estate works in this city? Because that is the tip of the iceberg, my friend. I was just doing favours. And you've got to admit, it's pretty funny. That old couple running the grocery store was so *fucking* stubborn, and then a little minor anarchy and they're selling for hundreds of thousands below asking."

"Pretty sure that's illegal, right?"

"So what if it is? You going to write a big exposé about it? For *Classical Modern*? First of all, there's no paper trail, you're just going off a hunch, and second of all, Fera hasn't put on a concert in more than two years, so good luck trying to hunt any of them down. Kilbride is completely clean — at least as far as Fera goes — and not a penny of the Great Lakes budget went toward their little productions. At least not a penny anyone can trace. Finally, and most importantly, no one fucking cares! It was a building with a disused theatre in it. Now it's a much bigger building with a theatre that can actually stage performances. You think anyone is going to see a downside?"

"Can I quote you on that?"

"No. And if you try to, Zimmermann won't publish it. And if he does, his magazine is going to be sued for libel so quickly you're going to be out on the street by next weekend. This isn't the United States. You can't just say whatever you want about people. Don't delude yourself, Alex. If you were a journalist, you wouldn't be talking to me — your legal team would be."

"Is that why you're telling me this?"

"No, I'm telling you this because you asked. And because it's funny watching you try to be a real journalist — it's hysterical, like a lemur trying to play the violin. But you like it when people make fun of you, right? Theresa said you get off on being humiliated."

"I wouldn't say I get off on it, no."

"You should try! If you weren't so repressed, you might enjoy shit like that. See? Not even half an hour with me, and I'm already expanding your sexual horizons."

"What do you get off on, Sean? Really. I'm trying to understand."

Sean poured more tequila. He didn't seem at all intoxicated yet. He pushed my glass across the table. "If you drink that, I'll tell you."

I drank, and the happy, familiar burn made me feel, for a moment, much worse.

"I'm a philanthropist. From the Greek. I love mankind, just like Rousseau: 'Man is born free, and everywhere he is in chains.' The problem is people get comfortable with their chains, so comfortable that if you take them off, they think you're stealing something. This city used to be such a pious shithole, backward, provincial — a real fucking bummer. Didn't mean people weren't fucking their brains out, they were just doing it to their kids or their servants or the immigrant whores in the old ward. Didn't mean there weren't rich cunts like the Standishes doing whatever they wanted to do in Rosedale. But it was all hidden away. People liked pretending they were virtuous so much they started getting off on the shame. I don't have time for that kind of hypocrisy, I want people to let it all out, let them fuck whoever they want, let them buy what they want, sell what they want, do what they want. Tear the old shit down, get out of the way of the people trying to build the future."

"That future doesn't have room for everyone."

"Of course it fucking does. You just have to nut up and take responsibility for your life. It doesn't bother me if you're happy making thirty-five thousand a year writing your articles, but if someone else is going to pay twice as much for the privilege of living in your house, why should you get to keep it? Because you were there first? Because you weren't willing to spend sixty hours a week building your career, and pissed away all your money at the bar?"

"You still haven't told me what gets you off."

"This!" Sean swung his arm in a gesture that encompassed the skyline. "Growth, development, new art, new experiences. I'm hard as a rock right now. I'm fucking jacked! You want to do some coke?"

"No, I think I'll be going, thanks."

"That's not what a winner would say, Alex. That look on your face, that's exactly what I'm talking about. This isn't personal, dude — you're the one making it personal. I'm just offering some constructive criticism."

"Goodbye, Sean."

XVI

I GOT INTO the office early on Monday morning and put my bag down on my desk. It had been a good desk, although it bore more coffee stains now than when I had first arrived. Outside the window, the shadows were still crawling down the brick wall opposite. I had grown attached to that brick wall. I felt a personal connection with each rusting hook and crusty nub of mortar. There were one or two things I needed to do before Zimmermann showed up, but before getting down to them, I wanted to enjoy a moment of serenity.

When he arrived a quarter-hour later, Zimmermann was in a cheerful mood, and chatted idly about his weekend while he took off his coat and put on the kettle. He asked how the opening had been, and whether I'd be able to get the piece done for the web that afternoon. I explained that I'd had written it up on Sunday and just finished posting it. He gave me a rare toothy grin and said something nice about how much I'd turned things around.

"Perhaps you won't need to become a lawyer after all!" he said, gliding into his office.

It was a chilly morning, one of those mornings that remind you of the treachery of September, the way it slides so imperceptibly into autumn. I checked my inbox while Zimmermann settled in. There wasn't much there that I actually needed to worry about. I deleted a good amount of spam, fired off a few responses on minor issues that would need to be sorted out by someone else, and waited for the call. It took longer than I expected.

"Alexander? Alexander, sorry, can you come here?"

I got up and walked into Zimmermann's office, which was as dishevelled and chaotic as always.

"Alexander, what the fuck is this, if you'll pardon my language?"

"It's my piece about the New Oren."

"Yes, I know. I am, after all, literate. It does not take great powers of perception to figure out what it is *supposed* to be. I mean, what is this you've written? I told you exactly what was required; I explained the, ah, connection we have to the individuals behind this effort; I provided, as I have so often needed to when giving you directions, an extremely clear gloss of the relevant information. And yet you have not only written, but posted to our public website, this … calumny. This *screed.* I don't think I need to tell you how inappropriate this is, how positively reckless. You sound like a conspiracy theorist. 'The Kilbride Development Corporation has collaborated with the Great Lakes Opera Company and an anarchic arts collective to pressure business owners into selling property'? 'Behind the philanthropist's smile lurks the rictus grin of the free-market fanatic'? 'Major arts organizations are conspiring to turn Toronto into a playground for the narcissisms of the rich'? What does it even mean for the rich to have a playground for their narcissisms? Do narcissisms now need playgrounds? How, exactly, does a narcissism *play*?"

"I have a source," I said, putting my digital recorder on his desk.

He pressed "play" and listened to the first couple of minutes. "Did you make a copy?"

"There's a digital file on my laptop."

Zimmermann deleted the recording with a click and looked up at me. "Did you really think that was going to work?"

"The story was shared on social media. Someone with the right skills might decide to pick it up, actually do something with it."

"The file on your laptop is the property of this magazine. You will leave your laptop exactly where it is, and you will leave the building." He leaned back in his chair and looked at me over his spectacles.

I had expected to feel a little bad, when the moment came, but it was the sense of shame that surprised me. The man sitting across the desk from me had tried to improve my life. I had spat in his face. And I'd told him one final lie: there was more than one copy.

"You're fired."

"I understand. I'm sorry."

"Don't lie to me, Alexander — we both know you're not sorry. Pack your stuff and get out of here. I'll send along the pay that's owed you sometime in the next week. Did you record anything else from Saturday?"

"I did."

"Good. We — I — need to fix this."

Zimmermann put his elbows on the desk and laid his head in his hands. I did not think of him as an old man, but looking down on the wispy hairs struggling across his age-spotted skull, I realized that this was what he was: an old, tired man trying to keep something going as long as he could.

He stood in the doorway and watched me pack up the few things I kept in the office, shoulders stooped, fingers digging into his eye sockets.

"I'm sorry, Mr. Zimmermann," I said.

"This is what I don't understand, Alexander," he said, looking up rheumy-eyed. "You can be so reasonable. And then ..." He shrugged his shoulders. "It's all very disappointing."

I reached out my hand. For a moment I thought he might shake it, but he looked at me with total exhaustion, and I let it drop to my side. I closed the door behind me and walked down to the street for the last time.

XVII

THE AIR WAS cold in the shadow of the tall buildings along King, but when I stepped into a patch of sunlight, it was summer again. The great rust bulk of Scotiabank rose like a megalith, flanked by the black standing stones of the TD Canada Trust and pale phallus of BMO. I walked past antique stores and Thai restaurants, cathedrals and parks and shops selling Persian rugs, and payday-loan companies, and ragged men urinating against trees. I walked past the warehouses on the rail line, where the slaughterhouses had stood when Toronto was still called Hogtown, past identical burger restaurants competing for business on opposite street corners, past grocery chains and ATMs and the old St. Lawrence Market, where people had been bought and sold, and the flatiron building that was the same as the one in New York, only smaller. I walked past a vodka bar called "Truth" and a park named for a colonial administrator and a café named for a hockey player and a performing arts centre built entirely of rubble, and in the colonnades I heard my own footsteps echo back into the centuries, back into Italy and Spain and the British Empire. In the windows of a building that used to be a bank were banners bearing the names of the great men, Gretzky and Potvin and Nedomansky, men who smiled at the stone face of the public building opposite with its columns and arches and the red-and-white flag flapping in the wind above. I walked on, deeper into the canyon of stone and glass. A sheer wall of golden crystal rose from the concrete, from where, every day, secret armies were commanded to march into humid jungles at night to rape and burn and dig the gold from deep in the earth's crust so it could hang from the wrist of a real-estate developer's wife. Above it all, the syringe of the CN Tower punctured the blue vein of the sky.

There was work being done on the road, and I stopped at a wire mesh barrier to watch the labourers hauling hoses and pipes up from the ground. The foreman was wearing a red hard hat with streaks of mud across the brim. He was joking with one of his crew members about something, but his words were lost in the wind. I knew it was a joke, though, because the crewman kept laughing, and the foreman was smiling wide enough to show his silver teeth. The ground was muddy and their boots were heavy with dried clay. There was drilling off toward the train station, and thick black wires were being unspooled from wooden bobbins the size of tractor wheels. A labourer with a sheaf of dreadlocks tucked into the back of his hi-vis vest was tenderly undoing a snag in a stretch of electric cable.

I crossed the street and walked across the windy cobblestone expanse between the Royal York Hotel and Union Station. The cabdrivers were idling in a long line, waiting for passengers. A stream of people walked out from between the columns of the concourse with their luggage trundling behind them, and I stopped by the station entrance. A train had just come in. Perhaps soon a train would be leaving, heading west to Detroit, Buffalo, Sudbury, Thunder Bay, Winnipeg, beyond the lakes with their shipwrecks and ancient inlets to the rolling prairies and the mountains and the Pacific. I could leave the city of pigs today, light out for the oil patch or the logging camps of the Northwest. You could float forever in this country; if you were careful where you looked, no one need ever pull you to the ground.

I stood there for a long time, feeling the bite of autumn in the wind from the lake. And then I started the long walk back up University Avenue. I couldn't stay in Sev's apartment forever. I needed to find somewhere to live.

Acknowledgements

IN EARLY 2017, the composer Joel Peters asked me if I would
write a story about an underwater organ for Earth World, a collaborative arts group based in Montreal. That story, "The Lower
Registers," became the basis for *Music for the Hydroörganon*, a
concert for organ electronics that premiered in Montreal in
2018. From it, the entire novel flowed; and so I must start
by thanking Joel, without whom this book would never have
been written. I also want to thank Adrian Foster, Noor Naga,
Bardia Sinaee, Jenny Berkel, Sarah Ens, and Vincent Lauzon,
who contributed compositions and poems to the concert and
helped make the hydroörganon come alive.

Thanks to Julie Mannell, who stuck her neck out for me,
and to Russell Smith, whose editorial guidance made this a
much better book than it would otherwise have been. I am

indebted to everyone at Dundurn Press, and especially to Vicky Bell, whose tireless copy-editing and fact-checking were a great comfort.

I am, as always, grateful to Naben Ruthnum, Noor Naga, Scott Bergen, and Paul Forget, who read early drafts of this work and provided the kind of fine-grained criticism no writer can do without.

The verses that appear in "The Laugh of Mephistopheles" are taken from Philip Wayne's translation of Johann Wolfgang von Goethe's *Faust, Part Two*.

Large parts of this novel were written in Yoshkar-Ola, Russia, and I would be remiss if I did not thank the Sadovins and the Ivanovs for their generous hospitality.

Finally, I want to thank Irina Sadovina, who understands that candour is the highest form of love.

About the Author

ANDRÉ FORGET was born in Toronto and raised in Mount Forest, Ontario. He is the former editor-in-chief of the *Puritan* and a contributing editor at *Canadian Notes & Queries*. His writing has appeared in a variety of publications in Canada and the United States, including *Maisonneuve*, the *Walrus*, and the *Outline*. *In the City of Pigs* is his first novel. He splits his time between Toronto, the United Kingdom, and Russia.